Beyond the Titanic

Mary Wernke

This is a work of fiction. The events and characters portrayed are imaginary. Their resemblance, if any, to real-life counterparts is entirely coincidental.

The main character in this book is based on a real person, a distant relative of the Mannion Clan on my mother's side. She really did survive the Titanic, but she didn't want to talk about it, so the entire book is FICTION, based on fact.

Beyond the Titanic © 2019 Mary Wernke
ISBN: 9781098847258

This book is dedicated to Emily Manion Roebken, my connection with Margaret.

Contents

Acknowledgements

I would also like to acknowledge two special people who made this dream happen. First, my husband Ed Wernke for giving me the freedom to pursue my dream, in traveling to Ireland twice and taking time off from other work to write this book.

I would also like to acknowledge my friend and mentor, Jen Ponce. Jen is one of those authors who knows everything, but doesn't act like a know-it-all *ever*. From adviser to editor to cheerleader, she pushed me through a first draft to a final edit that resembles what you see here. Thanks so much, Jen for listening to my worries and building my confidence.

A special thanks also to my cover designer Victorine Lieske, copy editor Jana Osborn, video trailer designer Melinda Wernke, beta readers and advanced reviewers, family and friends who allowed me to miss so many things in my single-minded pursuit.

Chapter One

For what must've been the twentieth time that day, Bridget scoured the rough wooden table her husband had built to accommodate their large family. The table was the heart of the small cottage, gathering the family and their warmth near the oversized hearth where she baked the bread, boiled the potatoes and warmed buckets of water from the well for weekly baths.

Lawrence's 75th birthday last month pulled all the children together again, perhaps for the very last time. Her children were all grown and with two off to America, the table was less often filled and more often a symbol of her aching emptiness. Despite her best efforts, she couldn't erase the memories with her faded cotton rag.

She shoved her hand into the pocket on her dress. Besides a twice-stitched hole, she found only her rosary and the ragged postcard burning a hole in her pocket for a week now. She pulled the card out and examined the drawing of the Titanic, the writing on the back once again, but there were no new clues from Margaret there.

It was time to attack the upstairs bedroom. On her way, she caught sight of the marks on the hand-hewn lumber in the door to the attic stairs. For nearly 40 years, Bridget had recorded each child's height on their birthday - John, Thomas,

Mary, Patrick, Ellen, Lawrence, Margaret and Cecilia. Only her namesake Bridget didn't survive the first year. The ache grew larger and her belly turned again at the loss.

Bridget had stopped measuring when the girls turned 18; Margaret was the tallest of the four girls when she left home. She and the baby — Celia for short — chafed at their mother's annual tradition. Mary left to be married three years ago, but Margaret and Celia remained to comfort her mother.

A gust of cool spring air tossed the flames as her husband barged through the front door, returning from his daily sojourn to the barn. Lawrence still milked the cows every morning and evening. His quiet presence as he settled into his easy chair beside the fire and lit his pipe usually comforted Bridget and set a pattern for their day.

"Any news from the boys?" he asked. The boys were actually grown men, but they would always be boys in Lawrence's eyes. Still a commanding presence at more than six-and-a-half feet tall, his shock of once-dark hair was now completely white. He was showing his age more and more every day.

Bridget only stared blankly into the fire again. "Nothing."

Her tight smile alerted him to something wrong with Bridget's mood, but Lawrence had a hard time reassuring her. He still wasn't sure what the problem was.

He leaned in and sought Bridget's eyes. With slow deep breaths, he rehearsed his next line from an oft-repeated litany he'd told Bridget day after day. "Didn't your cousin, Conor, work in the shipyards in Belfast? Isn't he a good boy and family man himself?"

Bridget bit her lip and continued to play with the rosary in her pocket. She was so very tired and desperate for good news from America. She pasted on a smile, picked up her dish cloth and changed the topic.

It had been days now and Bridget vacillated between

tears, hysteria and simply staring blankly at the wall. Her rumpled clothes hung loosely on her slight frame as she fed her family, but not herself.

The grandchildren played *Share the Ring* nervously at her feet, alternating between silly chatter and gripping silence, as their parents huddled closer together around the fire and Bridget. The slightest sounds seemed to provoke Bridget.

Earlier Sunday, little Noreen had dropped her dolly in grandma's lap with a huge gobbet of orange marmalade in her yarn hair. "Fix," the girl requested. Bridget proceeded to cut off the doll's wig, wash her sticky scalp and hand it back to Noreen's sister Maureen, prompting tears from both children. Their mother tried to explain Bridget's odd behavior in terms the girls would understand. "Gran's having a bad day."

Gran's salt-and-pepper hair and heavily creased skin gave little clue to her real age. She still worked outdoors alongside her husband, had raised seven children and kept the turf fires burning. The deep wrinkles around her eyes had more to do with worry than laughter, but Bridget was trying to keep her courage up.

It had been 10 days. Every day she baked a loaf of fresh brown bread and raisin treacle for the company trailing through like a parade on St. Patrick's Day. Lawrence spent more hours in the barn and in the village. He was distracted by the gossip at the pub in the village. Evenings, Lawrence came home later and later, after a few pints with the boys.

But today, even the easygoing Lawrence was keyed up. His foot tapped regularly as he sat down again, then rose and went to the window, watching for the post, as he did every day.

The postman came only twice a week to leave letters in a community mailbox at the end of the lane. Lawrence had been bothered with an upset stomach and a pain in his jaw all day, but the ritual kept hopes up.

"Any day now," he repeated, as he rubbed his unshaven chin. "Any day."

The couple were alone in the house — Patrick and Lawrence were in the barn and the girls had returned to school. Suddenly, there was a knock at the door and, without warning, a shop boy from Loughanbouy flew in. His eyes were wide, and he had a scrap of yellow paper in his hand with scribbles across one side.

"A telegram for you," he blurted out, panting between paragraphs. "From England." His eyes were wide.

Bridget was skeptical of telegrams; it could only be bad news. "Is it from Margaret?" she pleaded with the ink-stained ragamuffin. Her red-rimmed eyes searched his. The boy shrugged and handed it to her husband.

Slowly, Lawrence reached for the scrap of yellow paper. "It's from the White Star Line." His ruddy face whitened as he scanned the lines the operator had scribbled. "The Titanic has met with disaster," he recited, as if by rote. The tall, suddenly old man swayed, paused to catch his breath and struggled with the next few words.

"Get on with it, please," his wife begged, holding up her hand to ward off the awful truth. "Is there any word of Margaret?"

"The White Star Line regrets to inform you M. Mangan perished at sea."

Lawrence dropped to his knees. The paper fluttered to the floor, but Bridget simply stared. Then, a keen tore from her throat as she clutched at her rosary and pummeled her husband's shoulders, the small wooden beads whipping back and forth around his head.

She knelt before him. "Oh, God! Oh, God! Oh, God!"

Lawrence gathered his small wife into his arms, crying quietly as she wailed. His voice quaked. "My baby. Lord, why did you take my baby?"

Then Lawrence clutched his arm, collapsing sideways. He shook his head repeatedly and stared, glassy-eyed at his wife.

Bridget began to shiver uncontrollably; the errand boy ceased to exist — there was only her and Lawrence. *She* held *him* now and rocked back and forth on her knees, sobbing.

As the boy ran out the door, Lawrence remained silent.

"Eternal rest grant unto her, O Lord," Bridget whispered. "And let perpetual light shine upon her."

Lawrence's chest had stopped heaving, but he didn't respond with the usual, "Through the mercy of God, rest in peace."

"Lawrence?" Bridget prompted. "May she rest in peace?"

Still he didn't answer.

DAILY SKETCH TUESDAY
16 APRIL 1912

TERRIBLE DISASTER TO TITANIC

Feared Loss of 1,700 Lives in Mid Atlantic

----

655 KNOWN TO HAVE BEEN SAVED

Rush of Ocean Liners To The Rescue

On her maiden voyage the White Star liner Titanic, the largest ship afloat, met with a disaster as a result of which she sank.

Six hundred and fifty-five of the Titanic's passengers and crew are known to have been saved, says the Central News. It is feared that the others have been lost.

There were some 2,300 souls on board, and should the feared loss of life be proved true it will mean that about 1,700 human beings have perished.

The news of the sinking of the great ship was only received at an early hour this morning.

The intelligence was communicated by wireless to the New York office of the White Star Company by the captain of the Olympic.

In mid-Atlantic, shortly after ten o'clock on Sunday night (American time) she collided with an iceberg.

Wireless telegraphy messages were sent for assistance, and in a short time a number of liners were racing to her aid.

The wireless station at Cape Race first picked up the call for help, but very soon afterwards came the announcement that the Allan liner Virginian had received the same message, and was speeding towards the maimed Titanic.

Other great liners were reached by the same signals, and were soon hurrying over hundreds of miles of sea. Three of them, the Virginian, the Parisian and the Carpathia reached the Titanic almost together.

Meanwhile the Titanic had been sinking by the head, and an anxious night had been spent by those on board.

Passengers were put off in lifeboats, and fortunately the sea was calm. They were taken up by the liners without difficulty.

When she left Queenstown the Titanic had on board 2,358 passengers and crew, made up as follows: -

First Class 350
Second Class........... 305
Steerage............... 800
Officers and crew...... 903

This is the first disaster of such awful magnitude that has befallen a mammoth liner in the open sea.

Chapter Two

For the first four days of the crossing, Margaret had been the calm one among the five friends. Her best friend Ellie was nervous even at home, but on the ship, her worries magnified.

Tall, plain Ellie carried rosary beads in her pocket at all times and, back home, had attended Mass in the village every day. Father McCauley said Mass at four villages along his route — two each day — and Margaret believed Ellie might follow him to all four, if she didn't have a job in the village and a trip to America to pack for.

Margaret didn't really know Martin's two friends — the two Toms, as everyone called them, as one was never far from the other. Before they took off from home, she had only met them one time and had difficulty telling them apart.

Tom Kilgannon was the taller, more fair-haired of the two men. He seemed to be sweet on Ellie, never put off by her religious devotion and always following her around like an adoring puppy.

On the first day out from Queenstown, the five adventurers were playing cards in the dining room. Martin and Margaret were trying to teach the other three how to play *Rummy,* a new game he'd picked up in America.

Polished wood tables marched in five rows along the edges of the expansive area that doubled as a dance floor every evening. White-coated wait staff still bustled around the room and they could hear dishes and glassware clanking in the kitchen.

Margaret used her fingernail to flick off a bit of oatmeal stuck to the seat and tried to arrange the group evenly. Tom Smyth bowed out to bury his head in a book, leaving the two couples to play as teams.

The boat rocked easily as they churned through open waters, but luckily no one of their group had become seasick. Tom K *was* having a hard time grasping the concept of laying off three cards in sequence from the same suit, before discarding. He joked it was a seasickness of some sort.

Margaret had consciously paired Ellie with Tom K, still hopeful of making a romantic match. She knew Tom needed help with the game and Ellie needed help finding a husband.

Tom continued to fumble with his cards, frequently leaning toward Ellie to ask questions. More than once, he touched her arm — adding a King of Hearts on the three kings Ellie had played in the last round.

He beamed then, at everyone. A king of her heart, too, he'd supposed. Ellie didn't notice.

The Other Tom, as Margaret had taken to calling him was Tom Smyth, a newcomer to Galway. His sallow skin was the differentiating feature between him and Tom K. Smyth's hair was always a mess.

Margaret knew he was close to Martin, but she didn't like him. Besides his unkempt appearance, he mumbled when he spoke and seemed to enjoy dice more often than she liked.

She'd warned Martin about the man's gambling habits, but he was determined the two Toms would attend him at his wedding when they arrived in White Plains, New York, in May.

Below her bunk in their small cabin, Margaret kept a small trunk unopened. As she'd packed it with Ellie and

Bridget's help, she lovingly lay tissue between each piece. Now, she dragged the trunk out and opened its lid cautiously. She hoped there was no bad omen in examining one's trousseau on a new ship, weeks before the wedding day.

She pulled the white lawn wedding gown out first. The tiny pin-tuck pleats lined up evenly across the bodice. Tiny white rosebuds embroidered along the sheer sleeves and skirt made this the fanciest, and the most expensive, piece of clothing Margaret had ever owned.

She spread the dress out on her metal bed, taking care not to get it wet or dirty. It would be an heirloom for her daughters someday. As she patted and primped, Ellie came in on mouse feet.

"It's beautiful," she said.

"Maybe you'll wear it, too, one day," Margaret agreed.

She was no clothes horse, but as she touched each of the other pieces, she was emotional. She blushed when she lifted out a chaste white nightgown for her wedding night. Nearly 30, she knew about men's desires, but she wasn't prepared to manage her own thoughts and needs.

She fussed with the single ruffle at the neckline, closed her eyes and wet her lips. She felt a flutter in her stomach and put the gown aside. Best not to think too much, she decided.

The only other new dress Margaret had owned was the final item she withdrew. Her mother had sewn a blue and pink floral going away dress, for after the ceremony at the small country church near White Plains and a breakfast at his sister's home.

Bridget's tears had fallen when she tried the dress on the first time, perhaps even more so than over the wedding dress. The wedding gown wasn't handmade and a gift from her mother.

Going through the new clothes in the order she would wear them put Margaret in a dreamy mood. She was excited for what lay ahead in America — not just the wedding and being alone with her beloved. Martin had made a success in New

York already, with his small grocery store and two sisters living nearby.

Last night, she'd confessed to Ellie she was also looking forward to becoming a businesswoman. She *was* good with numbers, she told her best friend and bridesmaid-to-be, but she was also a people person with an ear for exciting new trends and a feeling for other's ideas.

"I'm 27 years old and I've never lived away from my parents' home," she confessed. "I want to work beside Martin in the store, make a home and start having children right away."

Martin had left for America in 1900 when he was only 17; she hadn't noticed him before then. But, on his return home to visit earlier this year, he was a grown man and she'd noticed him right away.

With both dark hair and a darker complexion, Martin was what her father described as Black Irish, descendants of survivors of the Spanish Armada. Of course, Martin denied any connections to Spain and spoke Gaelic better than most.

His curly mop was often hanging in his eyes, giving him a sheepdog look Margaret particularly admired. She also liked the trim beard and mustache he wore closely shaven. "It gives him an air of mystery and maturity," she told her friends.

But what really drew Margaret was the polite, almost shy demeanor she observed when they met in the village. At Mass, he smiled softly and turned his head when she looked his way. He could play the pipes quite well, but had to be begged to share a tune with others.

She started to despair of his ever asking her out, so she took matters into her own hands. She screwed up her courage and approached her older brother to ask a favor. "Patrick, I've seen you chumming around with Martin Gallagher. I'd like to meet him before he leaves for America. I don't know when that may be."

The next weekend, Patrick and Margaret spied Martin at a country set dance in a neighbor's barn. He was lurking behind the punch bowl when Patrick approached with Margaret. She assumed the punch was spiked with whiskey and worried Martin might be the culprit.

"He's much quieter than you, Maggie," Patrick teased. "Don't scare him off."

Margaret hated to be called Maggie. Patrick had better not introduce her to Martin that way.

"Martin Gallagher, I'd like you to meet my younger sister Margaret. Margaret," he turned to her with a flourish. "Meet Martin."

"You two are on your own now." He smirked and headed out to find a bottle or two of Guinness behind the barn.

Martin glanced up at Margaret, then lowered his eyes once again.

It would be like pulling teeth with this one. Margaret spoke first. "How long will you be staying in Galway?"

His voice was barely above a whisper "I'm only here for a very short time."

Margaret was resolved to draw Martin out. His rugged face and broad shoulders drew her in. His timid smile was a hurdle she longed to overcome.

"Tell me about America. What is it you do there?"

Martin brightened noticeably when Margaret asked about America. "I've been working a shop in New York. Stocking the shelves one section at a time," he offered. "Beginning with dry goods and tools."

"How do you decide what products to carry?" she asked. "Are there things for the ladies, too?"

For more than an hour, Martin regaled Margaret with tales of difficult clients and foodstuffs spoiling before they could be sold. "But you don't just want to hear about me," he finished. "Tell me about you."

"I'm next-to-youngest of eight," she said. "My older brothers and sisters are on their own, so it's just Dad, Mam and me at home. I have a job in the village, but I'm ready for something new. There's nothing in Ireland for me. I just think I could do so much more, given the chance. I'd love to try an adventure like America."

She smiled encouragingly and turned the subject back to him. "Does a store require heavy lifting?"

At the end of the evening, Martin asked if he might call on her at home the next day, a Sunday.

"Of course," she said. "In the afternoon. We attend Mass in the morning."

"Me, too," he said. "Maybe I'll see you there."

For the next three weeks they spoke daily, sometimes at her home and other times in the village. Martin's short time in Ireland accelerated their relationship and Margaret dragged her steps on their last day together, a picnic she'd suggested and prepared herself. She felt shaky when Martin took her hand on the long walk home.

He stopped as they neared her parents' home. "I know we've only known each other a short time. But I'll be returning to America in April and I was thinking... I mean, I was hoping... Dammit, Margaret, you know what I'm trying to say. Will you come with me to New York? As, As my wife, of course." His cheeks flared, but he didn't drop his gaze any longer and his hands held hers securely.

Margaret was tired of sleeping in the attic, sharing a bed with Celia and dreaming of a better life. She was not some teenage flibberty-gibbet like the girls in the village. She had dreams beyond the shores of Ireland.

"Yes," she answered at once. She leaned in for a kiss.

Martin blushed, but he drew Margaret closer. He knew he'd made the right decision. "She's bright, she's pretty and she's not afraid of hard work," he'd told his parents the night before, when he sought their blessing.

The kiss lasted longer than either had intended, breaking up only when they heard a bicycle bell jingle along the path.

"I have some savings I brought with me." His jaw was set

and his posture ramrod straight. His deep, brown eyes fairly danced. "I'm sure I have enough for two tickets."

The tickets were seven pounds, 14 shillings each, and had taken nearly all of Martin's savings. On the day he rode to Bally-gar to purchase the tickets, Margaret's father took him aside. "I think you're making a mistake," he told Martin. "It's unlucky to travel on any ship's maiden voyage and the Titanic was never christened."

But Martin and Margaret were not to be deterred. The huge, new ship was more than a pipe dream for the young couple — it boasted many features they didn't have at home, including indoor bathrooms in steerage.

The night before their departure, the families gathered at Peter and Kate Gallagher's home to say their goodbyes. Martin and Margaret's parents, brothers, sisters and friends were joined by the others traveling with them to America and their families.

But it seemed more like a wake than a celebration, Margaret thought. She clapped in time to the fiddle music and smiled as friends wished her safe travels. Her mother was melancholy - she was certain she'd never see Margaret again or get a chance to bounce more grandchildren on her knee.

Margaret tried to cheer her mother, but the feeling persisted through the night and she had trouble sleeping. Finally, as the sun peeked over the horizon in the east, Margaret dozed on Martin's shoulder as Ellie and the two Toms loaded into the Gallagher's wagon and headed south to Queensland with his father. They would meet the train at Castlebara.

Three times a day, without fail, Martin, Margaret, Ellie and the two Toms shared a meal in the common dining room in steerage. Margaret loved the raucous conversations in the room — mostly English, Swedish, Finnish and Irish, but she also heard languages she couldn't identify.

Martin said there were even some Orientals, but they kept to themselves. A large group of Irish men and women from County Mayo often ate at the same table, so Margaret and Ellie decided to introduce themselves.

On Saturday afternoon, Margaret and Ellie sat down for tea near two of the Irish women their own age. The Mayo girls were dressed similarly in simple skirts with white blouses, knit cardigans and black button boots.

"We're glad to meet you," Margaret began. "Where are you from in Ireland?"

"My name is Mary Mangan, and this is Delia Lynch," Mary offered. "We're from Lahardane in the parish of Addergoole. We're going to Chicago, where we'll stay in a rooming house with Annie's Aunt Kitty. She said she'll help us all find jobs."

"I'm Ellen Kelly," Ellie piped up.

"And, I'm Margaret Mannion," Margaret added. "Our last names are so much alike, Mary."

The two smiled at one another, as Margaret went on. "I'm also traveling with my fiancé Martin Gallagher. He's been in America for nearly 12 years and owns a store in New York."

She gestured toward Martin, sitting at the next table with Tom K. Martin waved in return, but quickly looked down to concentrate on the fresh fruit and warm tea. Margaret and Martin spoke frequently about the fine china and silver cutlery used on third class aboard the Titanic. The food and the accommodations were unlike anything they'd experienced in Ireland.

"That is such a coincidence," Mary said. "I'm also engaged to be married when I get to Chicago. And, I've been in America for seven years," she paused, unsure how much to share with her new friends. "My sister, Ellen, and I were home to visit my poor mother; she's been sick. Ellen decided to stay behind."

Ellie grasped Mary's hand. "I thought about not coming."

"I hope we don't come to regret the trip," Delia interrupted. "I met a strange man in Lahardane the night before we left for Cobh. He told me there will be a disaster, that hundreds would die, but I will survive."

Mary pointed at her old friend. "Stop with the gloomy stories, Delia. Let's talk about something more pleasant. Tell her about your hat."

"My mother took me to Hickson's Shop in Crossmolina for my first hat and gloves. She told me when we get to New York, to always wear them, as all the ladies in America wear hats and gloves."

Mary reached down to open the watch on a chain around her neck. Her diamond solitaire ring caught the electric lights and Ellie's attention. From inside the locket, Mary's photograph smiled back and her name was engraved in a fine script. "A gift from my beloved," she told Ellie.

It was hard to find quiet time alone with Martin on the huge ship. Ellie seemed pasted to her side during meals, and walks on deck were limited for third-class passengers.

Martin found an emergency crew ladder in the aft section of the ship, leading up to the shelter deck inhabited mainly by sailors. They spent hours there one day, wrapped in blankets and soaking up the sun. It had been a mild winter and the deep blue waters of the North Atlantic stretched as far as she could see.

"It's like another planet," she said, looking up at the narrow bit of a crescent moon. "I feel like we're all alone out here, not another person on earth but us."

"Don't forget, this is my third voyage across this ocean," Martin said.

"In just a few days, we'll be in America. My sister's husband will meet us at the dock and ferry us to White Plains. I can't wait for you to see the store!"

"I sold $300 in yard goods in January alone," Martin couldn't help but brag. "With you by my side, I'm sure we can pay off the mortgage on the building even sooner. You've such a head for numbers."

Margaret snuggled closer beneath the heavy White Star blanket. "I'm sure my papa would be glad to know my 8th grade education wasn't wasted on a girl."

Martin kissed the tip of her turned-up nose, then traveled up to kiss her eyelashes, one deep, ocean-blue light at a time. Their mouths lingered achingly long on one another until her lips parted and his tongue darted in to explore her teeth's biting edge.

Margaret had kissed a man before, but never like this. Her tongue lashed out to fence with his, as their bodies began to meld together.

Martin's hands, once firmly attached to his own belt, strayed across to her waist. They memorized each stitch in her blouse, circling up to find her breast. He kneaded softly.

The last 12 years alone in America had been hell, but Martin was no virgin. Tall and handsome, he'd never told Margaret he hadn't sown some wild oats before they met, but now he was ready to settle down. Three more weeks was a very long time to wait, when you were this sure.

Margaret's hands roamed across his broad back more urgently now. His weight atop hers shouldn't feel this good. She trembled as she felt his lips graze her shoulder.

She pulled her head back to gaze deeply into the eyes of the man who would be her husband. His scruffy beard tickled her chin. He'd let the beard grow out since departing Queensland and she liked it.

Her kiss was her solemn vow, to have and to hold. She drew a deep breath and withdrew. She had come so close, too close to let it go now.

"May 10th," she whispered into his ear. "Less than a month and we pledge our vows before God and family. Then, I'm all yours, body *and* soul."

Martin drew a ragged breath, then released his hold on her.

"You're so beautiful," he said. "Body and soul."

16

Saturday, on a walk about the ship, Martin and Margaret had sneaked into the public area normally reserved to first-class passengers on the main deck and their rooms below.

Martin had made friends with an Irishman in service to White Star, earning his passage as a steward, by waiting on the first-class passengers — offering trays of wine and sweet treats to the Sloanes, the Guggenheims and the gregarious Molly Brown.

Margaret had read about the first-class passengers and their accommodations in English newspapers. She loved the gossip below deck about the servants hired to walk dogs and the fancy food they ate up top.

"Meet Stephen," Martin said, when he introduced his fiancée to the server that morning, with a Cheshire grin. Margaret was surprised to see he had trimmed his beard and mustache much closer than she'd ever seen him wear it. "He needs some help with the cocktail hour in the main saloon. I've trimmed my hair to fit in."

Margaret tilted her head. "Saloon?"

"Salon," Stephen corrected his new friends. "Follow me."

He handed each of them a white jacket and black pants, indicating a dressing room hidden neatly behind the door to the kitchen. After a quick change, they scrambled up a ladder in the rear of the ship and followed Stephen's lead to pick up a tray of champagne flutes before entering the salon by the grand staircase.

The three weaved their way down the curving stairs from both sides. The stairs alone were dizzying, descending down seven of the ship's 10 decks, with oak paneling, bronze cherubs and paintings along the walls.

Margaret's hands trembled with the weight of the heavy tray full of drinks. Stephen sidled closer to show her an easier way to carry the tray, centering the bottle of champagne, pouring one drink at a time and offering glasses from one side and then the other to maintain balance.

Within minutes, the three servers met halfway down the stairs on a wide landing and took up their posts. Margaret stared up in wonder at the dome of wrought iron and glass that admitted natural light to the stairwell.

From behind her she heard a young woman's voice, "Jack, sweetie," she purred. "Be a darling and fetch me a drink."

Margaret whirled to see Jack Sloane and the much younger voice commanding his presence at her side. Madeline Sloane was as pretty as the newspaper accounts of her wedding described her. Dressed from head to toe in silver, her beaded gown swelled slightly below the waist when she turned to survey the crowd below.

Margaret drew in a sharp breath. "She's pregnant," she whispered in Martin's ear, just as Colonel Jack Sloane stepped forward to order a drink.

"Excuse me, young man," the business tycoon said to Martin. "Could you bring me a sparkling water for my wife?"

When Martin didn't hurry off, Sloane barked, "Now!"

Martin nodded obsequiously and took Margaret's arm. He nodded toward Stephen and shuffled her back to the top of the stairs and the hidden ladder at the rear of the ship.

"That was too close," he said, once they'd caught their breath three decks below. "Let's get these coats back to the dressing room before we get caught."

He and Margaret giggled at their adventure up top as he described it, for hours. But Margaret was left wondering, who were the Sloanes and what were they like?

She had seen one of their servants walking the Airedale pup Kitty and the young woman had bragged of the life her mistress led above deck. The cabins she described on the first deck were sumptuous — patterned after the Ritz Hotel in London, with sitting rooms and adjoining quarters for the richest passengers' servants. Other staff would room below in steerage, alongside the Irish, Russian and German immigrants.

"The food is like nothing you've ever seen," the dog walker

told Margaret. "I know we have three square and indoor plumbing below, but this dog eats better than that. The Sloanes choose from six courses at every meal, *seven* cheeses and *three* desserts."

That morning, Margaret had enjoyed stewed figs, a luxury she'd seldom had at home. At tea, there were cold meats and cheeses, stewed figs and rice. How could one person eat six courses? What a waste, she decided.

Her earlier admiration of Madeline Sloane began to sour, like the sumptuous meals they ate, too rich for her to stomach.

Chapter Three

Margaret snuggled deeper beneath the covers in her bunk, daydreaming about America — the store, the wedding, fine china and good food. She hadn't once looked back since boarding the ship.

Ellie's soft snore and the steady rocking of the boat lulled her to sleep. Just then, a grinding crash tore from the forward part of the ship where Martin was sleeping. It was as if they'd run aground — followed by a tearing sound. She jerked up when the ship let out a huge roar, shuddered and stopped dead in her tracks.

As she swung her feet out onto the cold floor, Margaret's thoughts raced, and she felt the first alarm bells go off in her head. She was determined not to panic. She stood up to check on Ellie in the upper bunk.

The usually staid Ellie looked confused. There were no windows and Margaret needed to see more. Suddenly, the cabin was no longer a refuge, but a trap.

Margaret scanned the room for her robe but couldn't see it anywhere. She panicked and seized a navy-blue White Star Line blanket to cover herself as she and Ellie rushed into the hall. Margaret frowned as they met Martin and the Toms coming from the men's cabins in the forward areas. Already the hallways were packed with bodies, and panic began to spread.

"Grab a proper wrapper and wait by the stairs," Martin

warned the girls. "I'll see if I can find out what happened."

But Margaret was too keyed up and too frightened to return to her room. Some of the passengers were congregating in the third-class dining saloon, praying, crying and asking God to help them.

An older man with whiskey on his breath leaned too close to Margaret, his eyes angry. "They lay there and yell, never lifting a hand to help themselves. They have lost their own willpower and expect God to do all the work for them."

Margaret waited anxiously by the bottom of the stairs for Martin to return. She turned to suggest to Ellie they start up the stairs, but she was nowhere to be seen.

The stairs were crowded with second- and third-class passengers trying to move upstream. Margaret searched frantically for her friend.

"Ellie! Ellie!" she called out. "I'm over here," Ellie was standing back in a hallway, clutching the hand of a small child.

"Whose child is this?" Margaret asked. "And why are you holding onto him?"

Ellie floundered. Just as she opened her mouth to answer, a mother with two other small children pushed her way through the crowd. "Thank you for holding Seamus' hand. I'm so overwhelmed."

She put out a hand, "I'm Mrs. O'Mara. We're meeting my husband in America," she told Margaret. The woman smiled weakly. "This is our first time apart and I'm not sure what to do."

Inwardly quaking, Margaret smiled and nodded at the woman, touched her shoulder and promised to see them to America safely. Ellie continued to nod at her sentiments, but Margaret could see she wanted to run back to their room.

Finally, Martin returned. "It's important we go up to the deck," he said. "The stewards are distributing life jackets back there. I brought one for each of you."

"Put them on, now," he shouted.

Margaret heard the concern in his voice. The third-class passengers began to argue among themselves. A lifeboat drill planned for that morning was canceled and no one was sure where to go or what to do. She and Ellie struggled with the bulky vests, as Martin located four more for the family they'd adopted. The three women helped the children with their vests as they looked around, unsure where to go next.

Water was beginning to pour into the lower levels. The two Toms were quick to mimic Martin's self-assurance and had already fitted their jackets tightly about them. The three men grabbed one another's hands and were carried up the stairs by the forward motion of the other passengers. Martin held tight to Margaret and she dragged Ellie and the O'Mara family up the stairs behind her.

Bells clanged furiously from the decks below, as they worked their way through a maze of hallways and staircases toward the lifeboats. As water rushed into the boiler rooms, the steam hissed and moaned from every direction.

Seamus stumbled as the crowd surged and his mother started to cry. "St. Michael," she cried out. "Save me."

Margaret slapped her. "You have to be strong," she said. "For the children." The mother's eyes widened, but she nodded and wiped away the tears.

Martin led his group away from the crowd, carrying Seamus on his back as he mounted the emergency ladders they'd discovered earlier. The two Toms carried the other children, behind Ellie, Margaret and Mrs. O'Mara.

Their arms and legs ached as they mounted the final stairway to the boat deck. Here, the gate was manned by two Titanic crew members with batons. One old and the other young, they were both broad-chested with military-style uniforms, White Star caps and badges.

"First- and second-class passengers will board the lifeboats first," the older one shouted over the din from the boilers. The harsh, deafening noise of high-pressure steam made normal conversation impossible.

"Lifeboats?" Margaret cried. "What's happening to the ship?"

The crewman responded with a slap of his baton against his palm. "Stand down!"

The younger crewman's chin trembled, even as he ordered the others to step back. He was frozen to the spot he'd been assigned, his eyes overly bright and his movements jerky.

Martin could see he was clearly afraid, but he didn't have time to talk. He reached through the gate and grabbed the man by his collar. "If you're boarding lifeboats, it's women and children first," he demanded. "Make way for these fine Irish women."

The boy blinked rapidly in the face of Martin's demands. His face was ashen, and his breath came in short bursts. He fought back tears with anger. "Women and children only." He gave in as he stepped aside for Margaret, Ellie and the others to follow.

The older crewman grudgingly agreed. He didn't want a fight with Martin. He was used to the third-class passengers stepping back and waiting their turn. Martin was different, assured-but-calm in his difference.

Mrs. O'Mara dragged Seamus and one lady carried an infant swaddled in a pink blanket. Margaret and Ellie each pulled one youngster along.

As the couples parted, Tom Kilgannon shoved his green cable-knit sweater into Ellie's arms. "Be safe," he said.

If Margaret weren't so frightened, she would have cheered for her friend. She stepped aside to make space for the other mothers and children as they swarmed onto the top deck.

She shivered as icy winds cut through her gown and the blanket she'd taken from their cabin below. As they worked their way forward, she saw a group of boys playing football with the ice chunks now strewn across the fore deck. Their cheers mixed with the shouting from every direction.

Surely the situation wasn't as bad as the stewards made it out to be. The children were still playing, not loading on to the lifeboats.

Just then, flares gave the night a festive appearance, like fireworks on New Year's Day. Another explosion lit up the sky bringing attention to the chaos below.

Seamus' fingers tightened on Margaret's hand with the flare's crash. He screamed wildly, as his mother ran ahead and was swallowed up by the crowd. "Seamus," his mother cried, as she fought against the crowd between her son and herself. "Please, someone help me."

Margaret dove into the crowd. "Don't let go," she shouted back at Ellie. "Don't let go!"

Margaret kept her eyes glued to the back of the woman's head—the woman she'd met only minutes earlier and promised so much. As the crowd surged and swayed, Margaret lost sight of her completely.

She stopped to get her bearings and the others pushed against her. She had to find the children's mother. She'd given her word.

Suddenly, Mrs. O'Mara was by her side in the crowd again, sobbing. "Seamus, Sarah. Stay with me!" she wailed, then pinched off her tears.

From near the boats, Margaret heard a new sound, one that hadn't carried to the decks below. The ship's bands played *Alexander's Ragtime Band.* The cheerful melodies were meant to ward off full blown panic among the passengers. It felt like they were dancing while Rome burned.

The front of the ship was tilting much lower in the water now. The family struggled to make it to the boats near the center of the portside. Her rubber-soled boots gripped the slippery deck as she fought her way forward to the middle. It went against everything she knew to walk away from the aft of the ship, as it lifted out of the water.

The smell of the ice reminded Margaret of an underground cavern she had explored as a child. The memories of the darkness and closed spaces made her shiver.

She held tight to her best friend's hand and herded the others along, as they pushed their way to the portside of the Titanic and waited in line. A false smile plastered on her face, Margaret's gaze darted from one side to the other. She started when she thought she heard someone call her name.

There was no music to be heard now above the whistles and screams from the ship and her passengers.

Just ahead, Margaret could see several first-class ladies boarding a lifeboat. There was room for about a dozen more, plus the baby, of course. With the mother and children now ahead of her, she and Ellie would not make the cut for this boat, but there would be others. She closed her eyes and prayed.

As they neared the front of the queue, she forced the more timid Ellie ahead, while she glanced back regularly for Martin and the other two men. She clutched the blanket tighter around her shoulders and toyed with the necklace Martin had given her on their engagement.

As the lifeboat hit the water, the crowd moved restlessly forward to board a second boat. Finally, it was the young mother's turn to board the lifeboat with her three children. As they stepped back to allow the family to board, Jack and Madeline Sloane quickly came forward.

They'd been waiting in the warm salon, sharing drinks and smoking cigarettes as Sloane devised the best strategy for survival. He was insistent they remain on the ship until the last minute. When an officer asked them to evacuate earlier, he told him, "We are safer here than in that little boat."

But now, Sloane could see the situation had changed dramatically. Above the waterline, there was little evidence of collision, but he saw where the bow of the ship was much lower, and the Titanic listed alarmingly to the starboard side. It was also becoming increasingly apparent there were not enough lifeboats for everyone.

As the crew delicately handed Madeline over to the man in the boat, Sloane shouted to be heard above the din. "I must accompany my wife. She's in a delicate condition."

First Officer Lightroller was polite, but firm. "Sorry, sir.

Women and children only."

Madeline gasped and tried to clamber out of the boat and return to her husband on ship.

"Oh, for God's sake, be brave and go!" he admonished. "I'll get a seat in another boat!"

Sloane stepped back into the crowd, but he kept his eyes on his young bride.

Margaret and Ellie were next. As they clambered aboard, they saw Delia Lynch from County Mayo.

"I forgot my hat and gloves," Delia said. "I have to go back." She climbed out of the boat and ran back down the stairs toward the lower decks.

As she left, some men attempted to rush the boat to take her seat. Lightroller fired three warning shots in the air, but two men jumped on board as the boat was dropped in fits and jerks to the glassy sea below.

Margaret jumped at the shots, but she held her place on the middle bench. While the crewman wanted to force the men out of the boat, she and Ellie fought for their position.

"We can't force them into the water," she argued. "They'll die."

Already, Margaret was shivering in the frigid night air. As the yeoman worked to loosen the lifeboat's lines from the doomed ship, the women struggled to maintain balance in the rough waters beside the doomed ocean liner.

Just then, a giant wave washed across the boat deck, sweeping two collapsible boats into the sea. Lightroller abandoned his post and dove from the top of the officers' quarters into the water after it.

He felt the cold of a thousand knives being driven into his body as he entered the sea. All around him, he could hear every emotion amplified and mingled — fear, despair, agony, resentment and blind anger. Most of those around him died on impact, but he made his way into the collapsible.

The crewman in Margaret's boat shouted for help in getting away from the Titanic, before they were drawn down into her vortex. The two men, Ellie and Margaret helped to row away toward still waters. Their arms and their lungs ached with their labors and the bitterly cold night air, but they rowed frantically to save themselves and the others with them.

In the inky blackness of the North Atlantic, those in the boats watched helplessly as the Titanic continued to disintegrate. Margaret watched as the forward deck dipped into the water and the stern rose, like the lighter end of a child's seesaw. The three propellers hung there, inarticulate buzz saws levitating above the ship.

Margaret searched the boat deck frantically for Martin. She saw a large knot of men gathered 'round the Catholic priest in the stern, clinging to the ship's rails as they clutched their rosaries.

"We have to go back. We have to save them," she cried, but the crewman on board was afraid the lifeboat would be capsized.

One by one, the boilers exploded out the ruptured sides of the ship. Ellie clutched her friend's arm as the Titanic's lights flickered once and then permanently went out.

Suddenly, the ship shuddered and split loudly into two pieces, cracked down the middle like a giant egg. The hull split, the boat bellowed and burped up her dead from within.

The women watched the bow of the ship go down into the roiling black water in minutes, but the stern remained afloat for a few short minutes, rolling to one side as if to protect their eyes from the awful spectacle that followed.

Margaret looked away from the spot where Martin had stood only minutes earlier, pulling Ellie's head into her shoulder. She heard a huge gulp, as if a giant sea monster had swallowed a whale. When she looked back, the Titanic was gone.

The waters were filled with debris and hundreds of people who had jumped or fallen into the frigid waters. As the Titanic broke up below them, huge chunks of debris bobbed to the surface — beams, doors, furniture, paneling and chunks of cork from the bulkheads.

The dismal moaning sound came from all sides as the throng of victims called for help. It was both horrifying and supernatural. Slowly, the splashing of those in the water lessened and died.

The women in the lifeboats at a distance were silent. There was no way they could look away and no way to escape the tragedy playing out before their very eyes.

"We have to go back," Madeline cried. "Perhaps we can save someone."

"No!" the crewman said. "It's too dangerous."

Margaret and Eleanor huddled next to Madeline, as the younger woman wept. "It'll be okay," Margaret said robotically. Deep in her heart, below the frozen soul that had watched Martin die, she knew nothing would ever be okay again.

Within minutes, Margaret was shaking uncontrollably. Tears were frozen on her cheeks; her lips were numb and she felt faint. She moved from side to side on the boat's bench, trying to avoid frostbite.

Ellie had worn a wrapper into the hall when the women first recognized something was at odds. Without a robe or a wrap, Margaret had only the life vest, the blanket and the other women's bodies for warmth. She began to cast about for another chance to escape the cold; a way to escape the dark treachery of the midnight ocean.

Margaret could see Madeline was agitated; she moved restlessly on the seat next to her. The younger woman's pale skin was clammy, sweating despite the frozen temperatures. She moved closer to Madeline and put her arm around the girl, singing softly and speaking tenderly as she would've comforted Celia from a bad dream.

"I'm pregnant, not an invalid," came Madeline's sharp retort. "I've been treated like a child most of my life. I don't need that from you, too."

She stopped for a moment. "I'm not sure I can go it alone. I shouldn't have to."

"You're going to be fine," she said. "You're also not alone in this world." Her eyes dropped to Madeline's belly.

Madeline sniffled and rubbed her eyes. "I want to be strong; I really do. Cosseting wasn't my choice; it was my mother's."

"Well, your mother isn't here," Margaret said. "You are an adult and about to become a mother. Your life is your own."

Now Margaret's lip began to shake in earnest and the hand she held with Madeline's was sweating.

"I'm s-s-sorry to scold you in the middle of the o-ocean," she smiled weakly. "Let's make a pact, to be strong together."

Madeline slipped a smaller fur wrap from beneath her beaver coat and offered it to Margaret. "Deal," she said, but Margaret demurred.

"We are Sloanes," Madeline insisted. "Jack's grandfather was a fur trader, so it's no skin off my back."

She grinned in wicked black humor. "Please, take it."

It was no time to stand on false modesty. She wrapped the fur tightly around her as the women huddled together, their arms interlinked. It was hours before they saw more flares explode in the night sky miles away.

"It's a ship!" Ellie shouted. "They're signaling they've seen us!"

But it was another hour before the Carpathia neared the lifeboats, crowded together like a hungry flock of birds. The three women waited anxiously as two other boatloads were rescued from the icy ocean.

Madeline was one of the first taken up from their boat. As she was hoisted up in a sling, another passenger jeered. "La-de-dah, the rich ladies are still first-class."

Margaret turned on the attacker. "Give her a break. She's only 20 years old and she's pregnant. There'll be room for everyone."

By late morning, all of the survivors had been rescued

from the lifeboats. Ellie and Margaret didn't see Madeline again as the Carpathia returned to New York.

The captain had given Madeline his own quarters while the remaining passengers were shown to spaces on deck, handed a blanket and a bowl of lukewarm porridge.

While others celebrated small reunions with others they knew from the Titanic, most were mourning their dead who failed to appear on the rescue ships. Now that she had a warm wrap and warm food in her belly, Margaret thought she would be okay, but she continued to tremble. She couldn't stop crying. Ellie held her close and mopped at her tears.

Then, as the sun rose higher in the sky, the two friends dozed quietly against one another.

Margaret pulled the fur stole closer as the two women huddled on a bench near a brightly burning fire for warmth. The Carpathia had made a brief stop at Pier 59, owned by the White Star Line, to drop off the lifeboats from the Titanic, then traveled a few blocks south to dock at the Cunard Pier, Pier 54.

Margaret gawked at the throng of people gathered to meet them. Details of the disaster were still scarce, a reporter told her as he begged to hear her story. Madeline refused to talk to anyone.

As the thought of Martin's death settled like a giant boulder on her heart, she withdrew from the pier to a world of her own making. Her mind was still reeling from the events of the last four days, but she could not yet form words around the experience. She doubted she ever would. Within minutes, sleep overtook her.

"Miss?" A tall stranger in a uniform paused before them. His height blocked the sun.

"Miss Mangan?"

Margaret didn't reply.

"Are you Miss Magnan and Miss Kelly?" The man bent

down toward Ellie now.

Ellie's soft voice barely carried up to his ears, with the wind at her back. "Yes, I'm Ellen Kelly. This is Margaret Mannion."

"We are with the Travelers Aid Society and the Women's Relief Committee. We're taking a roll call of the survivors. We need to speak with and confirm your identity."

Margaret looked up at Ellie and shook her head. "Where are we?" she asked. "Where is Martin and the two Toms?"

"Can you spell your names for us?" The worker repeated.

"Kelly, K-E-L-L-Y. Ellen, E-L-L-E-N. That's me."

Ellie glanced at Margaret. When her friend didn't respond, she placed her hand gently on Margaret's and looked up.

"This is Margaret Mannion. M-A-N-N-I-O-N. Margaret, M-A-R-G-A-R-E-T."

The officer looked puzzled. "Margaret Mannion? Not Mary Mangan?"

"I haven't seen Mary," Ellie replied for her. "Oh, God, no! Mary wasn't on our boat. I haven't seen her since teatime yesterday."

From across the pier, Ellie heard someone calling out to her. It was Delia Lynch.

"How did you get here?" Ellie asked. "I was frightened when you left the lifeboat for your hat and gloves."

"The water had filled the deck where Mary and I were staying," Delia said. "I rushed back up to the boat deck, but all the lifeboats were gone. I climbed a rope and fit into the last lifeboat to leave the ship."

The smaller, swarthier worker turned to Delia. His breath smelled dark and damp - a whirlpool of stale fish and whiskey.

"We're going to need you to speak to us, miss," he mumbled. "There's been some confusion. We show two third-class passengers, Mary Mangan and Margaret Mannion. One is missing and we presume this is the other. Do you know the whereabouts of Miss Mangan?"

Delia nodded and started crying again. "I haven't been

able to find Mary."

"Thank you. Miss Lynch, was it? We've reported her missing and notified her family of the loss."

Ellie shivered again, but not from the cold. She felt as if a ghost had walked over her grave. "We spoke to Mary yesterday, Margaret. Don't you remember?"

Again, a head shake and a dull nod. Ellie turned to the ship's officers. "Is there a doctor nearby?" She asked. "I think we should have someone take a look at my Margaret."

Darkness was settling over the city as Margaret and Ellie found a bed at St. Vincent's Hospital. The nurses brought each of the women a fresh, white gown and tucked them in between clean sheets, plumping up a real feather pillow behind their heads.

Then they checked their temperature and blood pressure, brought more warm food and insisted the women rest quietly.

By the time she fell asleep again, Margaret was completely out of tears. She had seen Martin on the ship, praying the rosary just before the Titanic cracked in two and plunged to the bottom of the sea.

She knew he was dead, but she still hoped his body would be recovered, so she could give him a proper burial. When the McKay disgorged the last of the bodies in Halifax, Martin was not among them.

She slept fitfully, imagining Martin just below the water's surface, reaching up to her. His arms were cold and wet and grasping.

Margaret woke up from her nap to see Ellie in the bed next to hers.

"I know I need to write to my parents and Martin's family," she said. "But I just can't bring myself to put pen to paper. It's as if writing it down makes it real."

"We can wait until we get out of the hospital," Ellie consoled her. "My family is expecting us in a week's time. I'll help you with the letter to Martin's parents then."

Margaret hadn't heard Ellie's plan. "Maybe we should return to Ireland right away. What do we have to look forward to here with no husbands, no jobs, no friends?"

Ellie stared straight ahead. She had no husband or plans for one in the first place. "I planned to live with my sister's family all along."

She pressed her lips together tightly to stay quiet.

"I didn't mean anything," Margaret began. She swallowed hard and bit down on her lower lip as it began to tremble. Nothing she said anymore made sense. "I only meant... I was only thinking of myself. I'm sorry."

Ellie sighed again as she stared down at her feet, but she didn't apologize.

"I feel terrible that you've lost Martin. Of course, I wish it had never happened. But, it's too soon to make any big decisions. Let's make a pact. We'll live together and work hard to make money to send back home. If one of us were to marry, the other is free to go back home."

Weeks later, a representative of the White Star Line visited each of the survivors. He assured Margaret that Martin received a proper burial at sea. "There were not enough embalming supplies to bring everyone who had died back to America," he said. "As a sailor, I'm sure that's what I would've wanted."

Margaret's heart broke again. She would never again say goodbye to her beloved. Her chin quivered and she rolled away, hiding her face in her covers once again.

The next morning, Ellie marched to the front of the line near the nurse's desk and spoke briefly with the representatives of the survivor's charities. When she returned, her positive outlook seeped across the boundaries Margaret had erected around herself for protection.

"I've brought some documents the White Star Line would like us to sign," Ellen said. "They've offered $25 each to replace some of our things."

"In two weeks' time, we'll have a room downtown for as long as necessary," she said. "The senate has convened a hearing into the accident and requested all the survivors remain available until the investigation is complete. We may have to testify."

"No!" Margaret said. "I never want to talk about this again. With anybody, even you."

Margaret and Ellie glimpsed Madeline only one other time, as she was greeted at the pier in New York by a handsome young man in a three-piece suit. Beyond the suit, his facial features and coloring reminded her vividly of Martin. Probably because of the loss, she groaned inwardly. Every man from this point forward would compare unfavorably to her Martin.

The young man with Madeline strode forcefully ahead and looked the White Star officials in the eye. He spoke fast and louder than necessary, so everyone around could hear.

Margaret thought he looked to be about her age, but his manner made him appear much older. He was obviously too old to be Madeline's son — perhaps a brother or a cousin, she wondered aloud.

"That's Vincent Sloane," a bystander told her. "His picture is in all the newspaper accounts of the ship's sinking."

Margaret liked the young man's cut. He wore a well-tailored suit like he was born to wealth, but his face was strong. She decided then and there to swear off men altogether. It was the only way she could see to salve a broken heart.

DAILY SKETCH THURSDAY
19 APRIL 1912
OUT OF TOUCH
Long Period of Waiting for News of the Carpathia
THE STEERAGE PASSENGERS
NEW YORK WEDNESDAY NIGHT

To-day brought little fresh news of the survivors from the ill-fated Titanic, and the American continent is waiting with the most intense interest for the arrival of the Carpathia. According to an official statement issued by the Cunard Company the Carpathia is due here at eight o'clock to-morrow night, and not until un-looked for passengers have landed will it be possible to obtain reliable information as to how the great liner met her end.

Various imaginative stories have been printed here only to be contradicted or disproved by the shipping companies and the Marconi Company, who have been able to show that no such wireless messages have been received. The only real news to-day was of a negative character, and further emphasized that there can be no hope for anyone who is not on board the Carpathia.

For some time, there was considerable anxiety felt for the Cunarder's safety, for after yesterday's message from her commander, saying that he was groping his way cautiously through ice floes and bergs, communication with the ship ceased.

This proved to be due, however, to atmospheric disturbances and the fact that the Olympic, which had been acting as a relaying station between the Carpathia and the shore, had got out of wireless range. Eventually a reassuring message was received from the Sable Island wireless station stating that they had been in communication with the Carpathia, and later the White Star Line Company received the following message: "East of Ambrose 596 miles 11 p.m. Tuesday, all well."

Chapter Four

Vincent Sloane was the colonel's only son and heir apparent. He cared little for Madeline's grief. As far as he was concerned, she was a little gold digger.

Standing on the wayside a day later, the Sloanes boarded a private train, waiting to head south after the devastating news Jack Sloane was one of the first bodies to be identified by the captain of the McKay.

Colonel Sloane was dressed in a tailored suit, with monogrammed cuff links, *JJS*. He had $2,500 cash in his trouser pockets and a watch, engraved, "All my Love, Madeline," in his vest pocket. The watch was stopped at 2:28.

Vincent's smile began to waiver and he struggled to find the right words to address his stepmother. The loss he felt was his own. He quickly found a seat in the train's well-appointed private car, as far from Madeline as he could.

As the train picked up speed, Vincent leaned back in the velvet-covered seats. He ran one hand through his dark, curly hair and looked around. The accommodations were more luxurious than a commercial car and heavy drapes shielded his view from others, a feature he'd always found valuable in preserving his privacy.

Solitude was a trait Vincent valued. When he was a child, he spent a lot of time alone at their country home with the servants, while his parents traveled, often in opposite directions.

He had grown not only accustomed to being alone, he preferred it.

Now, staring at his shoes, Vincent forced himself to face the inevitable. When he first read of the Titanic's sinking, he tried rationalizing his loss. "No!" his secretary heard him shout from the inner office. When the pretty, young woman tried speaking to him about the telegram from the White Star Line, he asked to be left alone. Now, *the memories came flooding back.*

As a small boy, Jack and Vincent had been close. Since his parent's divorce just over a year ago, the pair had traveled, hunted together, planned for Vincent's ascension to the throne of Sloane Enterprises.

A slight young man, Vincent was never athletic, but his father didn't allow him to be bullied. Vincent learned French from his governess and self-defense from the under-butler.

His formal education at Eton was his mother's contribution. Sometimes, if he didn't score well on his reports home, his mother would not allow him to come home on holiday. She was a strict taskmaster, but Vincent felt he was a better man for it.

When he returned to New York in 1909, he was a firsthand witness to the rows between his parents. Ava Sloane's fiery temper was the polar opposite of his father's easygoing manner. Her decision to return to England and seek a divorce a year later was no surprise.

It was a surprise when his father started seeing a debutante named Madeline LaBlanc, from a new money family only months after Ava's departure. Vincent voiced his disapproval to his father, but only once. Jack Sloane became a man of wealth and power by taking charge of his future. He was tired of his harpy ex-wife, he told Vincent, and ready for someone younger, prettier, fresher.

His father was nearing middle age and thinking of retirement in 10-15 years, Vincent knew. If his father wanted a dalliance with a pretty little thing, he was entitled.

Their marriage was another setback. But it was the news of Madeline's pregnancy that blew Vincent back on his heels. Another heir, especially a boy, could pose a threat to his position, his father's love and especially to his inheritance.

Vincent leaned forward in his cushioned seat and turned his back to Madeline's sniffles. His eyes were cold and flat. If there was one thing Vincent couldn't stand, it was a weak woman.

Feeling as if he might vomit, he left the car quickly to stand on the platform between cars outside. He spit the burning saliva from his throat, but disgust left a sour taste in his mouth as he imagined his father's last hours.

Shivering in the biting spring air of the east coast, he rubbed the back of his neck and arms as if to erase the chill within. Then, he slammed his fist into the iron railing and began to sob.

Alone on the train, Madeline Sloane pretended to be sleeping to avoid conversation with anyone, especially her stepson, Vincent. She was sick and tired of being sick and tired. The clickety-clack of the train car's wheels against the track gave her a sense of security, and the covered windows gave her privacy. She pulled her fur coat tightly about her and withdrew into its familiar cocoon.

Only 20 years old, she had grown up as an active woman with interests outside her home, much to the dismay of her mother. While Madeline played tennis, Sylvia LeBlanc set up French lessons, dress fittings and tea parties. When Madeline suggested a year abroad, her mother took to her bed for three days.

Sylvia knew her daughter would be likely to find a husband in a year, or perhaps even two years, but society was all about coming out socially at the *right* time and snaring the *right* husband. When she heard Colonel Jack Sloane was on the market, she arranged for him to be at the parties her daughter attended and to dance with Madeline at her debutante ball.

Alone in her room, still carrying the doll-like, pink vestiges of her childhood, Madeline prepared for the ball in tears. "I feel like a walking wedding cake."

Festooned with white organza, yards of pink and white ribbon and topped with a large floral piece on the bodice, Madeline shrunk inward, trying to make herself less obvious. The elaborate gown already overwhelmed her small, trim body. Her lady's maid had spent hours with an iron fresh from the fireplace, pressing strands of hair into recalcitrant curls draped down her back.

Later, seated alone near the edge of the crowd, she tapped her foot out of time with the stringed quartet playing in the background. As she clenched and unclenched her fists, she took a deep breath before answering the frequent questions of a man lingering near her elbow all evening.

Jack Sloane was old enough to be her father. The silly grin on his face belied the fortune Sylvia had described to her in excruciating detail before the ball began. He leaned into her every word, and when they sat down for a light supper, he sat so close their knees touched.

Madeline was daydreaming about the cute new tennis pro at the private court where she played, when the Colonel spoke up, "Madeline? Would you like that?"

She looked up just in time to catch her mother's knowing glance. She had to step up her game to escape her mother's iron fist. She broke into a wide smile and plumbed the depths of her brain for some witty commentary that wouldn't give away her complete lack of what he was talking about.

A flush crept up her face as she touched Sloane's arm. As she raised her eyebrows and tilted her head toward his, she felt a sense of power. She dropped her eyes a second time and toyed with the diamond droplet that dangled near her décolletage. He was smitten and with very little effort on Madeline's part, they were engaged to be married in less than six months' time. The 19-year-old had found an escape hatch from her mother.

Jack petitioned the church for an annulment of his first

marriage, so he and Madeline could be married in the church. Image is everything, he had agreed with Madeline's mother. All his life, Jack had been schooled in maintaining the family's reputation in society and in the Episcopal Church. Madeline was adamant the ceremony be held in a church, any church as long as it wasn't Catholic. In the end, considerable force, applied by a heavy stack of money in one minister's hand, did the trick.

Sloane was ready to have some fun, stepping out with a pretty young thing on his arm and spending money like there was no tomorrow. He was thrilled to rid himself of the shrew he'd married as a young man and pleased Madeline seemed to find him attractive.

The couple was married in a quiet ceremony in the bride's home within a year of their meeting. The teenage bride wore white, of course, but the dress was vastly different from the one she'd worn only a few months earlier at the debutante ball. The gown was form-fitting and ended just above her ankles. Silver sandals glittered on her toes and a tennis bracelet, a gift from the groom, reflected like diamonds in her eyes.

Her dark hair was now cut short in a fashionable bob and she wore a sequined headband around her forehead, attached to a short veil.

During the reception, Madeline toyed with her wedding ring, a simple gold band. At one point, it seemed restrictive on her finger, so she removed it and looked inside. A script circled the inside, "Yours alone, always and forever."

Suddenly, the ring was less restrictive and more about freedom. Madeline was quite sure she could control Jack Sloane with a wiggle of her ring finger. At that moment, she vowed to retain a power she'd never had with her mother.

Men were so much easier to manage, she thought, as the honeymoon began on Jack's yacht and extended into six months in Europe. During the entire time, Madeline learned to enjoy her freedom and the leisure time at her command.

She stretched luxuriously in the bridal suite atop the five-star Ritz Hotel along the Champs-Elysees in Paris. The feel of Egyptian cotton sheets and silken comforters topped with heavy velvet robes against her bare skin heightened the appeal.

Her much richer, much older husband seemed to enjoy her surprising sexuality and delighted in her charms, if she offered, never when she did not. In this new world, Madeline learned, sex was power, and she held the cards in this relationship.

But, when Madeline became pregnant, Jack became more recalcitrant. "A Sloane heir must be born in New York City," he had insisted. The colonel booked passage on the largest, most expensive steamship available, the Titanic. Madeline quietly acquiesced, as she did with chosen few things her husband suggested, knowing her strength lay ahead with Jack's heir.

Madeline chafed at the confinement of her pregnancy. She'd celebrated the ability to travel at her leisure, drink champagne until midnight and sleep until noon. Carrying Jack's brat inside her ended all that.

The night the huge ship shuddered to her last stop, Madeline was alone in her room, uncomfortable with her growing belly and grating at Jack's over-attentive manner. The four walls of the luxury suite paneled in a heavy wood and the canopy across the bed she now shared, were closing in like a prison cell.

She couldn't say she was glad her husband was dead, but Madeline was certainly happy to be both independent and independently wealthy. On Thursday afternoon, Madeline knew she would meet with Jack's attorney for the reading of the will and, on Friday morning, she would be rid of Vincent. The ungrateful bastard, she thought bitterly.

Since their return to the city, the two had constantly been at odds. Madeline needed a new wardrobe, all in white French crepe. She was a young, rich widow, so she refused to wear black. Her pre-pregnancy wardrobe, the one her mother had delivered to their Fifth Avenue mansion, no longer fit her burgeoning belly. And, the many lovely pieces she'd bought in Europe for the summer in the city, were at the bottom of the ocean.

A dressmaker and a milliner had been to Sloane House already. The dressmaker suggested she break with convention, especially to alleviate discomfort in warm weather. "Surely if someone of such social standing could break with conventions, others will follow," she said.

The milliner agreed. "Mrs. Sloane, I can design for you a becoming widow's cap, with lighter combinations of black and white, with dull black roses and a dull black draw hat, trimmed with white crepe or tulle. Veils may also be trimmed with white crepe while in mourning."

Madeline was quick to agree, ordering various nets for pretty summer gowns in combination with thin silks and muslin. Unfortunately, the lady's maid didn't agree with her choices and had a hard time hiding her misgivings. Madeline's mother had chosen a lady's maid Madeline despised heartily. She avoided direct eye contact with the maid and tried to eavesdrop on her every conversation with Sylvia LeBlanc. She'd have her replaced immediately, but she was hamstrung until the funds from Jack's will were released.

With Jack's death, his assets were frozen, and Madeline was unsure how she might pay for the items she so desperately needed to continue her position in polite society. As the manager of the estate, Vincent had appropriated funds for a small party at the house for the officers and some higher-level crew members of the Carpathia to thank them for their timely rescue of 12 April.

Unsure of herself for the first time ever, she frowned as she looked down at her belly. She wrinkled her forehead and moved again to a more comfortable chair in the boudoir Jack had hired a designer to complete while they were absent on their honeymoon.

Because Madeline's mother told the designer her favorite color was pink, the comforter and bolsters were pink, the walls were lined with pink silk and the draperies gauzy fabric was the color of ripening strawberries. She felt like a little girl in her mother's home again, drowning in a strawberry milkshake.

Madeline had borrowed a larger dressing gown from her married sister and had a seamstress take it in on the top and let out the hem. But she was not willing to accept her sister's charity or her mother's orders for long.

"If I take a dress, next it will be a coming-out party and then another engagement," she told her maid. "Soon, she'll have me married again." She stomped her slippered foot.

As Madeline's Bentley pulled up in front of the lawyer's office, summer heat bore down on the pregnant girl. She was now eight months pregnant and wasn't feeling especially charitable in the close heat NYC was famous for. It was no wonder most of the Fortune 400 left the city for their country homes in the summer.

Vincent met Madeline at the lawyer's office. He'd arrived an hour earlier to consult with an attorney of the same firm, who handled the Sloane Enterprises' legal matters. James Bartlett, Esquire was agreeable with sharing the details of the will with the younger man before the reading.

Vincent smiled, like a cat with a saucer of cream, as he greeted his stepmother at the door. He was anxious to conclude the day's business so he could call his mother in England and report the good news. Often, on Vincent's weekly calls with his mother, she asked about Madeline and her bastard baby. Today, he hoped to let his mother know the usurper was put in her place.

Waiting for the secretary to bring coffee, Madeline shifted uncomfortably in her chair. Her eyes bore into the top of the Bartlett's head, as he shuffled the papers, hemmed and hawed. Finally, he looked up, first at Vincent and then, less warmly, at Madeline.

"The will was written about a year ago," Bartlett intoned. "Jack left everything to his two children, Vincent and Alice, with a codicil for future spouses and heirs, if they were to survive him."

Uneasily, he glanced again at Madeline. "As his wife at the time of his death, you will receive an annual allowance of $10,000 and may continue to occupy the mansion, commonly known as Sloane House. However, ownership of the home will remain with Sloane Enterprises, under corporate management. The allowance and the mansion revert to Vincent Sloane, if you were to remarry."

"For the love of Pete!" Madeline blurted out. "What about our baby?"

"Colonel Sloane allowed for guardianship of any future children to be vested in Mr. Sloane and within the same terms as the allowance, aforementioned."

Madeline found it difficult to catch her breath. Was she to be treated like a child once again? Under the care and tutelage of Jack's son, the insufferable Vincent?

As Jack's only son at the time the will was written, Vincent was awarded the lion's share of the Sloane fortune. He was also named chairman of the board of Sloane Enterprises and given full guardianship of *any* of his father's other heirs, including his sister Alice and the baby Madeline was carrying.

Bolting upright, Madeline whirled to leave. "Ass!" she hurled at Vincent, sitting calmly across from her. "This is not the end of my claim to Jack's estate. My son will not stand in line behind anyone, least of all you!"

"A good day to you, Madeline. May I offer you a ride home?"

Madeline's hand shot out and slapped his face. She stormed out the door, red-faced and seething.

As her handprint rose up bright and red on the cheek visible above his trim beard, Vincent struggled to maintain his cool. His smile tightened as he straightened his collar and pulled loose the crease in his pants.

He rose from his chair and turned to Bartlett. "Thank you, good sir. You've earned my father's recommendation in knowing which documents to bring forward and which ones to lose. Send me a bill."

Doors slammed and tempers flared, as Madeline returned to the mansion. A housemaid knew enough to get out of the way, but she wasn't fast enough. "You're fired!" Madeline yelled. "You probably helped set this up! Get out!"

She stomped up the stairs and into the master suite at the rear of the house, slamming the heavy door behind her. The windowpanes shuddered and a nearby Louis XIV chair rocked on its delicate white-painted legs.

Madeline threw herself down onto the blush-pink coverlet and began to sob, beating the pillow top and not even trying to stifle her cries.

"You stupid, blind, son-of-a-bitch," she screamed at the ceiling, hoping Jack was listening up there somewhere. Where were you when we married? Why didn't you think of me and our baby?"

Within hours, Madeline was all cried out and resting comfortably in her room, but she was determined to make things right. Her version of right, anyway.

She pulled a bell near the bed to call for the pretty, young Irish girl she'd hired a few days earlier to take care of the baby, when he arrived. She knew it would be a boy and she knew Jack would have wanted him to be properly provided for. She'd chosen the Irish girl, Emily, as a nanny. Her mother had always liked Irish servants, Madeline recalled. Her mother knew how to hire the right girls, the girls who knew how to serve a real lady.

Emily tapped softly at the door to Madeline's sitting room. "Yes, ma'am," she murmured.

"I'm in labor with the baby," Madeline said quietly. "Have

Roebken bring the car around."

Margaret lay back in bed as the nurse adjusted the feather pillows behind her head. Her room was filled with flowers, freshened on a daily basis by the nurse assigned to her care.

Two of the bouquets were from the Sloanes, a large bouquet of summer blooms, pink and blue carnations from Sloane Enterprises and Vincent had sent two dozen pink roses on his own. Madeline asked the orderly to remove the pink roses.

"What would Madame wish me to do with the flowers?" he asked.

"Throw them in the trash for all I care!"

Thank God, the room at Saint Joshua's was nothing like those at the public hospitals Madeline had visited with her mother for various charity events. There, two to three women shared a room while they labored to give birth. Babies roomed in with their mothers alongside an iron bedpost and chipped cradle.

Madeline's room was luxuriously furnished in heavy, dark wood and thick white linens, the bedding filled with the finest goose-down and crystal chandeliers hung at its center. A smaller, more antiseptic room served for Baby Jack's birth, but the minute the nurse whisked him away to be weighed and measured, Madeline was moved somewhere she could be more comfortable.

Just then, one of the nurses brought Baby Jack into the room. He was all cleaned up from the horrible, bloody birth process and his little bald head fairly shone. As the baby nestled close to Madeline's body, he made mewling noises and pursed his lips.

The nurse looked up at Madeline. "Will you need help learning to breastfeed?"

Madeline looked at her with dismay. "Do I look like a wet nurse?"

"I'll be right back, then." The nurse left the room for a bottle.

The baby began to cry, a weak gasping sound that alarmed his mother.

Madeline eyes darted around the room. She quickly fluttered her hands near the baby, hoping to distract him from his woes. Her pained stare only seemed to increase Baby Jack's unhappy tears, as he stiffened, and his face turned beet red.

Madeline's voice shook as she attempted a lullaby. She watched the clock nervously for the nurse's return, pulling her wrapper away from the baby's clutching fists and tearful sobs.

The nurse rushed in minutes later to take the baby to the nursery and a warm bottle. When his mother was more rested, she would return for diapering instructions. She doubted Madeline Sloane had ever seen a baby's bare arse, patted their back waiting for a burp or wiped up dribble.

Nurse Ansley shrugged and asked a secretary to ring up the Sloane mansion to have Madeline's nanny return. But, on arriving in the waiting room outside the nursery, she found Emily pacing anxiously.

The pretty, young woman had accompanied Mrs. Sloane to the hospital and seemed a common-sense type of girl. She told Ansley she had a child of her own and asked if she should remain until the baby was born, to give comfort to the young widow.

"Only immediate family are allowed in delivery," she told her. "Mrs. Sloane doesn't seem like the type to show weakness, but I think she'll need some help when they are dismissed."

"Why don't you come back later in the day, to see if there's anything else you can bring from home for the lady?"

On the floor near Emily's chair was a large carpetbag, packed with a personalized layettes; the baby's initials **JJS** embroidered in blue thread on each gown. His mother had not chosen a girl's name to match John Jacob Sloane VI's initials, as she was determined to give the colonel another male heir. Madeline had never forgiven Jack's cousin for naming their Son John

Jacob Sloane V before her own son was born.

Ansley handed Baby Jack and the small bottle of evaporated milk to Emily and waved her down the hall. "Room 12, on your right."

The Brooklyn Daily Eagle
Saturday November 9, 1912
THE SLOANE BABY'S
FINANCES

Brother Will Support Son,
Leaving His Millions to
Accumulate

Surrogate Fowler yesterday afternoon appointed Vincent Sloane, at his own request, general guardian of John Jacob Sloane VI, posthumous heir of the late Colonel John Jacob Sloane IV, for a period of fourteen years.

The young man, in his petition sets forth that it is his intention to mainly support his brother during his minority, and asks that only $10,000 per year of the income of the baby gets under the will of the Titanic hero, be paid to him for this support during the next three years, and that after three years no further sum be paid him. He also asks that the remainder of the income be allowed to accumulate, and reinvested until his brother reaches his majority.

The surrogate signed a decree authorizing an accumulative fund from the interest of the funds as petitioned for. At the end of fourteen years, Mr. Sloane may ask to be appointed guardian for a longer period. Under the law a guardian may only be appointed for a term of fourteen years at a time. At the end of which period the court has to review the guardianship.

If the baby's fortune, estimated at $3,000,000 at present is invested at four percent, it is estimated that young John Jacob Sloane will be the possessor of more than $6,000,000 when he reaches the age of 21.

Chapter Five

I t had been three months since Margaret and Ellie arrived in the city. Their move into her sister's apartment had not gone without its hitches. Cathleen welcomed them with open arms and showed them around the apartment with obvious pride. The pair followed her from a small living room into an even smaller bedroom.

"The children's pallets are rolled up in the closet there," Cathleen told Ellie. "If me and Robert aren't home at bedtime, just have them roll them out in the living room. Robert's gone out, scouring the neighborhood for a mattress you two can share."

"Where's the bathroom?" Margaret asked cautiously.

Cathleen opened the front door and pointed down the hall. "We share a bathroom with the others on this floor. The lock on the door works most days, but there's an old blue scarf hanging on a nail by the door. If the room's occupied, the rag's on the doorknob."

Robert and Cathleen O'Dey were raising six children on the fourth floor of a six-story walk-up in the Lower East Side. Margaret especially hated rolling out the old mattress Robert had found on the curb. There were large stains on the backside, making it apparent it was used hard by someone before her.

Bobby, the oldest O'Dey child, frightened Margaret. Nearly as tall as his father, Bobby hadn't seen the soapy side of a washcloth in weeks. He bragged about skipping school nearly every day and always came home reeking of tobacco.

Ellie was concerned Bobby might be running numbers for a loan shark at the corner shop, near the newsstand, but Cathleen would hear nothing of it.

The little O'Deys ran wild in the neighborhood after school, as well. Cathleen worked at a market more than a mile from the apartment building, leaving early to walk to work in the opposite direction as Robert's deliveries. Often, she wasn't home until after dark, only to spend hours in the kitchen, trying to feed 10 hungry mouths on two small salaries.

Dinner consisted of potatoes, an unidentifiable gray meat-like substance and cold gravy. If everyone was at home, they crowded 'round the dinner table in a free-for-all unlike anything Margaret had glimpsed growing up.

Dirty hands grabbed for a share of a sweet, if there was one. One time the youngest O'Dey -- Margaret could never remember all their names -- got an elbow to the eye, reaching for a dinner roll. Since Bobby was the biggest, he often took two and dared the littles to say anything about it.

"Dammit, Bobby!" Robert's voice boomed and everyone stopped moving. "If you don't keep your bloody mitts off the food, I'm gonna whup you."

Margaret swallowed hard and she looked over at Ellie. Her friend's chin trembled, and she blinked rapidly, but was rooted where she stood near the stove.

Ellie had hinted at problems at home between her mother and father, but Margaret didn't want to pry. Was Robert's outburst with his children, a regular occurrence at the dinner table Margaret witnessed, a reminder of Ellie's troubles at home?

Later that night, after the children were all asleep, Margaret tried to coax more information from Ellie. "Are you happy here? When we find jobs in the city, I think we can get an apartment of our own. Without so many people underfoot, I think things will quiet down for Cathleen and Robert, too."

Ellie drew her body closer and her face tightened. She couldn't meet Margaret's eyes. "Men like Robert, like my dad, they, um, they don't quiet down."

She sighed heavily and shrugged. "The reason I came to America was to get away from the shouting and the hitting. Now, we're smack dab back in the middle of it."

Margaret felt a heaviness in her chest. She reached over and hugged Ellie. "It's going to get better, soon, hon. Our luck has to turn, soon."

When they arrived in America, Ellie and Margaret had sworn to stay together, but Margaret was having second thoughts. The idea of living in a small apartment with this family was worse than her situation at home. Her only hope was for both women to find employment that would allow them to have a place of their own.

Cathleen suggested the two try to find a job at a biscuit factory on the edge of the West End. They traipsed two miles to the cold, dark factory the next day to find there was only one job available.

As they walked into the foreman's office, he apprised the pair -- his eyes traveling up and down from their head to their toes. "What are you girls here for? Didn't they tell you we need someone to do the hard work of a man?"

Ellie piped up. "Give us a chance, sir. We're both farm girls and used to working hard."

The foreman spit a wad of tobacco in the general direction of the spittoon in the corner. The shitty brown spit ricocheted off the baseboard and stained the wall and floor. "I like big girls who know how to work. Come by again in the morning and I'll give you a chance to prove yourself."

"But, what about my friend?" Ellie implored.

The foreman leered at Margaret. "The floor is full. We don't usually hire Irish girls. I'm making an exception for you because I don't think you'll be leaving to get married right away."

On the way back to Cathleen's apartment, Ellie was quiet. "I don't have to take the job," she said. "I can wait, and we'll find something together."

She was appalled at the foreman's behavior, but she knew he was right about two things. Ellie was a big girl and had strong arms to handle the heavy batters, thick with flour, cream and sugar. And Ellie wasn't looking for a husband, like Margaret.

Ellie's experiences with her own father had likely scared her off men forever. "Nonsense, Ellie," Margaret said. "We have to take the jobs we can find. I'll keep looking."

Walking to work alone gave Ellie a lot of time to think about living in America, finding an apartment with Margaret and the prospects for marriage. She'd seen her own parents' marriage nearly destroy her mother.

Ellie's father liked to drink and after he lost three fingers in a farm accident when she was a little girl, he took to spending much of his time drinking away the small salary he used to bring home for his family.

On the days Matty Kelly was at home, Ellie's mother suffered all the more. The tiny house full of kids got smaller and smaller as the large, angry man woke up like an angry bear whose sleep had been interrupted. At first, Matty just screamed at his wife, but one day, he started yelling at the children and raised his hand to slap Ellie.

"They're just little ones, Matty," her mother pleaded with her husband. "Let me get your pipe and slippers, while I pick up a bit."

"You're home all day with the brats," he ranted. "Why don't you pick up after them then? Why don't they pick up after themselves? And, where's my dinner? I've been working hard all day."

A ghost of a smile formed on Nora's lips before she could seal them as she'd learned years ago.

"Are you laughing at me, woman?" He raised his good arm,

holding his cigarette and pointed at his long-suffering wife. "Aw, c'mere." He spread his arms; a hasty grin plastered on his face. "I didn't mean nothing by it."

Nora backed up, looking at Matty for a hint of his temper. "Come here!" he demanded.

As she came into his arms, Matty's cigarette descended onto Nora's neck and Ellie heard her mother scream, even as her skin sizzled.

"Now, get my pipe," he said. "This cigarette's ruined."

Margaret didn't want to be a single woman in America. Since she was a small girl, her mother had taught her she needed to marry a good man. Her only job, as a wife, was to support his endeavors and raise his children. She had all but despaired of marrying well before she met Martin.

Five months younger than Margaret, Martin had often teased her about being an older woman or "robbing the cradle." But he was secure in himself and, from the beginning, Margaret knew they were evenly matched.

Both were from Galway; both wanted a family, and both were willing to work hard to become successful. His older brother had gone to America in 1900 and written home, praising the land of opportunity. Martin was convinced and wanted to start their marriage securely, so he went to America to create a new life for the two of them. Now he was gone.

At 27 years old, Margaret was worried her best years went down with Martin and the ship. Her future appeared bleak without a husband to care for her.

"You could consider a vocation," Ellie told her. I've been praying about it more and more since we left home. I'm nearly convinced taking the veil is the way for me. The Lord saved our lives back there on the ocean for a reason. I'm open to becoming His bride and teaching all His children His ways."

Margaret loved the Lord, she told Ellie. But she wanted

children of her own and a man beside her. The only part she wasn't sure about was the degree of servitude in the marriage vows her mother described.

Margaret was a modern woman on her own in the city. Before, she had big dreams of running the grocery store with Martin at her side, as equals. Both would put in a hard day at work and go home to a warm cottage with beautiful children. Martin would read stories to the children, while she prepared dinner by firelight ...

Daydreaming was the only escape Margaret could find the strength to do nowadays. She hadn't slept well since arriving in America. Whenever she closed her eyes, she saw Martin's face peering up at her from below the dark seas. His eyes were open, and he seemed to be begging her to return to his arms.

Many nights, the screams of the people in the water around the lifeboats woke her from a sound sleep. As she glanced around the dark room, she reached out to be sure Ellie was still asleep by her side.

In the dream, Ellie didn't get on the lifeboat. She was struggling in the icy water as Margaret tried unsuccessfully to haul her into the boat. Her pillow was sodden with the tears she shed for her inability to save those she loved.

As daylight filtered through the fly-speckled windows, Margaret struggled to start her day. Wearily, she rolled to the edge of the dirty mattress and came up on to her knees. In the time it took to bring herself to her feet, she'd rattled off two Hail Marys and the Lord's Prayer. She knew she had to hurry to get into the bathroom down the hall before the hefty Russian man down the hall made his daily visit. The time and the smell would keep her away and she'd have to hold her piss or find a chamber pot.

A quick wash with a clean rag and some cold water and Margaret was back in the O'Dey apartment. She started a pot of coffee, extra-strength like she and Robert liked it and put a cup of cream and a pot of sugar on the table. Ellie had left for work an hour ago and it was Margaret's turn to wake the children and get them ready for school.

As they fought over the bits of bacon and jam in the cupboard, Cathleen came out of the bedroom. "You kids! Shut up, now! Your father's under the weather today and needs to get some sleep. Margaret, is the coffee nearly ready?"

With their mother awake, if not alert, Margaret took her first chance to slip into her shoes and scoot out the door. Today was they day she'd find her first job in America, she was sure.

Day after day, Margaret walked up and down the streets of the city, looking for work. She was amazed at the huge variety of people and carriages on the streets of the city. Carriages of every sort filled the street, from the lowly wagon Ellie's brother-in-law drove for deliveries - when he wasn't "under the weather" — to a high-class landau with liveried footman and driver. The clatter of the horses' hooves battled with the rumble of tires from the newfangled automobiles crowded behind. In New York, it seemed every third vehicle was gas-powered.

Margaret had seen far fewer automobiles in Queensland when they'd boarded the ship for America, but before that day the opportunity to see and hear the noisy machines in County Galway was limited. The county councilman drove an automobile when he visited the area near her village, but those times were few.

Blat! A horn sounded behind her, breaking her reverie and pulling her back to the job hunt. She scurried over to a bench near the corner to scour the secondhand newspapers left behind, scanning for job advertisements.

Many of the ads for jobs in shops or eateries said outright, "No Irish Need Apply." More than once, Margaret had walked to a storefront miles away, only to be greet with a placard in the window echoing the same sentiment. For days, she wandered up and down the areas where the finer ladies shopped, tired, hungry and footsore.

After one particularly difficult day, Margaret was especially discouraged. Her back ached from sleeping on the floor. At the last shop, a red-faced woman had thrown her apron in Margaret's face.

"Get outta here, Mick!" she screamed. "Go back to where you belong."

Margaret put a shaking hand to her forehead and clutched her shawl tightly around her. Her voice shook with tears, as she spent her last dime on a newspaper. "I'm willing to work hard," she told the newsie, a young Irish boy with smudged cheeks and holes in his shoes. "But I can't get a chance here. Back home, I worked in service for years because that was the only option. I wanted something better for myself here."

The boy turned to his next customer, calling out, "Armory Show opens on Lexington Avenue! Get your newspapers here!"

Perhaps it was time to consider returning to Ireland, Margaret thought as she trudged up the dirty, muddy hill past the biscuit factory. She turned wearily toward the O'Deys, shook her arms at her side and squared her shoulders. There was only one small personal chore to handle.

In the morning, she would return the fur stole to Madeline Sloane, from the lifeboat. Perhaps she'd had her baby by now and would welcome a visit from a friend on the Titanic.

30 July 1912
New Rochelle, New York

Dearest Dad and Mam,

I am sorry I have not written sooner. As you have likely heard, there was a catastrophe on the ship we had booked passage. Ellie and I are fine, but Martin, and the two Thomases perisht at sea.

We are living with Ellie's sister for a short while.

Tomorrow, I will make a last effort to set my affares in order. If I can work a few months at the factory with Ellie, mayhaps I can earn a return ticket.

Your loving daughter,
Margaret

Chapter Six

Madeline was ecstatic to play hostess for the captain and the first officers of the Carpathia. She'd been cooped up inside the Sloane House on Fifth Avenue for months now, except for the three weeks at Sloane-Kettering Memorial Hospital with Baby Jack.

She cinched in her white English crepe gown, adjusted the black and white feathers in her hair and admired herself in the cheval mirror in the corner of her room. "Not bad, for a widow and a mother."

Her previous maid used to constantly harp on her not to add dazzles like the feather, a diamond or other jewels while she was in deep mourning. "Baubles wouldn't hurt him now," Madeline had insisted. The casket had been burnished with gold and a jewel-encrusted coat of arms, just as she ordered.

For the funeral, Madeline had worn black pearls at her wrists and throat, with the large solitaire diamond and gold band on her left hand, over elbow-length gloves. A gauzy white veil trimmed in white crepe blurred her features, but did not detract from her beauty.

Madeline took comfort in being a rich woman in her own right. She'd shed her mother to a large extent and considered herself an attraction for many men closer to her own age. The Mrs. Astor's list of *The 400* aristocrats in fashionable New York City society included several marriage possibilities much younger than Colonel Jack Sloane.

In the four months since the funeral, Madeline was always pushing at her mother's boundaries. The white mourning clothes were a big sticking point between the two. Madeline's anger and guilt played off one another, coming to rest on the baby's nanny, the cook and, more often than not, her own lady's maid.

Caroline was an older, English woman her mother had insisted on hiring while the Sloanes were still on their honeymoon. Madeline didn't want someone young and pretty, like the nanny she found after she arrived home in New York City.

Emily's porcelain skin and dark, luxurious hair drew admiring gazes from any man with two eyes. She'd keep that one in the nursery or the kitchen today, that was certain.

Just then, a knock at the door signaled Caroline's entrance. She always appeared silently outside the boudoir and occasionally Madeline didn't even hear a knock at the door before the woman was behind her.

"Does milady require assistance with her hair?" Caroline asked, a sophisticated British accent still thick in her voice. The 62-year-old widow worked soundlessly and tirelessly each day to help Madeline with her morning meal, her toilette and then dressing for the day.

"I think my hair is suitable for an afternoon party in my own home, Caroline." As Madeline twirled, the ruffle at the bottom of the gown billowed out and the feather in her hair dipped and bowed. She was like a little girl, dressed up for a costume ball.

Caroline frowned carefully, couching her suggestions in propriety she thought befit her lady's station. "In the old days, madame, a lady didn't wear anything but the most severe cut and no adornments until a full year had passed from the burial."

Madeline stomped her foot. "This isn't the old days. Those days are dead and buried and I'm not! I'll wear a feather and a ruffle, if I want to, and you'll keep quiet about it."

She pirouetted on one black and white slipper and

flounced into her chair. "Please, my jet necklace and earrings with the smallest drops. Hurry it up, too, the captain and his officers will be here shortly."

Madeline knew there were going to be problems with the staff, but things were already beginning to get out of hand. The little party she was planning for the captain of the Carpathia already had the kitchen staff upside down. She'd convinced Vincent to include party expenses in her household budget, largely because she'd spent her monthly allowance on new gowns for late summer and early fall.

"I need you to help in the kitchen," she told Emily, when the girl brought Baby Jack down from the nursery the evening before.

Emily was a good replacement for the nanny her mother had hired while she and Jack were in England. She had a kind, loving manner with children — not just her baby Ryan.

Each evening before dinner, Emily brought Baby Jack to Madeline so his mother could appear attentive and enjoy his company. The baby wasn't much for conversation, Madeline noted, but she supposed that would come with time.

She was hopeful the mothering instinct would kick in soon, as well. Emily was a natural with Baby Jack, but Madeline knew as his mother, she needed to show a deeper concern. When he turned 21, her son would inherit three million dollars from Jack's estate, but Vincent was acting miserly toward his half-brother until then.

"Baby Jack will need a tutor in another year or two," Madeline had told him last week, carefully measuring her smile. "I'd like to begin interviewing candidates to find the right one."

"We can easily agree on Jack's wishes to provide for his son_s._" She leaned on the plural. "Both you and Baby Jack, correct?"

Vincent's head tilted to one side and he snorted softly.

"Your baby doesn't need a private tutor. He can attend the academy when he's of age."

A vein throbbed in her forehead as she recalled the conversation. It wouldn't do for Vincent to see Baby Jack not well attended by his mother. But she didn't want baby spit up on her gown today. She had guests arriving in less than three hours.

As Madeline handed Baby Jack back to Emily, she smiled prettily and asked about progress in the kitchen.

"Ma'am, I'm not able to help much in the kitchen, with little Jake here," she said.

"Jake? The baby's name is John Jacob Sloane VI. I want to call him Baby Jack to honor his father," she admonished. Without turning around to acknowledge Emily's nod, Madeline went on. "Put the baby down in a rocker near the kitchen," she said. "You can listen in while you help with the canapes."

Madeline stopped Emily as she turned to go. "Ask Cook to see about hiring another serving girl for the party. If my wicked lady's maid hadn't left me in a lurch, she could have stepped in to help."

She turned away and plopped down at her dressing table. The woman looking back at her in the mirror was red-faced and her lips were pinched. She smiled stiffly and picked up a comb. "I guess I'll have to finish dressing myself."

As Emily and the kitchen staff put the final touches on the champagne punch, tiny buttery croissants, strawberries dipped in chocolate and petit fours, Baby Jack snored contentedly in a wooden rocker near the stove. Emily felt guilty for complaining, but she was short-tempered from staying up so many nights with the baby, while his mother dozed peacefully a floor below.

"I'm glad someone's sleeping this afternoon," Emily said to no one in particular. She loved children and hoped to have more of her own, very soon.

Emily had come to Sloane House with her husband Todd,

who was Colonel Sloane's driver. The two had emigrated to America from Ireland only a year earlier with a tiny baby and Todd had quickly found employment.

The kitchen door banged open and Todd stepped in. He wore a uniform of navy-blue trousers and a jacket with a stiff collar and epaulets. His cap was also a dark blue with a black band, a white bill and a gold badge with an "S" facing the front, as if he were an officer in the Sloane navy.

Emily smiled when she saw him. In the garage, Todd's wardrobe took a more common turn. A coverall jumper with the same gold crest embroidered on the chest covered his dress uniform and took the greatest hits from oil, grease, dirt and bird droppings on the garage floor.

"Mrs. Sloane mentioned we could ask Jarvis to look for more housemaids and a lady's maid," Emily told the cook as she smiled across the room at Todd, pilfering a fresh cookie.

DeeDee was one of two housemaids in the kitchen today. "Yes!" she said. "Madge and I are surely overworked trying to keep up this big house."

The cook, a stout, florid English woman, shoved DeeDee aside. Sadie's frizzy brown hair was a halo around her melon-shaped face, the hair color and her tempter likely from similar bottles to the one she kept in the back of the cupboard. "You need to work harder and spend less time making cow eyes at the delivery boys," Sadie barked. "Get to work, now, you!"

DeeDee frowned, slamming the door on the icebox a little too hard when she'd covered the finger sandwiches and set them inside. Sadie liked to pick on her because she was young and new in the house. Emily saw where DeeDee was younger than the rest, but she worked hard and had some good ideas.

She echoed the girl's comments. "I could sure use the help. I'm not comfortable acting as three servants in one."

"Milady yelling at Caroline all the time may have made the rounds," DeeDee offered from her post in the corner. "You're going to have a hard time finding people willing to work for her. Women have more choice now."

A knock at the back door to the kitchen caught Sadie's attention. "Here's the boy from the bakery or the florist, she said. "Let him in, Emily. Not you," she looked pointedly at the housemaid.

Margaret was fortunate to ride along with Ellie's brother-in-law to an area of town near Fifth Avenue. Each day Robert delivered coal to the homes along the lesser avenues. Each evening he came home coated in black dust, as if he'd just stepped out of a Ballingarry coal mine. Her mother's father was a coal miner in County Tipperary, and she was always talking about the dirt and the dust he brought home with him.

Uncertain how she would make it home that evening, Margaret had carried sensible shoes in her bag, in case she had to walk the entire distance. She only had one good dress for job-hunting and a possible work situation. She couldn't afford to have it covered in soot.

When she arrived at the mansion, he dropped her at the rear entrance. "Are you looking for work today? We don't run a charity, you know."

Margaret bristled. "I'm taking one last turn through the shops and eateries on my way home," she said. "I just need to see Mrs. Sloane."

Robert continued to needle her. "Don't rise above your station, little Maggie Mannion. It's for sure Mrs. Sloane will not even meet with the likes of you."

No one except Martin had called her Maggie since she was a child. She certainly didn't appreciate the familiarity of Robert using her childhood nickname.

As she clambered down from the buggy, Margaret pulled the paper-wrapped bundle with the fur inside closer to her chest. She'd considered keeping it for the winter or even selling it to make her way for a few more months. But in the end, honesty won out over charity.

Cathleen had found the wrap folded neatly and wrapped in paper among Margaret's belongings she kept on a chair in the corner of the living room. "The Sloanes aren't going to miss one little beaver stole. There is a hawker on the corner who's willing to buy used goods, no questions asked. I can introduce you Saturday after work. The money would make a nice contribution to your free room, here."

Margaret narrowed her eyes. The tension in her neck and shoulders was visible. "The wrap is not mine to keep. I'll return it tomorrow. To the rightful owner." She grabbed the package away from Cathleen and slept with it that night.

Walking up to the house, Margaret smoothed her dress and flicked away an imaginary piece of lint, rapping sharply at the heavy wooden door. She could hear the chatter of female voices behind the door and was cheered by their apparent camaraderie. She longed to be one of many women again, working alongside each other and making their way.

She knocked again, more loudly this time. A tall, dark-haired woman answered the door with a surprised look on her face. "You're not the florist or the bakery boy," she said. "I'm sorry, I was expecting flowers and petit fours. May I help you?"

Margaret stepped back, ready to hand the package to the girl and apologize for the interruption. "I met Mrs. Sloane when we took to the boats on the Titanic. This wrap is hers and I've come to return it."

"Come in and take a seat, but just for a minute," the young woman offered. "We're very busy."

"Oh, no, I can't stay," Margaret stammered, as she stepped into the kitchen. "I need to keep moving. I'm looking for work."

Sadie was at her side in a moment. "If you're able to stay and help in the kitchen, I can give you a day's wages. I can't promise any more, but if you're a good worker, I can put a word in with Jarvis. He manages the house."

"I'd love to work in this kitchen," Margaret glanced about her. The large, spacious room sparkled with light from windows on the south side. White cupboards, counters and floors were spotless — covered in every sort of delicacy she could imagine.

"Hand me an apron and put me to work," she said. The wrap was set aside and forgotten.

It was hours later when Emily, Margaret and Sadie, the cook, collapsed on stools near the pantry. The flowers had been ushered in shortly after the new girl arrived. They were hothouse beauties, rivaling anything Margaret had ever seen in her limited time in America.

The florist's arrangements of roses, carnations and daisies appeared out of season, like a snowflake in summer. Margaret carried three huge bouquets, towering above her head, into the entryway and dining room, following puppy-like behind Emily until she learned her way.

At odds with her curious nature, she spent just seconds in the wood-lined entry, gazing up at the portraits of American fur traders, swathed in pellets and big fur hats. The Sloane women were gowned heavily in every painting, smiling faintly except for the last matron in the line.

"That's Caroline Sloane," Emily said. "Colonel Sloane's mother was known as <u>the</u> Mrs. Sloane in this city. She was the queen of society and hosted many a dance party in the ballroom at the rear of the house."

"More than 400 people were here in one night. She passed on and left the house to her son, Colonel John Jacob Sloane IV."

Margaret's eyes filled with tears. "I saw Colonel Sloane on the Titanic. He looks so much younger in this picture."

"Yes," Emily replied. "Mrs. Sloane was heartbroken and Baby Jack's left fatherless. She's hardly more than a child herself," she whispered conspiratorially. "The walls have ears," she said, nodding in the direction of the stairs.

As if on cue, Madeline Sloane glided down the stairs. The beautiful society woman was dressed head to toe in layers of sheer black, gray and white gauze. Her gown plunged at the neckline and her hair was bedecked with dozens of tiny white flowers.

Margaret gasped, drawing Madeline's attention and perhaps her ire.

"We're on our way back to the kitchen, ma'am," Emily offered, backing out.

"Just a moment," Madeline cut her short. "Is this the new girl?" She glanced closer at Margaret, a hint of recognition in her eyes. "Have we met?"

"Yes. Um, yes, Mrs. Sloane." Margaret was nervous again. "I don't want to bring up bad memories, but we shared a lifeboat on our hurried departure from the Titanic last spring. Congratulations on the birth of your son."

Emily eyes widened. She hissed at Margaret under her breath. "We'd best get back to the kitchen, Margaret."

She took the other woman's hand and began to withdraw. She tried to keep her voice light as she nearly dragged Margaret backwards. Madeline's temper was famous among the household staff. But Margaret wouldn't budge.

"Of course, I remember now," Madeline looked her directly in Margaret's eyes now. "Are you long in New York?"

Margaret tripped over her words. "No, I'm sorry ma'am. I'm thinking I will have to return to Ireland as I'm alone myself, now. My fiancé drowned."

"Please, stay after the reception and we'll talk," Madeline offered.

"I'd be delighted," Margaret stammered. As the two women walked quickly out the hall, Emily trembled. Margaret turned to her. "Whatever is the matter? You seem so nervous around Mrs. Sloane."

"Just you be careful. Because we're Irish women, both of us, I'll warn you. She's not your friend."

Now that the party was over, Margaret helped Sadie,

Emily and the rest of the staff pick up the dishes and wash them up. There was enough food left over to feed an army and Margaret desperately wanted to ask to take some home with her to Ellie's sister's house.

This was the kind of treat Ellie's family hadn't seen in a lifetime in Ireland or America. What the littlest ones wouldn't give to feast on chocolates and fresh strawberries!

She had just about screwed up her courage to ask Sadie for a box of leftovers, when an older, dignified gentleman came into the kitchen. Margaret had seen him opening doors and ushering guests into the mansion earlier in the day. He was dressed in a serious black and white suit with tails and wore gloves when offering Mrs. Sloane, the captain and the others their light refreshments.

"Is there a Miss Margaret Mannion in the kitchen today?" he asked, casting about for a possible stranger among the staff.

Margaret thought he appeared to have a broomstick up his back. "It's me. I'm right here." She gave a small wave.

"Indeed," the butler enunciated each syllable, while looking down his nose. "Follow me. Mrs. Sloane would like to see you in her sitting room."

Margaret fetched the fur and followed the butler up the back stairway from the hallway near the back door she'd entered this morning. This stairwell was dim and much narrower than the one she had seen earlier.

"Are you presentable?" the man asked when they'd reached the top of the stairs.

"I wore my best dress and was careful not to spill," she replied. She wondered if there would be an inspection before she was let in to meet Mrs. Sloane.

"What is the bundle you carry with you?" he asked.

"When I met Mrs. Sloane last spring, she loaned me a wrap," Margaret replied. "I wanted to return it."

She hesitated to mention the circumstances of her meeting with Mrs. Sloane. It was obviously not a welcome subject in polite company. She and Ellie were reticent to talk about the disaster with any of the curiosity-seekers around them.

The butler — Margaret thought she'd heard someone call him Jarvis — knocked softly on the door to Mrs. Sloane's suite. Margaret didn't hear the reply, but he opened the door and stepped in, motioning for her to follow.

She was puzzled by Jarvis' formal introduction to Mrs. Sloane. Hadn't they just met again a few hours earlier? After he left the room, she stood rooted to the heavy, dark maroon carpet. She felt like she'd been planted in the corner near the door and dare not move.

Madeline was arranged comfortably on a chaise lounge, also upholstered in a heavy, claret-red tapestry with gold brocade trim, near the fireplace. A small fire crackled cheerily in the large marble firebox. Photographs and flowers dotted the mantle and there was another large portrait, this one of Madeline herself, above the massive stone edifice.

The young widow held a large glass of wine in one hand and a slim cigarette in the other. Margaret had never seen a woman smoke before. Her mother would have been livid.

According to the newspapers, Mrs. Sloane was five years younger than Margaret, but she looked so much more sophisticated. After the Titanic disaster, New York newspapers recalled her entire life story — her family's wealth, how she'd attended the best schools and had made her debut just two years ago.

So much had happened in her life since then — a marriage, a honeymoon to Africa and Europe, the loss of her husband and now, the birth of her son.

"Come, take a seat in the chair, there," she pointed to a delicate chair near the fireplace, upholstered in the same tapestry and brocade.

"Are you living in the city? With family? How are you getting along?"

Margaret was taken aback each time Madeline addressed her. On the boat, they were thrown together by fear and calamity. Earlier, in the hall, she tried to know her place and act the servant girl she was for the day.

Now, with a glass of wine and a warm fire, Madeline wanted to chat like old friends. How should she respond?

"I need someone I can trust," Madeline confided. "I want someone close to me to watch my back. I'm alone in this house, just as you are alone. I don't trust the servants my mother hired while we were on our wedding trip."

"Would you like to come to work with me? I have enemies, but I feel I can trust you, like a friend."

Margaret gasped out loud. She tipped back her head and took a deep breath before answering. "Yes, ma'am. Thank you so much. This means so much to me."

Her eyes glowed as the two women discussed Margaret's daily responsibilities, when she could report back to work and possible living arrangements.

Madeline wanted Margaret to live at Sloane House. "I'd like to have you live here, on the third floor. That way you're available early for breakfast and late if I'm out for an event."

"I'm really beholdin' to my friend Ellie and her family, Mrs. Sloane. I must repay them also for their kindness. They took me in when I had nowhere else to go."

Madeline backed down, for now. "Very well, then. I will see you bright and early in the morning. I'm usually up by nine."

"Thank you, Mrs. Sloane. Thank you, again." Margaret began bowing, as she backed toward the door.

Madeline raised an eyebrow. "I only ask one thing, Margaret." The maid stopped in midstep. "Complete and utter loyalty. In this house, you belong to me."

It took all the strength Margaret had left in her, not to hug Madeline. She did dance a tiny, little jig in the hallway outside the suite, after she'd accepted the generous offer.

Madeline had asked her to be her friend, but Margaret was doubtful. She'd seen wealthy women on the ship and in the stores since her arrival. Women like Madeline were accustomed to having their way <u>all</u> the time. Margaret was unsure how far her new employer would go in her demand for utter loyalty.

Besides, her best friend Ellie was at home waiting for her. She'd all but begged Ellie to find her a place at the biscuit factory. Wouldn't she be surprised to see the plum position Margaret had snared?

Head in the clouds, Margaret didn't see the brooding young man standing close to DeeDee in the kitchen. He looked very familiar — dark, curly hair, trim facial hair — but she couldn't place him from the luncheon or her searches around town for work.

Dressed in a well-tailored suit of summer-weight cotton, he was about the same age, but towered over DeeDee in height and bearing. He was smoking an unfiltered light brown cigarette. "What was it with these Americans and their cigarettes?" she wondered.

Quickly, she scoured her memory of the chatter about the afternoon's guests. Closely shaven, the cut of his suit said money, not sailor. Perhaps this was the manager she'd heard Sadie mention earlier. Someone Mrs. Sloane had hired. Vincent, was it?

His hand lingered on DeeDee's arm, then she turned sharply and disappeared up the stairs, past Margaret. "Excuse me, miss," Vincent said. "I'm waiting for a Maggie Mannion. Would that be you?"

"Yes," she replied. Her smile wavered as she struggled to find the right words. "I'm Maggie. Margaret Mannion, that is." His familiarity with her name grated on Margaret's nerves.

"I'm glad to meet you," he said, offering a hand and a reassuring smile. "Cook tells me you might be available to help out around the house. Kitchen work, laying the fires, tidying up, that sort of thing."

"Honestly, Mrs. Sloane has just asked me to stay on as her lady's maid," Margaret said. "Helping her dress, drawing her bath, that sort of thing."

"Needs help dressing, does she?" Vincent's voice was venomous. "Does Mrs. Sloane need help with her hair, too? Is she some sort of child?"

Margaret swallowed hard. "Her hair? I'm afraid I don't . . .

Who was this guest with all the questions? Mrs. Sloane had asked for loyalty. She'd show him loyalty. "Mrs. Sloane is the lady of the house and I'm her employee. If she asks for my help, I'll give it. I owe her so much."

"Well, what *Mrs. Sloane* wants, *Mrs. Sloane* gets," he spat out. He pivoted, stomped out his cigarette on the shiny kitchen floor, turned and left the room.

"Well, he's a bit cheeky." Perplexed, Margaret turned to find Emily watching them.

"He's really the master of the house, now," she answered. "Since his father died. That's Vincent Sloane, Colonel Sloane's son and heir to the bulk of his estate."

On his way back to his townhouse, Vincent settled back in the car. His father's chauffeur, Todd Roebken, found the way easily. He'd have to consider hiring the man away from Madeline now that she had returned a widow.

As they crossed the intersection of Broadway and Seventh Avenue, the aptly named Times Square lit up the night. The Gothic fortress was the tallest structure in the city, housing The New York Times — the newspaper where Vincent owned a great deal of stock. The Times inspired the city center's name, but it might soon be moving. The business had outgrown the tower and Vincent could not be more pleased with the profits.

The glow of the city lights cut in and out on Vincent's face as his mind turned to the day's activities. He'd accepted Madeline's invitation to honor his father's memory, but the day had reaped unexpected benefits.

The captain of the Carpathia offered an interesting tidbit that might come in handy if Vincent decided to sue the White Star Lines. The captain told the younger man the waters were filled with icebergs and six warnings were transmitted the evening she sank. Vincent was determined someone would pay for this travesty and he was sure nothing could be recovered from Captain Smith, who'd gone down with his ship.

Also, during the reception, Vincent spotted Todd's wife. Unsure what the nanny was doing serving hors d'oeuvres to guests, his curiosity nearly got the better of him. Months ago, he'd trained his mind to disregard her. She was, after all, a married woman. He'd never let that stop him before, but he liked Todd.

He asked Madeline about the other young Irish girl he thought might be new. She was tall and dark-haired, but her hair was knotted in a bun atop her head and she didn't smile often, like the nanny.

"That's Margaret," Madeline told him in passing. "She was on the Titanic. Her fiancé died."

Vincent was doubly curious now. "How did she end up here?"

But Madeline was tired of talking to Vincent already. "She borrowed my fur and decided to return it. End of story."

Vincent made a mental note to get better acquainted with the new girl. A man could get lost in those eyes. And, he could always use an extra pair of ears in the mansion.

"Mr. Sloane?" Todd's voice brought Vincent back to the present. "We're coming up to your place. Vincent had leased the entire penthouse floor of the Waldorf-Astoria from his uncle. The luxury hotel was built in two stages and played host to dozens of political and business conferences involving the rich and famous. Its lofty exterior featured a conglomeration of balconies, alcoves and loggias beneath a tile roof bedecked with gables and turrets.

Vincent loved the opulence and the location, but he especially enjoyed the popular restaurant — the chef there was familiar with Vincent's culinary favorites, a Waldorf salad with Thousand Island dressing and a flan with blue raspberries.

As he went to step out of the car, he poked his head back in the driver's window. "Just a word of warning, Roebken. I met Mrs. Sloane's son today and he looks nothing like my father. I doubt he is a legitimate heir. Watch yourself with that one!"

Dearest Dad and Mam,

Good News! I have been offered a position in a large house on Fifth Avenue in New York City!

The Sloane House was once owned by a Colonel Jack Sloane who died on the Titanic, like my beloved Martin. Mrs. Sloane was on the ship as well, and escaped with her life, as did Ellie and I. A kind lady, she gave me her fur wrap whilst we were on the lifeboat and I returned it earlier this week. She offered me a job as a lady's maid.

As nearly as I can tell, I am to help Mrs. Sloane with her toilette and to dress and arrange her hair each morning and evening.

I will remain living with the Kellys, as the Sloane's driver is available to take me back and forth each evening and Ellie's brother has a wagon route near the Sloane House each morning, delivering coal.

Keep me in your prayers, Mam, as I do for you.

Your faithful child,
Margaret

Chapter Seven

Margaret walked Emily back to the apartment and introduced her to Todd and their toddler Ryan. Todd offered to give her a ride home. "I've just returned from the Waldorf-Astoria, where the captain and his mates are staying on Mrs. Sloane's dime. The car's still warm. Can I give you a ride home?"

Back at the O'Dey apartment, it was quiet as a tomb. The children were all outside or at the neighbor's playing. Cathleen was working in the sewing room at a local milliner and Robert was still out on his route.

She could hardly wait for Ellie to get home from the factory. As she'd left the mansion, Sadie gave Margaret a small box of treats to share with her family. The servants didn't quite understand the relationship between Margaret and the large, boisterous group back at Robert and Cathleen's. So, Margaret just called them family.

She opened the white cardboard box now, slipping a bright red berry out of its nest and biting down decadently. The juices dribbled down her chin and she giggled as she mopped herself with a fresh hankie.

"Well, you're certainly in a good mood."

Margaret jumped when she heard the voice from behind her. Ellie moved on mouse feet, often stepping into the apartment without anyone even knowing she was home. Her equally quiet demeanor served Margaret, the talker of the pair, well, too.

"I got a job!" she exclaimed. "Madeline Sloane asked me to be her lady's maid! Do you remember Mrs. Sloane from the Titanic? She was with us on the boat. I went to her mansion on Fifth Avenue to return the fur she gave me on the boat. There was a party, and, well, one thing led to another." Margaret stopped suddenly from her chatter. Ellie had an odd look in her eyes. "What is it?" she asked.

"I was let go at the factory," the girl said. A single tear traced down her cheek, joined by another and then a flood. Ellie collapsed onto the mattress on the floor near Margaret's feet and her friend lay down beside her. She gathered Ellie into her arms.

"There, there," she patted Ellie's back and handed her a handkerchief. After several minutes, Margaret asked again. "What happened? Was there a problem in the shop?"

"The floor m...m...manager asked me into his office and said, 'How, how bad do you really want this job?'"

"I said, 'I really need this job. I'm alone in America, except for my sister.'"

"And you, of course," she added.

Margaret took her hand. "Why the tears, then?"

"Margaret," she cried, "he touched me on my, my bosom. And, he said, 'prove it.' And then, he kissed me. On the mouth!"

Suddenly, the two women were in each other's arms again. Margaret struggled to restrain her temper. She was ready to fight for her dear childhood friend. She'd go back to the biscuit factory, by God. She'd have it out with the man. Perhaps it would come to blows, but she didn't care.

Ellie sniffled and tried to pull herself together.

"We'll go after him together," Margaret told her.

"Oh, no. I couldn't," Ellie replied, tears starting anew. "It's my word against his and he's not just a man, he's the floor manager. When I bit his lip, he shoved me and told me not to come back."

"You bit him?" Margaret crowed. "I'd like to see him explain the fat lip to his wife."

Ellie continued to cry quietly.

"Are you worried about a job?" Margaret understood her friend's dilemma. "Perhaps I can speak to Sadie or Emily at the Sloane House. There's definitely something there for a good worker like yourself."

Ellie was quiet for several more minutes. Margaret began to wonder if she'd panicked or was just ashamed of what had happened to her.

"Ellie? He didn't, he didn't *hurt* you, did he?" Margaret stumbled over her words now. Ellie was not married, after all. She'd never had a boyfriend and likely had never been kissed before today.

"No," Ellie finally said, near to a whisper. "I've made a decision. I'll go to the Sisters of St. Francis in the morning. I'm ready to give myself to their order. I want to pledge myself to Jesus."

"It's not as if you have to go to the convent today," Margaret begged. "Can't you wait and see if something better comes along?"

Ellie searched her friend's eyes. "There is nothing better. This is something I've always wanted to do. Don't try to talk me out of it. I love Jesus."

Margaret was already late for her first day at Sloane House, so she couldn't stick around the apartment to try to talk Ellie out of leaving. "Promise me you'll wait until I get home," she said on her way out the door.

Margaret rode into the city with Robert. Some days his deliveries took him close to the Sloane House. Other days, Margaret had to walk the last mile or two.

Today's walk was sodden, like Margaret's mood. Ellie held true to her word and marched down to the motherhouse of the Order of St. Francis the very next day. Margaret snarled under her breath, as she trudged through the rain. "I love Jesus, but I loved Martin, too. It's a different kind of love, one I will likely never find again."

She stepped into a mud puddle and swore. "Good Gravy! What next?"

Not only had she lost her fiancé, but now she'd lost her very best friend. She was alone, a stranger in a strange land, without any family. She began to wonder if she'd made a mistake in taking Mrs. Sloane's offer of employment.

Madeline Sloane wasn't her friend and she certainly wasn't family. Ireland started looking better every day. By the time she arrived at the mansion's back door, Margaret had talked herself into a snit.

She stepped into the clean and warm, large-but-cozy kitchen. A big fire was roaring behind the stove and she melted into its warmth and the aromas of baking. Sadie's cinnamon rolls brought heaven to earth every Friday — Margaret wanted to lie down beside them and bask in their mouth-watering comfort.

Emily was in the kitchen this morning, as she always was when Margaret arrived. Baby Jack was such a happy little boy, and was getting very active, as well. Margaret and Emily had grown up around children, so they weren't surprised when the baby started crawling at only six months old.

"His mother isn't so fond of all his energy and his mobility," Emily said. After she fed him, dressed him, cleaned him up and showed him off to his momma, Baby Jack crawled all over the kitchen for the remainder of the day.

It was a Wednesday, so Margaret reviewed Madeline's usual plan for the day in her head, while she carried up the breakfast tray. Most of Margaret's day was spent following Madeline around the house and about town, catering to her every need and listening to her deepest confidences.

Most often, Madeline talked about herself.

"Does this dress make my hips look wide?"

"I'm worried my short hairstyle may be going out of fashion."

"Mrs. Gould called three times this weekend. What do you think she wants?"

Madeline seldom mentioned her male friends, but Margaret knew she was developing relationships with more than one man among her friend's families. She knew better than to ask too many questions. The friendship Madeline professed stopped at the bedroom door. She stayed in her room a good share of the morning, taking breakfast while still in her nightclothes. She literally couldn't dress herself or comb her hair without assistance.

Margaret didn't mind Madeline's helplessness. She felt like the woman truly needed her and perhaps even cared about her personally. It was an honest living and most days, Madeline was kind and generous. Once or twice, she'd discarded a perfectly wearable frock to the side, because she didn't like the color or the fit.

"Take it, Margaret," she said. And, the very same day they were out shopping to replace the dress with two more just like it, in different colors or a newer fashion. Margaret carried the boxes and opened doors.

Today, Margaret went quickly to Madeline's room. The evening before, her young mistress had told her she wanted to visit friends this morning and would be staying for lunch with Mrs. Vanderbilt.

The Vanderbilts and the Sloanes were both members of the gilded circle that dominated New York City society for nearly 40 years. The circle was peopled with old money blue bloods and captains of industry. The nouveau riche, Madeline's parents among them, fit in too, albeit uncomfortably.

After lunch, Mrs. Sloane wanted to take a ride in Central Park. The first time she'd mentioned an afternoon ride, Margaret made the mistake of laying out riding clothes. Madeline laughed merrily, making Margaret feel stupid.

"We'll take the car," she said, looking down her tiny little nose. "Ask Todd to bring the Bentley around at 11."

Todd, Emily's husband, drove Madeline everywhere, even if it was just around the block. Sometimes, when Madeline was visiting a friend, Margaret waited outside with Todd. He liked to fill Margaret in about the foibles of the Sloanes, the Vanderbilts, the Goulds, the Belmonts and the others. But Todd was nothing if not loyal.

He'd been with Mr. Sloane before the colonel remarried. Sloane had promised Todd, on his retirement, the car the chauffeur drove every day.

Young and dashing, Todd was the perfect serious foil to Emily's sweetness. Many evenings, as Margaret stayed behind to tend to Madeline after her social engagements, she caught Todd and Emily in the kitchen with their baby Ryan. Emily sang softly to the baby, as Todd rocked him and stared lovingly at his wife.

Ryan had Todd's red hair and Emily's flashing dark eyes. His chubby cheeks and roly-poly legs belied his quick little temper. When Emily paid too much attention to Baby Jack while Ryan was around, he cried unmercifully.

Today, Todd joked with Margaret, trying to draw her out of her doldrums.

"Mags," he said. "Why don't you move into the Sloane House? Emily and I are in the apartment over the garage and I know she'd love to have you close. Ryan thinks of you as a second mother already."

"It's something I'll have to think about," Margaret replied. "I'm not one to be beholden to anyone."

That evening at dinner, Ellie cleared her throat loudly. "Cathleen. Robert. I've made a decision. I will be going to the Sisters of St. Francis tomorrow. It's the right decision for me."

Robert threw his glass at the wall and the couple next door started shouting. He put his face directly into Ellie's. She could smell the stale beer. "Your responsibility is to this family! We paid for your trip to America, not so you could join the convent. You have to pay us back."

Ellie started to cry again, and Margaret put her arm

around her friend's shoulder.

But Robert wasn't finished. "Why did you have to leave the factory anyway? Couldn't you find a way to work with the foreman? A little tickle now and then?"

Ellie left the table in tears and when Margaret woke the next morning she was gone.

As the weather in the city worsened, each day's trip to and from the Sloane House grew more difficult. One morning, the sun finally decided to shine on the snow and ice-covered streets along the dingy street where Robert and Cathleen live.

Robert was more than his usual sullen self and Margaret was relieved to have him continue the silent treatment. But the rough roads and Robert's bad attitude made for a late arrival at the Sloane House.

Margaret hurried to carry the tray Emily had arranged for Mrs. Sloane up the back stairs. The lid on the teapot jiggled as she jogged up the steps and the china cup rattled.

Madeline was already sitting up in bed, reading a magazine. "You're late. I need you to pack for a quiet weekend in the country. The Goulds have invited me to travel with them to the Hamptons. Barbara has a cousin, Richard, visiting from Boston and we're all tired of the dirty, cold, wet city streets."

"There'll be sleighs, hot chocolate and a big fire. Be sure to pack warm woolens, my riding outfits and furs. It's going to be a lark and Barbara tells me her cousin is a doll. I'll be leaving in the morning."

As soon as Madeline was off to the Hamptons, with Todd at the wheel, Margaret tried visiting Ellie at the convent. The heavy, dark doors of the abbey itself were hidden behind a stone wall with a locked gate and a long trail through a forested garden of imposing evergreens.

She was met at the door by a foreboding older woman

with a long gray gown and starched white wimple, wrapped tight about her pinched face. "Sister Mary Ellen is in formation. She needs to spend her time in prayer and meditation to be sure she has chosen the right path. Please respect her privacy."

The doors, carved crosses on both sides, closed softly in her face.

So many doors kept closing in Margaret's face. Ellie was cloistered. Robert and Cathleen were grasping — the drive to the Sloane House was impossible. Margaret needed to make a change.

Maybe she should consider looking closer at the friends Emily and Todd had tried to introduce her to from their circle. Most were widowers with children; all were from Ireland and, of course, each was Catholic. Emily was nothing, if not determined Margaret would marry in the faith.

When Margaret arrived back at Cathleen's, Robert was in the kitchen. She was surprised to see him out of bed, since he'd been ill when she left for work. "Hair of the dog," he chuckled, lifted his chipped cup in salute.

Robert was unshaven as usual, but his face was paler and more haggard today. He blinked at the sunlight filtering in through the apartment's single window. "Home early? Taking a little holiday, are you? I hope you get paid for all your days off."

Margaret turned back into the living room area, still littered with pallets and the crappy mattress in the corner. "Mrs. Sloane left early for a weekend in the country."

Robert sneered. "Well, la-dee-dah. A weekend in the country. If you cared for this family, you might have gone along and earned some extra money helping around the es-tate." His emphasis on the two syllables was comic.

Margaret ignored his continued harangue. "I thought I would visit Ellie at the convent, but they wouldn't let me in to see her."

"That's a good thing," Robert answered. "She's dead to me."

Margaret whirled. "How can you be so mean? She's your sister."

"She's not my sister. She was Cathleen's, but not anymore. I've told Cathleen and the kids never to mention her name again. The same goes for you."

Margaret held back tears, as she rustled through her meager belongings in a dresser she shared with Ellie and the children. She turned on Robert. "Something is missing. I had $12 saved up I was going to send to my mother for Celia. Did you take it?"

"You've been here for nearly a month," Robert shot back. "It's time you carry your fair share. If you don't like it, get a place of your own." He spat into the sink and slinked back into his bedroom.

Margaret clenched her fists. She clutched at the bits and pieces she'd salvaged from the charity of the donations to Titanic survivors. It was all she had in the world besides the savings she'd pulled together for Celia. She swallowed hard and shook her head, trying to pull together a plan.

Moving to the kitchen, she opened the icebox, but the block of ice had melted days ago, and Robert had neglected to replace it. Fumbling through her purse, Margaret found two pieces of paper currency — dollar bills they called them — and a large collection of coins, silver and copper.

Rather than start a new cache in her dresser drawer, Margaret carefully counted out the money and returned it to her purse. Back outside the apartment, she turned left and marched to the corner grocer three blocks away. Because it was the end of the day, Margaret was able to haggle with the grocer for some wilted vegetables, a tired soup bone and two tins of brown bread.

By the time Cathleen returned from work, she had put together a beef and barley soup — made thicker with chopped vegetables and more attractive with the addition of the bread. There was only lard and a little sugar remaining in the cupboards, but the children were overjoyed. By stretching the few items Margaret was able to barter for at the grocers, the children were satisfied for the first time in weeks.

Robert rolled out of his room just in time to shovel two bowls of soup and thick slice of bread into his piehole. Without so much as a smile or a thank you, he left the apartment to meet with his friends at the neighborhood pub.

"Good riddance to bad rubbish," Margaret muttered.

Cathleen slapped her. "We've put a roof over your head for months now and that's the thanks we get. More than once you've woken the children and us with your cries. Robert deserves some time with his mates in the evenings."

Margaret carried the dishes to the sink and began washing up. The day had only magnified her homesickness for Ireland and dashed any hope of bringing Celia to America to live with her and Ellie. As she rinsed the last mismatched bowl, dried it and stacked it in the corner cupboard, she trailed tiredly to her corner.

Under the pillow, she found a book she'd borrowed from the library at Sloane House, *The Call of the Wild*. Maybe by immersing herself in the Klondike Gold Rush, she could escape the confines of the dirty city apartment, where she'd never felt welcome.

Every Sunday, Emily, Todd and Ryan attended Mass at St. Michael's. Most Sundays, Margaret was home with the O'Deys and went to their church across town. But, once or twice, caught late on a Saturday night, Margaret stayed at the Sloane House and attended Mass the next morning with the Roebkens.

Her greatest treat at the Mass was hearing Emily lead the choir. She had heard her young friend hum and whistle in the kitchen and she knew Emily sang lullabies to Ryan and Baby Jack, but the full throat of her voice in the choir loft was a quality Margaret had only heard in recordings at the Opera House in

Galway City.

"*Ave, Ave, Ave Maria,*" Emily's voice rose high and sweet above the others. "*Ave, Ave Mari-i-i-a.*" Margaret closed her eyes and floated along in the softer moments. Then, as the music swelled, she was drawn to the sounds of voices lifting her up in song.

As the music ended, Margaret began to cry. Why was the music so moving? Was she missing the Mass at home or simply drawn to Emily's talent? When the family joined up after church, she peppered Emily with questions. "Why don't you sing professionally?" Margaret begged. "You could be a star."

"My life is with my children, Ryan *and* Baby Jack. You, too, Todd." She poked him. "My songs are a prayer and that's what they'll always be. When I sing to my babies, I'm turning their faces toward Him, as well."

Margaret didn't dare disagree, but she made other excuses to attend Mass with the Roebkens and to ask Emily to sing around the house at every opportunity.

She remembered Todd's kind words outside the Sloane House last week, when he encouraged her to move into the mansion. The answer was suddenly crystal clear. Celia must be her first priority. Since Robert O'Dey had stolen her initial savings, Margaret was forced to start over.

She'd speak to Madeline about moving into the Sloane House on Monday. Tomorrow would be her first day with her American family at the Sloane House.

Madeline returned from her trip to the Hamptons late Sunday evening in fine spirits. Her cheeks had a rosy glow, but Margaret didn't think all the good humor was about fresh air and sunshine in the country.

"Barbara's cousin Richard plays tennis and fences. His favorite wine is deep red, but I think he likes rose, as well. He's a banker."

"Thank God, I don't have to wear black anymore. This weekend, I was able to wear my new red cashmere sweater with a woolen skirt. Next summer, I'll be wearing white again on the tennis court."

Madeline's mother Sylvia didn't think it was proper for a widow to leave her house for at least six months after her husband's death, but Madeline stepped out more often than her mother would ever know. A new romance might give the old woman a heart attack.

"Mrs. Sloane," Margaret jumped in when Madeline's chatter about Richard trailed off. "I've had second thoughts about your offer to live on the third floor, as you suggested. As you may be aware..."

"Of course," Madeline jumped in. "I'd love to have you under our roof. "I know I keep you here late many evenings, preparing for bed or after a party in the city. I do know Todd can take you back to that awful apartment you share with your friend, but I'd really prefer having you here. It would be better for both of us."

Margaret was relieved. Despite Emily's encouragement, the women weren't sure if Madeline's fickle nature might prevail. What Madeline had originally described as a friendship certainly wasn't one.

The younger woman was willing to loan books and donate discarded dresses, but the conversations centered entirely on Madeline's whims. On Mondays, she was giddy from the weekend's adventures. On Tuesdays, her temper flared over Vincent's visits. On Wednesdays, she was introspective and spent the day examining her future. On Thursdays, she had bridge club and on Fridays, she made plans for the weekend.

This morning was a prime example of Margaret wanting to talk only about herself. She didn't want to hear anything about Margaret's life, nothing about Martin and little about the staff and their needs.

"Thank you, Mrs. Sloane." She picked up a brush and tamed a few stray tendrils escaping from Madeline's upswept hairstyle. "I'll try to bring a few things each day from the O'Deys, but I think I can start staying here within the week."

"Stuff and nonsense," Madeline sputtered as Margaret tucked ribbons in her chignon. "I'm staying in much of the day. Perhaps Todd can take you around and bring all your things in one trip."

"Later, we can make a night of it! After Emily gets Baby Jack off to bed, you can set the fire and make some hot chocolate. We'll sit by the fire and you can brush my hair. I can't wait to tell you more about Dickie."

It took only a single trip in the Sloane's long black car, to move Margaret's meager belongings into the mansion. She carried the slim cardboard case each of the Titanic survivors was gifted by benefit at the hospital. It was light enough with the two dresses she'd gathered from Madeline's generosity.

Emily moved from room to room, pulling Ryan from the stack of toys and ragged clothing piled in the corner near the dresser. Before long, she was straightening up and worrying about the O'Dey children. "How many live here?" she asked. "Are they all in school?"

"Six. Yes." Margaret replied despondently. Margaret fingered the necklace she'd worn when she left Ireland. She felt she was leaving the last vestiges of home with Ellie's family.

She wanted to wait until Cathleen returned home from work, but she was worried Robert might arrive first and she would have to explain. Or get into another argument with the man.

Instead, she found a pencil stub under the chair and wrote a short letter to Cathleen on the back of an envelope. "I appreciate you took me in when I arrived in America, penniless and alone. You and your children are like family to me," she wrote. "If anyone inquires about me, I will be staying at the Sloane House to save time going to work each day. You are in my prayers."

As they walked down to the car, Margaret felt less burdened with each flight they descended. Her case bounced against the walls, leaving paint marks at each turn. The light bulbs on the landings were broken out years ago, but some light sifted in from cracked windows. Others were covered with plywood.

Todd carried the second box, loaded heavier with Margaret's books, her most prized possessions and the only things she had gathered since all her volumes, poetry and folklore by Irish authors were lost to the ocean floor.

Since arriving in America, she haunted the used bookstores and carefully rationed her pennies for the likes of C.S. Lewis and thrillers by Bram Stoker. The Sinclair novel was on top, unread.

Emily brought up the rear, holding Ryan's hand as he took the stairs one at a time. Her painstaking good humor was worn thin by the time they reached the bottom.

Like a snake shedding her old skin, she wiggled into the back seat between the boxes and sighed contentedly in the warm sun of Indian summer. Emily turned and smiled at her new friend while Todd pulled slowly into traffic. Ryan was asleep before they reached the Sloane House.

29 October 1912

Dearest Dad and Mam,

I am writing to let you know I have moved into the Sloane House, so you may address letters to me here, in care of Madeline Sloane. Mrs. Sloane's stepson, Vincent, is the house manager, but I don't care for him and would prefer to receive my mail from Mrs. Sloane's butler who takes the messages from the postman.

I have not heard from you since I wrote to you upon receiving this job. I hope all is well. I still miss Martin terribly and, of course, my family more than I'd ever imagined. In coming to America, I always believed I would be comfortable here with Martin and to see Ellie on occasion. Now that Ellie has become Sister Mary Ellen, those hopes are dashed.

I will still make a go of it here and hope to be able to save more funds for Celia's travel, now that I am not sharing my meager salary with the O'Deys. Mrs. Sloane is glad to have me under the same roof and I've made friends here, too.

Please, take care of yourselves and write to me soon on Fifth Avenue.

Yours forever,
Margaret

Chapter Eight

When Margaret returned to the house with her things, Emily helped arrange the few trinkets, the dresses and a pair of shoes in the attic room's wardrobe. The house manager, as Margaret referred to Vincent Sloane, had decreed all ladies on staff would wear black dresses, white aprons and mob caps at work. It looked more professional and befitting Sloane House, he said.

Margaret was actually quite grateful, as her dresses were becoming worn and faded from repeated washing and wear. Ellie had offered her one of her own dresses when she moved out of her sister's house, but they were much too large for Margaret. The money Ellie had left behind on the kitchen table the night she left disappeared with Robert. He came home a little less steady that night, reeking of whiskey and sweat.

It was late when Margaret and Emily finished putting things away and making up the bed. Margaret had left Madeline's company as soon as possible earlier in the evening, but her mistress wanted to go on about a possible beau and a new hairstyle she'd spied in a ladies' magazine.

"Walk me down," Emily asked. "We'll make tea in the house kitchen and I'll take a pot and some cookies to Todd, as a thank you for putting Ryan down tonight."

They'd arranged a few cookies on a plate and Emily left for home. Margaret was ready to climb the stairs to her new room, when she heard a man's steps in the hall.

"I'm glad to catch you here this late." Vincent Sloane stepped into the kitchen and Margaret's mood quickly soured. "Madeline mentioned you were moving into the house today and I wanted to welcome you."

Margaret was taken off-guard by Vincent's kind words. The few times she'd seen him at Sloane House during the past months, he was always frowning. She had heard him and Madeline argue on a regular basis. But, in the candlelight, Vincent seemed softer all around. A single, dark curl dragged across his forehead.

He smiled engagingly. "You're up late. I hope Madeline isn't taking advantage of your good nature. I'm afraid she's still a child at heart."

"She's young and pretty and all alone in this house," Margaret said. "She simply needs a friend."

Vincent stepped back. "I guess she is young and pretty. But, she's hardly alone." His brown eyes shone brightly in the flame of the candle Margaret carried.

"Is there anything I can get for you? I was about to retire," she asked.

"No, thank you," Vincent said. "I'm here to help. I want to be sure you're happy at Sloane House. I hope we can be friends and I'd like to speak with you more often, now that you're living here. I visit each Tuesday and I'll be certain to seek out your counsel in matters regarding my father's widow."

"Good night," he said, with a slight bow. "Sleep well." Quickly, he strode out of the kitchen.

"Sleep tight," she corrected him under her breath. "Don't let the bed bugs bite." She muttered under her breath and mounted the back stairs, Vincent Sloane's admonitions already forgotten.

The days at Sloane House quickly fell into a pattern. Rising before dawn, Margaret had coffee in the kitchen and prepared Madeline's breakfast tray. It made less work for Sadie and the housemaids if Margaret put together Madeline's breakfast and took the tray up to Madeline's suite. It also gave Margaret a chance to gauge her mistress's mood and plan her day.

Madeline woke up slowly and enjoyed English tea with two lumps of sugar, toast lightly browned with butter, cinnamon *and* sugar. One morning, during the second week, she made the mistake of entering Madeline's room after she knocked, but before she Madeline responded, "Enter."

Madeline was obviously still abed, but the neat braids Margaret had plaited just 12 hours ago, were wrapped across Madeline's face and one was tucked into the front of her sleeping gown. Her eyes were glued shut and wrinkles adorned her brow.

Margaret had slept with her sisters in Ireland and with Ellie on the ship and at the O'Deys. But she'd never seen Madeline in disarray. Certainly not like this.

"Did you sleep well, ma'am?" Margaret inquired.

"No, I didn't," she snapped back. "What business is it of yours?"

"I'm sorry, ma'am. Let me set this tray aside and bring you a warm cloth from the bathroom."

Madeline sat up, but her puckish mood didn't brighten when Margaret pulled the drapes open and let the low winter sun into the mistress' suite.

"What would you like to wear today, miss?" Margaret asked.

"It's Vincent's day to inspect," Madeline rolled her eyes. "I always wear my least attractive frock on inspection day. You should know that by now."

"How about trousers? Are they suitable for a day at home?"

"I'll wear them whenever I want. Let the old biddies complain. As a matter of fact, today's a good day. They're warm, like me and rather severe, like Vincent."

"Yes, ma'am," Margaret replied and scooted to get the gray

suit and a white silk blouse with a bow at the neck. While Madeline picked at her breakfast, Margaret set out the lotions, powders and creams Madeline wore daily to protect her complexion.

After she'd set the breakfast tray aside, she brushed out Madeline's braids and wove her waist-length blonde hair into an elaborate plait down her back. It would have been impossible for Madeline to do it up herself and Margaret welcomed the quiet, introspective moment to start their day. When she'd tucked the last comb and pin into the elaborate confection, she patted stray bits into submission.

Madeline smiled, nodded and yanked one tendril along her temple loose. "Mustn't be too perfect for Vincent," she said, as the two went downstairs to greet the day.

Todd was struggling with a belt on Vincent Sloane's car one Saturday, as Emily played with the boys and Margaret tended the kitchen garden. Vincent appreciated Todd's service on the car, as his chauffeur was not especially gifted under the hood. In addition, his car ran more smoothly than Madeline's and he liked Madeline *and* Todd to know that.

As he hovered in the background, Vincent was careful not to get grease on his trousers. He didn't mind getting dirty, but he wasn't interested in getting into the mechanics of things. Greasy fingernails made him uncomfortable in general.

"Damn!" Todd swore as the wrench refused to tighten.

"Everything okay?" Emily moved closer to the garage while the boys tossed a ball back and forth on the lawn. She had one eye on them and the other on Todd and Vincent.

"I could sure go for a glass of lemonade," Todd told his wife. "Could you bring a pitcher for the four of us and cups for the kids?"

Emily left the boys in Margaret's care while she went inside. Vincent sidled over, feigning interest in their ballgame.

"Great day to be outside," he began. "Are you a picking something for today's lunch?"

"I'm not much of a gardener," Margaret said. "Sadie just asked me to pull some weeds."

"I'd offer to help, but I'm really not dressed for it," he countered. "That's why I'm stepping back and letting Todd fix the car. I'm not good with my hands. Can I carry your basket?"

Margaret just stared at him, incredulity apparent on her face. Time to slow it down a notch, he decided. Whistling, he turned back to the garage, just as Emily returned with the drinks. She and Margaret joined the men in the shade of a large oak tree near the garage door and called the boys over.

Margaret poured the pale pink lemonade over ice in the tall frosted glass tumblers. She handed a pair to Todd and Mr. Sloane first, Vincent's hand barely touching hers as she handed him the cup.

"Whoa!" He acted pleasantly surprised at the addition of muddled strawberries. "This is delicious."

"It's Emily's specialty," Margaret said as she handed small plastic cups to the children and lastly served Emily and herself.

Quiet reigned as the adults sated their thirsts, then the children dropped their cups and began racing about again. "May I?" Vincent asked Emily and turned to haul up both boys about the waist and twirled them like a carousel.

Emily looked at Todd in surprise. "He loves children," her husband replied. "He's told me he wants sons of his own someday."

Most days, when Madeline received guests, Margaret found an excuse to busy herself elsewhere. Often, there were clothes to launder, mend and iron. Madeline didn't like the housemaids washing her things, especially her delicates. She thought they were too rough, perhaps damaging a bit of lace or even absconding with a small item.

Other times, Margaret joined Emily and Jack in the kitchen while Madeline completed correspondence or visited with friends in her parlor. Jack was a happy baby and most mornings he and Ryan were cheerful mates, playing 'round the fire while Emily kept a close eye and helped Sadie with the morning's chores.

But today Madeline's sour mood continued. "I don't like the brown trousers for a little boy," she told the Emily. "I want him to wear blue tops and bottoms every day."

"His blue trousers were in the laundry, Mrs. Sloane," Emily replied. "I'll speak to the laundress right away."

"You do that. And, call up Macy's to have them send over three more pairs. He's growing like a weed, so measure before you call."

As the two friends stood to leave with Baby Jack, Madeline pulled Margaret back into the room. "Please, stay with me," she pleaded. "I can't take another hour alone with that man."

"Do you mean your stepson, Mrs. Sloane?" Margaret asked.

"Who else do you think I meant, stupid girl?" Madeline snapped, then looked down. "I'm sorry to be so short with you, Margaret. It's not your fault. I'd need to ask for an increase to my allowance. My year of mourning ends soon and I'll need an entire new wardrobe for spring."

Margaret flinched at Madeline's words. "I, I understand." She shook her head slowly. So much for friendship.

"You don't know Vincent," Madeline continued, without a glance at Margaret. "He's trying to cut me *and* Baby Jack out of the will. I called a lawyer, but it's hopeless for a woman to contest."

Margaret could only nod. Her mother had taught her early on, a woman's place was in her husband's home. Without a husband, Madeline was cut out, just like Margaret.

"Just mind your P's and Q's," Madeline cautioned further. "Vincent is a slick one and he's out to take my portion of Jack's estate. Listen to how he speaks to me and, if he asks you any questions outside of this room, just play dumb. That shouldn't be too difficult."

When Vincent arrived at Sloane House later in the morning, he was his usual charming self. Dressed in a navy-striped suit and tie, his light brown hair was cut short and combed to one side with a bit of a cowlick at the back of his head.

As Margaret handed him a cup of black coffee, she examined his hands. They were smooth and his nails buffed to a shine. "Two sugars and a splash of cream?" She tried to make small talk to cover Madeline's bad mood.

Vincent shredded Madeline's budget. "You really need to make some cuts. I will say, the household has been humming along more smoothly since Margaret's arrival."

Madeline smiled invitingly. "I *neeeed* to talk about my clothes. Spring is fast approaching and by mid-April, I'll need to move out of my widow's weeds and into something more becoming a woman of my station. I thought I might visit with some designers this week to begin work on a new wardrobe."

"Has it been a whole year since we lost my father?" Vincent replied thoughtfully. "It seems like yesterday. Indeed, the pain is still raw."

Madeline was quick to agree. "Yes, yes. I feel the same way, of course. But Jack would want us to move on. I'm still a young woman and you are a young man. Have you considered marrying after the year of mourning is over?"

"Are you proposing?" Vincent grinned. "I'm busy learning the ropes at my father's office. I'm not ready to marry."

"Don't be silly. Your father would want you to marry and have children. He would have loved for you to give Baby Jack a little niece or nephew to play with. Someone for him to mentor as they grow up together in the city. Have you spoken to your mother?"

"Mother has decided to move back to England," Vincent said. "She thinks Europe is a more civilized country. My sister's introduction to society and her subsequent marriage are paramount in Mother's mind."

"Oh, do stop being a pill," Madeline finally snapped. "I just want a new dress for the spring parties. You have millions and I have, I have, nothing." She burst into tears and stomped out of the room and up the stairs.

Vincent gazed after her in amusement. "You see what I'm dealing with," he said to Margaret. "A spoiled, petulant child. My father coddled her, and she expects me to do the same."

"Mrs. Sloane is having a bad day. She didn't sleep well. Please, just give her a few pounds for some new dresses," Margaret said.

"Oh, I fully intended to allow for some new gowns this season. I just want her to recognize my father ahead of her frocks. And, I wanted to needle her a bit. You might tolerate her puckish moods. I cannot."

He fell silent then, his gaze on her. Margaret wanted to squirm as his eyes roamed, first to her cap, then to her face, then lower. When his eyes finally met hers again, she could feel the heat in her cheeks. "You have such lovely hair, it's a shame to cover it up with that awful cap."

"And the shapeless dress does nothing for your figure. You might ask Sadie if one of the housemaids is handy with a needle and thread. They could take it in to fit your shape better."

Margaret stared, mouth open, as Vincent left the room, without further comment. She was rooted to the spot, thinking of Martin's rare compliments and the year without him. Her lips parted and she became aware of her pulse, jittering somewhere around the 150 mark.

What was he up to? She lingered near the door by the hall and swallowed hard. Margaret bit her cheek as she drew in a sharp breath and blew it out. He's up to something. She hurried into the kitchen to report to Emily, and then up the back stairs to attend to Madeline.

Vincent stood stock still as Margaret walked back into the kitchen. Her refusal did nothing to dampen his spirits and sense of the game. He'd simply have to learn to sharpen his game play to impress the pretty Irish girl.

13 December 1912

My dearest Margaret,

This is the hardest thing I've ever had to tell. Your father died in his sleep last week, so he didn't suffer. The funeral was Tuesday. I don't think he ever recovered from the wrong news of your passing when the ship sank.

I did not want to use a stranger's phone to call and there is nothing you can do to help him now. I do not want you to return to Ireland. You are better suited for America and the money you send home is so helpful.

I will be okay here with your brothers and sisters. Please continue to write to tell me of your adventures in America.

Your loving mother,
Bridget Mannion

Chapter Nine

Emily heard Margaret gasp, then a soft moan. "Papa."

She pulled a rocking chair, usually reserved for Sadie, near the fireplace and helped Margaret sit down. "What is it, Margaret? Bad news?" She reached for her friend.

Margaret held up a hand, warding off a hug. She was afraid she would crumble into pieces if anyone even touched her. "Papa, papa, papa," Margaret moaned, wrapping her arms around herself as if to stop her heart from beating out of her chest.

Emily could see Margaret was having trouble breathing and she couldn't focus to answer her questions. She began to sob, then lifted her eyes to Emily's. "I killed him. My father is dead, and I killed him."

"No!" Emily rubbed Margaret's back in tight little circles. She wanted to hold her close, but the tension in Margaret's body warned her off. Instead, she stroked her arm while attempting a clumsy smile.

Finally, she sat down across from Margaret. Their knees touched as Emily spoke. "My mother used to say, when a parent dies, you bury them in your heart. He'll always be right here with you, now." She carefully touched Margaret's shoulder again and the two dissolved into one another's arms, Emily absorbing some of Margaret's hurt.

Finally, the tears slowed, and Margaret simply sat and

rocked back and forth by the fire. Emily didn't say, "It's okay. Stop your crying." Instead, she told Margaret, "It hurts. Just let it all out."

Finally, Emily plucked the once sleeping Baby Jack from the cradle and set him in Margaret's lap, while she fixed lunch for the two little boys.

Margaret held the baby close and stared into the fire. The flames licked higher into the chimney. Other staff members came and went. Sadie noticed the chair, Margaret and the baby. She raised her eyebrows into a question mark toward Emily. But Margaret took no notice. She rocked the baby to sleep once again and with his light snores, she began to doze herself.

Emily took the chance to visit Mrs. Sloane in her sitting room. Madeline was writing letters and making phone calls. When she heard of Margaret's father's death, she wanted to help. She suggested a return ticket to Ireland, but she was afraid Margaret would not return.

"The funeral is already spent," Emily told her employer. "I think Margaret would be better served by keeping her busy. A kind word and perhaps some extra quiet time with our family in the evenings?

"Yes, of course." Madeline was also especially close to her father. He'd tried to slow down the wedding plans Madeline's mother had set upon, but he was no match for the strong-willed woman.

Madeline slowly climbed the stairs to her bedroom. She had in mind a special memento she wanted to share with her lady's maid and friend. Her social circle didn't include anyone like Margaret, and she wanted to be sure her new friend felt included.

That evening, as Margaret began dressing Madeline's hair, her eyes were red-rimmed and her cheeks blotchy. The younger woman put her hand to the top of her head and stopped Margaret's brushing. "I know you received bad news by post." she began. "I won't pretend to understand your loss, so soon after our shared losses in April. I want you to have something to dry your tears in the days ahead."

Madeline pulled the Irish handkerchief from the drawer of her dressing table. The ornate white *M* was stitched with a special flourish Margaret had seen only in some of the finest shops of Galway City. The lace was soft and full.

"You're so kind, Mrs. Sloane. I mean Madeline." Margaret touched the hankie to her cheek. "Thank you for this lovely gift and the time you've offered to grieve my father. I would like to spend the day with Ryan, Emily and Todd tomorrow. Have a Mass said for my father's soul at St. Joshua's, maybe light a candle."

"But I'd really like to return to work on Monday. Busy hands... you know...," A single tear escaped from behind the eyes she thought had gone dry.

Madeline turned, rose to her feet and hugged Margaret, but the gesture felt forced. They broke apart quickly and Madeline sank to her stool in front of the dressing table. As Margaret gathered up her employer's clothing off the floor, Madeline spoke up again, "Take as much time as you need, Margaret."

"Thank you, ma'am." She liked Madeline well enough, but she knew where the boundaries lay, and hugging was outside the line.

For the rest of the week, Margaret went about her work like a robot. She'd read about robots in the Wizard of Oz and humanoid robots were in the newspapers, which were always strewn all over the floor after Madeline had finished her breakfast tray. Mrs. Sloane had the bad habit of leaving much of her food uneaten on the tray and her coffee cup half-hidden behind a book or a bit of bric-a-brac.

With war brewing back in Europe, newspaper editors were discussing remote control weapons, based on the work of a Nikola Tesla who had built an electrical boat that could be remotely controlled by radio.

Margaret was a robot now and Mrs. Sloane carried the radio controls. She trudged through her duties at Sloane House, picking up Madeline's dainties, dressing her for her excursions and listening to her blather on as she brushed out her hair each evening. After the first mention of Margaret's father's death, Madeline never mentioned him again.

By the end of the second week, Margaret was beginning to wonder if she might ever recover from the loss of her father. He encouraged her to come to America, with the understanding he would always be there in Ireland if she had to return. But he wasn't in Ireland any longer and she might never return.

She shouldered much of the blame for his death, too. Her mother said her father's heart was broken by the mistaken news of her death. And now, Margaret would never see him again. She had lost a fiancé and now her father.

"How *can* I go on, Em Gem?" she asked her best friend. "I wish I had died instead of him."

Emily stopped in her tracks. She set Baby Jack down and wrapped her arms around Margaret. "How can you not go on, my dear Margaret? Your father wanted you to be here. He wanted you to live a good life and to help your family. Your brothers in Ireland are there to help your mother. Your responsibility is to help provide for Celia's passage here."

It was Emily's quiet tone and common-sense manner that pulled Margaret from the dark place she'd been living. Emily was the friend who let you cry when you needed to, rail against injustice when it struck too close to home, but to rein you in when either mood had gone on too long.

"You're right, Emily. I'll try to put on a happy face."

"Happy isn't necessary, dear Margaret. Grief comes in waves; tomorrow you may feel human again and the next day it will wash over you. I'm here for you to talk to, whenever you need me. Please, try to carry on just a little bit and perhaps your work will help to distract you."

Margaret straightened her shoulders and smoothed her apron. Emily had spoken from the heart, she decided. If she were to keep extra busy, she hoped some of the sadness would subside.

Margaret felt drained. Despite the aches throughout her body, she knew it was time to return to work. As she left the kitchen and moved into the main hall on her way to Madeline's sitting room, Vincent appeared, as if out of nowhere.

"Margaret." He stood between her and pantry door. "Madeline mentioned your loss and I wanted to offer my sympathies. I know how difficult it is to lose your father."

"Of course," she answered. "I'm sorry to have acted so harshly. I should be more respectful, Mr. Sloane. Does it get any easier with time?" It had been only eight months since she'd lost Martin. Life had a way of rubbing salt in her wounds.

"I can't say it gets easier," he replied, smiling softly. He placed a hand on her arm and leaned in. "It's more like you just get accustomed to the hurt."

Margaret pulled back from what was fast becoming a tender moment, but Vincent continued. "Every day, I think of something I should discuss with my father, some little bit of business or a story I heard at work. Unlike Mother, Father loved crazy stories. He'd like to have traveled into space or under the sea." He stopped short. "Sorry! I didn't mean to bring up past wounds for either of us."

"Please, Mr. Sloane. It's just... It's just when I thought I was starting to get over the loss of my fiancé, something new strikes me down. Todd thinks I should start seeing other men."

"Todd, the driver?" Sloane asked. "Are you close to Todd? I know you are friends with his wife, Emily."

"Todd reminds me of my brother, Larry. They have the same red-blonde hair. And, he treats me like a sister, always looking out for me and seeing I make it home safely."

"I've always liked Todd," Sloane replied absentmindedly. "My father hired him before he remarried. I don't know if he knew Emily would be such a good nanny. The new baby was a surprise to all of us."

"Well, I had best get back to work," Margaret moved toward the door. "Your mother is expecting me."

"Stepmother." Vincent bristled. "My mother is the Honorable Baroness Ribblesdale. Her parents were members of society for many years, unlike Madeline's family. This home was a wedding gift to my parents."

He stepped aside and Margaret moved quickly up the hall toward Madeline's parlor at the front of the house and away from Vincent's newfound kindness. She was uncomfortable with his compassionate manner. It felt sincere, but she couldn't imagine where it had come from. If it was real, he might have feelings for her.

She stopped again to examine her own feelings. With her insecurities laid bare, she needed advice, but wasn't sure which way to turn. Emily was an obvious choice, but she'd made her opinions of Vincent clear already. Perhaps DeeDee, the opinionated housemaid with the short dark hair. Margaret liked her common-sense approach to life and, based on gossip, she certainly had the experience with men.

As Madeline finished with her phone calls in the hall, Margaret arranged the coffee service in the sitting room. At the sound of heavy footfalls from the foyer, she whipped around, coming face-to-face with Vincent.

"Excuse me, sir." She backed up, nearly overturning the polished silver teapot. As she grabbed the pot, one hand on the handle and the other on the base, heat singed her fingertips and she instinctively popped them in her mouth.

"I'm so sorry, Margaret. Are you hurt?" Vincent appeared contrite, but there was a playful smile on his face. He took her hand and looked directly into her eyes, measuring her reaction even as he placed a gentle kiss on her reddened palm.

Slowly, he let go of her hand and moved to his chair. He leaned back and put his hands behind his head. "Feeling better, now?"

Margaret struggled to bring the conversation back around to the tea service. She could still feel his lips on her hand, their softness against the burning pain.

Vincent's jacket tightened across his shoulders as he leaned in toward the coffee table and poured himself a cup of the strong black brew. He held the heavy pot up toward Margaret in invitation, the muscles in his arm flexing with its weight.

When she didn't respond, he set the teapot down, added sugar and cream and sipped luxuriously. His dark lips curved over the cup's rim and caressed its edge, but his eyes never left hers. Then he set it down again and put his hands together, forming a steeple with his fingers.

"Cook has laid out some cakes, baked fresh this morning," she said. "Is there anything else I can get for you?"

His grin spread a bit wider. "What do you have in mind, Margaret? You don't mind if I call you Margaret?"

Margaret jerked up. She noticed his hair was not as carefully combed to one side as usual and his suit coat was left unbuttoned. She pressed her lips together and swallowed. Then, shaking her head, she answered professionally. "You may call me Miss Mannion or Margaret, as Mrs. Sloane prefers."

She felt a tightness in her chest, weighing the pros and cons of responding to his first question without betraying her conflicting emotions. Instead she gave him a distracted nod and hurriedly returned to the kitchen to regroup before Mrs. Sloane returned.

Margaret stood in the pantry, bouncing one foot against the polished floor and rubbing her hands against one another, as if to dispel a chill in the air. Listening carefully for the bell from the sitting room, she darted a glance into the kitchen to see if Emily had returned from the nursery with the baby.

She was certain Mr. Sloane's flirtatious comments were completely innocent, but she wasn't prepared for his kiss or steering the conversation away from his ribald comments.

She startled as the bell rang again, loudly, from the sitting room. She picked up a towel and wiped her brow, drying her hands again and picked up another tray with the tiny cakes Sadie had so carefully prepared. She tossed a clean towel across the tray top to prevent the dishes from rattling as she made her way back to the meeting.

Margaret was beginning to hate Tuesdays. They started out tense and only got worse from there. As she cleared up after Madeline's meeting with Vincent, complaints were all around her.

"The stove is too hot." Sadie.

"The coffee was weak. I hate weakness." Madeline.

"That cute bakery boy's late this morning." DeeDee.

"Baby Jack is teething, again." Emily.

"You're over budget on furnishing." Vincent.

"Sloane Enterprises is short on staff." Vincent again.

"The city's going downhill fast." Vincent *again*. His face was pinched, and a vein was throbbing in his temple.

After three months of silly smiles, flirtatious glances and mocking looks, she'd had it up to her eyebrows with the spoiled rich, both Vincent and Madeline. She set the coffee tray down in the sitting room with a decided bounce. Madeline and Vincent looked up from their paperwork.

"Margaret!" The pair spoke in unison, probably the first time they'd ever done anything together willingly. Margaret nodded a quick apology and turned to leave the room.

"Is there something you wanted to see me about, Margaret?" Madeline asked.

"No, Mrs. Sloane. It's nothing. My hands are just slippery from the kitchen." She returned to the butler's pantry.

"I've forgotten a napkin," Vincent excused himself and followed her into the hall. "Do I make you nervous?"

She whirled to face him. "You don't make me nervous. You make me angry. You're not some silly schoolboy and you're not my beau."

"Your beau?" He chuckled softly and touched her elbow. "Is that what you'd like me to be? Your favorite beau?"

Margaret frowned. "No. I don't want a beau of any stripe, but especially not one of yours. I lost my fiancé less than a year ago, so I'm still in mourning. If you can't respect your stepmother's loss, please respect mine."

Mrs. Sloane had been absent nearly every weekend since April. When Madeline was gone for a weekend, Emily would take Baby Jack to their apartment where he would sleep with Ryan. The anniversary of the Titanic loss, while inspiring newfound gaiety in Colonel Sloane's widow, forced introspection on Margaret.

She spent most of two weekends huddled alone in the bedroom at the top of the stairs. "It's time to reexamine my life and my priorities," she decided. "If I'm not be a businesswoman, a wife and a mother to Martin's children, what are my next steps?"

Years earlier, Margaret had posed nearly the same question to her mother. Since she was a child, Bridget had told Margaret motherhood was not just the highest calling, but perhaps the only calling for a woman. Her mother was 65 years old and had been raised in a rural area of a poor country — she couldn't see a career for any of her daughters. A career in service was an option Bridget may have considered for an unmarried daughter, but for Margaret it was only a fail-safe measure if she couldn't find a husband.

She and Emily had several lengthy conversations about marriage in the past months. "Marriage isn't just a way to share a home and children, Margaret," Emily said. "It's something much deeper. A sacrament, both literally and figuratively. The love Todd and I share is blessed in the church."

The puppy eyes Todd still turned Emily's way each time she came into the room were a signal true love was still alive.

When Martin died, Margaret wanted to die, too. But, twelve months of sunshine, bustling city life and good friends who really cared had brought her back to life. Even Mrs. Sloane brought a smile to her lips now, as Margaret vicariously enjoyed the food, the clothes, the jewels and the nightlife Madeline pursued.

Leaning back on the bed, Margaret picked up the worn copy of *Pride and Prejudice* she'd inherited from Mrs. Sloane. The light banter of Jane Austen was always a pick-me-up for Margaret, but the simple-minded pursuit of husbands for the Bennet daughters only reminded her of home. Perhaps her Mr. Darcy was still out there somewhere.

Reading was always her pleasure and her escape, even as a child. As an adult, she gobbled up books from the Loughanboy library and her father indulged her wherever he found books for her that he could afford.

Margaret's older brothers had enjoyed the penny dreadful series, Margaret recalled. The awful, serial stories focused on the sensational exploits of detectives, criminals or supernatural heroes. The illustrations were crude, and the paper made from cheap wood pulp. They weren't just dreadful. They were awful.

Thoughts of country homes, neighborhood dances and the Bingleys and the Bennets lulled her back to sleep.

At least two nights each week, Madeline spent the evening with Richard Gould. Margaret knew the visits were entirely innocent, but she was still doubtful a young widow should be spending time with a man, single or married, without a chaperone.

"Perhaps I'm old school," she'd confided to Emily while preparing Madeline's breakfast tray. "I'm still mourning Martin. That's why I told Todd I won't be seeing any of his friends until this summer."

"It's precisely because you weren't married, Todd has suggested seeing some eligible young men. In our circle and in our home, of course. We would never allow any harm to your reputation, Margaret," Emily said.

"I'll try to be less a stick-in-the-mud," Margaret answered hesitantly. "I've had a young man here and there offer a smile or a word of encouragement. It's my own heart that's holding me back."

As she finished the tray and turned to go up the backstairs, Vincent stepped into the room. "Madeline's baby is getting fussy," he said to Emily. "I think you should see to him right away, before Madeline sets him down and forgets about him. He *may be* a Sloane, after all."

Emily scurried to Madeline's suite, leaving Margaret alone with the man, heightening her nervousness. Not only was he her boss, but his friendly demeanor made her suspicious of his motives. After all, he was so very rich, and she was simply poor.

"Margaret, may I speak frankly?" he asked. "I feel a certain connection to you. When I learned of the loss of your father, I mean."

"Yes, sir, Mr. Sloane." She replied.

"Please, call me Vincent," he answered.

"No, sir, I mean Mr. Sloane. I could never address you by your given name. It would be disrespectful."

"Margaret, please. I am asking you again to call me Vincent. As I said at the outset, I feel a special kinship between the two of us. So close in age and circumstances, such as it is. We may have more in common than you think."

Margaret's cheeks flamed. The teacup rattled in the dainty, pink-flowered saucer on the tray she carried. She could think of nothing else to say that didn't sound impertinent.

"I'll remember your kind words," she said, moving toward the door. "I do think of you as a strong force in this home. And, you sir, are *nothing* like my brothers."

"I'll take that as a good sign," Sloane said, and wheeled

about. "I'd hate to have you think of me as a brother."

Saunterings
Town Topics

June 23, 1913 What playboy about town has been out of circulation lately? Town Topics hears one man, heir to a large fortune and son of a Titanic hero, may be off the market ladies. Vincent Sloane, owner and manager of Sloane Enterprises, took over the reins of the company from his father last summer. Before and after the young man became immersed in his father's business, he was more well-known as an extra single man at large parties. A graduate of Harvard Business College, the younger Sloane has been seen on City Streets with various young woman — some known to society and other actresses and singers on City Stages. Has young Sloane attached himself to a fair maiden of our city? He is of marriageable age and his father's widow is near to his same age, as well. Sloane's mother is in England and rumors are she's engaged to marry a baron. Does this make Vincent royal? What do you think, fair readers?

Colonel William d'Alton Mann

Chapter Ten

On Sunday, Margaret and the Roebken family followed their usual routine. After Mass, Emily roasted a small chicken — the skin was golden brown and the meat succulent. Juices dripped down Ryan's chin as he chewed on a drumstick. There were boiled potatoes to remind them of Ireland, green beans and an apple pie. Emily was an excellent cook, but Todd was the baker in the family. He'd put up the apples last fall from a tree near the garage and garnished the pastry with cinnamon and sugar around a large A for apple.

"A, apple," he repeated to Ryan over and over again before they dove in. "P, pie."

After the meal, Emily rocked Ryan to sleep. "Too-ra-loo-ra-loo-ra! Too-ra-loo-ra-li. Too-ra-loo-ra-loo-ra! Hush now, don't you cry."

After half a dozen versions of the same melody, the youngster finally nodded off. Emily passed him to Todd and turned to Margaret. "What did Mr. Sloane want coming into the kitchen Wednesday?" she asked.

"You were there." Margaret squirmed. "He wanted you to look after the baby."

"I think it was more than that," Emily said. "He has no good intentions."

"Don't be silly!" Margaret was shocked by Emily's idea. Her cheeks blazed and she turned toward the fire, wanting to blame their color on the flames.

"I just don't want you to think he's sweet on you or, even if he was, that it could go anywhere. Sloanes don't marry lady's maids and lady's maids don't marry rich playboys. Think about your own future, your family responsibilities and your father's expectations."

Margaret was livid. "Don't talk to me about my father's expectations!"

She turned toward the baby's room. "Sorry, I don't want to wake Ryan, but I have to think of what's best for my life. It's not Mr. Sloane, if that's what you're thinking. But it doesn't hurt to exchange a kind word with the man. He's been through a lot lately, too."

"Vincent Sloane will marry a socialite," Emily said. She attacked the table with broad strokes of rage. "His future was mapped out for him from the day he was born. He'll run his real estate empire for a few years, marry and start a family, then go into local government. I wouldn't be surprised if he's a candidate for governor or even president by the time he's 50."

Margaret sighed. "Now you're talking marriage. I've barely exchanged a smile and a nod with the gentleman. I'm not so naive as to think there's a future Mrs. Sloane for me other than to fetch and carry for his wife someday. He's nice and he smells good, that's all."

"Pfffft," Emily bit her bottom lip and pushed the oath out in a rush of hot air. "Don't fool yourself!"

"April 16 is just around the corner," Todd added, having overheard the end of the conversation as he came out of the small bedroom. "I'll speak to Kelly, John and William this week. We can go with you, if Sadie will watch Ryan."

For the rest of the week, Madeline was fit to be tied. Margaret spent hours listening to her spew venom about Vincent. Her employer was short with staff and ignored Baby Jack completely. Margaret would never understand this spoiled young woman. She was happy one day and angry the next.

On Thursday, she entered the dining room to pick up Madeline's lunch tray. She'd barely touched her watercress sandwiches, tea cakes and coffee. Madeline was having an animated conversation on the telephone. She held the plastic handle in one well-manicured hand and toyed with the dial on the base with the other. Margaret had never ceased to be amazed by the sheer number and ease of phone conversations in the Sloane House.

Back in Ireland, only one or two businesses in Loughaunboy had commercial telephones and they were the candlestick variety. She knew nothing had changed since her departure, because her father had called the O'Dey home once when she was living there. Dad had to go to the village office to make the call and it cost him a pretty penny, so he was short with the one conversation they had there. Margaret realized now that was the last time she spoke to her father.

Madeline, Emily and Sadie were on the phone all of the time. Emily and Sadie only made calls to order groceries or baby items, but Madeline chatted with friends on a daily basis, sometimes for hours. If they weren't able to visit each other's houses, meet for coffee or lunch at one of the bistros downtown or take a ride in the sleek, black autos they all owned, they were on the telephone.

But Margaret could tell Madeline's current conversation was not with one of her usual friends. Her tone was more measured and hushed than the usual quick wit and bawdy laughter she displayed with her friends.

"Now, Richard. You mustn't be so bold. I'm still in mourning."

Margaret cleared her throat loudly and Madeline cut the conversation short, "Talk to you later."

"I was just checking if you wanted to take the car out this afternoon, Mrs. Sloane. Todd is having some difficulties with a drive shaft, whatever that is."

"I did want to go out this evening to the theater. Please draw a bath and set out my claret velvet evening gown. Dickie Gould, Barbara's cousin from Boston, is in town for the weekend and he will be picking me up at eight."

"Will the Goulds be joining you?" Margaret asked.

"Don't be impertinent, Margaret. Dickie and I are old friends. I may be late, so don't wait up."

It had been more than a year since Margaret survived the Titanic. She no longer had vivid nightmares of screaming passengers, exploding boilers and a ship split in two on a daily basis. But, at least once a week, she woke up crying and calling out for Martin.

In her dreams, Martin's face had begun to fade. His dark good looks were still there, but his hair was shorter, and he had a full beard. Martin always wore his hair long and only shaved his full beard on this mother's request. On the ship, he had shaved the beard completely off when they helped serve drinks in the main salon.

Margaret smiled softly, dreamily, as she came fully awake. Even more unusual than Martin's beard in her dreams, she noticed his mannerisms had become more forceful, less polite and more self-assured. She shook her head twice and snuggled back under the quilts, hoping for a few more minutes sleep.

Under the eaves, early sunlight had not yet peeked through the third-floor windows. Usually, Margaret tacked a light blanket across the windows when she hoped to sleep late. As she began to doze off again — it was a Sunday and she planned to skip Mass this week — the image of the man in her dream rose up from the ether.

Margaret sat up in surprise. It was Vincent. The man in her dream was the stuff of nightmares — Vincent Sloane.

Margaret had been consciously avoiding Vincent when he

visited Madeline at Sloane House. His attention to her problems was not welcome, despite her friendly response that summer. No good could come of what DeeDee called a harmless flirtation.

Vincent *was* a flirt and a tease, she thought. The next step, if she let this infatuation go forward might be a not-so-harmless tussle between the sheets, DeeDee-approved.

She sighed softly. Vincent did look a lot like Martin. He was tall, well-mannered and friendly. She enjoyed visiting with him and that's all there was to it.

She rose from the warm bed covers. If she were to come across him in the next week, she would make it a point to ignore him or pick an argument. That would put a stop to any more bad dreams.

Margaret rushed headlong from Madeline's bedroom, heading for the back of the house and the stairs to her room. Rounding the corner, she met Vincent coming down from the servant's quarters. She dropped a bundle of Madeline's things she'd been taking to mend and launder.

"Sorry, sir. I didn't expect to see you here. Are you looking for Mrs. Sloane?" Margaret blushed as she gathered up the fine French lingerie Madeline favored. Her dream from the night before still fresh in her mind, she was convinced he could see right through her.

Vincent stumbled over his words. "No, I was just, um, inspecting the third floor for evidence of leaks in the roof. Jarvis mentioned there were some water problems up there."

"My room is at the rear of the house," she said. "I was just going up, if you need to see one of the rooms there. I believe you'll find my quarters in order."

The color in Vincent's cheeks rose to meet her own. "Actually, the housemaid — DeeDee, I believe is her name — happened to be in her room this morning. She'd run up to get her hat and gloves, so I took a glance in there. All's well."

He held the stairwell door as Margaret passed through. As she went up the stairs, her form was silhouetted by a large window at the top. Vincent waited until she turned the corner. His smile tickled the fringes of his mustache as he returned to his inspections of the upper floors.

It was a Thursday and Mrs. Sloane always hosted her bridge club on Thursdays. Bridge Club was also an opportunity for Emily and Margaret to spend quality time together in the kitchen.

Mrs. Sloane wanted Emily to parade Jack in front of her society friends, so she had to stay near the sitting room while they played cards and near the dining room when the luncheon was served.

Sadie made a special effort regarding Thursday luncheons, as well. The card game was interspersed with canapes — cut into hearts, diamonds, leaves and three-leaf clovers and garnished with red peppers and black olives.

When the ladies had retired to the dining room, Margaret served Sadie's famous chicken salad with bites of celery and grapes and, for dessert, a baked Alaska with coffee ice cream. The ladies oohed and awed, while Madeline ate it up, acting if she'd had a vital part in the preparation of the meal.

Margaret helped serve the food and take it away. Madeline trusted her more than the housemaids to be circumspect with the society friends she invited into her home. One time, she had caught DeeDee snitching canapes from the serving tray on her way through the butler's pantry.

In contrast, Margaret always waited until the ladies were gone for the day and Madeline was resting up in her room, to enjoy leftovers from the luncheon. Mrs. Sloane encouraged the staff to finish up the leftovers after the party was finished.

Margaret enjoyed bridge club for this very reason. Her

tastes had changed from her childhood days of beans, brown bread and mutton. Wolfing down the tiny salmon bites and a soggy sandwich, she was surprised to hear a man's voice behind her.

"Enjoying the ladies' foods?" Vincent asked, stepping closer. "Did you win at cards as well?"

Margaret jumped and dropped a mayonnaise-laden grape down the front of her apron. "You startled me," she turned an angry eye on Vincent.

Emily had taken Baby Jack up to the nursery while his mother was napping. Vincent moved closer as she hurriedly finished her meal. "Please, Mrs. Sloane isn't available today. I'm sure you have better things to do than to pester the help."

She turned to face him, and he was much closer than she'd imagined. She could see his long eyelashes, his glowing brown eyes and his mustache — it looked very soft. She melted just a bit, as she contemplated the close quarters where she was trapped.

Vincent's smile grew less restrained as he pulled a handkerchief from his breast pocket and dabbed a bit of mayonnaise from the corner of her mouth. "You missed a spot," he teased. "Please inform Mrs. Sloane her clothing allowance has been increased at her request. Have a good day."

Vincent's charm followed him out the door like a favorite cologne. "See you Tuesday."

Saunterings
Town Topics

August 27, 1913 One Madeline Sloane has been sighted about town with none other than Richard Gould of Boston. Earlier discussions intimated Mrs. Sloane may have become infatuated with her own stepson, but this rumor puts to rest any such attachment, un-incestuous as it may have been. Gould is a banker and is not married. His family is part of The 400 in New York City and would have been frequent party-goers at Mrs. Sloane's home when her late husband's mother, Caroline Sloane, was the social hostess of the season. Madeline Sloane was a small heir to JJ Sloane IV's fortune, as the bulk of Colonel Sloane's money went to his son Vincent. Her son JJ6 is set to inherit $3 million from his late father at the ripe old age of 21. Poor little rich boy? I think not!

Colonel William d'Alton Mann

Chapter Eleven

Spring blossomed into summer and Margaret grew weary of the gentleman callers Todd brought to the apartment above the garage to meet her. Kelly didn't wash his hands before the visit; John had terrible bad breath and William couldn't even look up when they were introduced.

Finally, Emily spoke to Todd about the quality of attractive suitors for her trusted friend. His solution was to ask Margaret to join the choir at church.

"But my singing voice sounds like a drowning cat," Margaret complained.

"With that sound, you're more likely to scare men away than attract a husband," Emily said. "Let's take a break and let nature take its course."

Margaret was relieved. She was tired of feeling she was always on display for the men her friends thought she might marry. Her parents had always told her she must marry before she was thirty. Hopefully things were different in America.

If she were to judge by Mrs. Sloane's appearances, it was time to throw off the shroud and start frolicking. Madeline was out to dinner or the theater two or three times a week, often staying out well past midnight. On one occasion, Margaret stumbled over Madeline coming into the house just as the sun peeked over the horizon.

"This is probably the type of activity Mr. Sloane warned

me about," she thought. "He'd probably like me to report this to him, but I have no intention of doing so. I don't want to get caught up in the middle of that dust-up."

Madeline's activities did give Margaret ideas of another sort of conversation she might not mind. She missed intelligent, male companionship and she didn't see any harm in speaking with Mr. Sloane — or Vincent, as she had taken to calling him when no one else was within earshot. She often dawdled in the hallway outside the parlor after Madeline's weekly contretemps with Vincent. While she continued to wear her hair tied up atop her head, she more often added a ribbon, or a comb Madeline had given her.

For his part, Vincent made no secret of his attraction to the pretty, young Irish woman. One week, he brought a small box of chocolates in his briefcase with the papers for Madeline to sign. Another time, there was a nosegay of fresh spring posies from the corner market on Seventh Avenue.

Emily didn't miss the coquettish smiles, the chocolate on Margaret's breath or the nosegay in a small water glass in the kitchen. She shot Margaret an arch look each time her friend waited quietly in the hallway. Her concern for Margaret was a concrete worry she took home to Todd that evening.

Things came to a head for all concerned in the fall of 1913. Vincent always made it a point to stand in a corner of the hallway, shielded from view of either the kitchen, the pantry, the parlor or the front door. He told Margaret he'd been raised in this house and knew of secret passages and hideaways they could explore together, if Emily's admonitions became bothersome.

Vincent was a flirt, Margaret decided, and there was nothing wrong with flirting back. She tried to avoid Emily's gaze however, when Vincent arrived at the house on Tuesdays.

It was a bright fall day in late October when the other shoe dropped. The sun was shining through trees heavy with red and yellow. But in the house, Margaret couldn't see past her own nose. The tension had been building for weeks – her mind was buzzing with images of Vincent strolling in the door, Vincent bowing deeply, Vincent winking at her.

Madeline was still upstairs when Vincent arrived, and Margaret was pretending to be busy fussing over the tea service in the sitting room when Vincent sneaked up behind her with a playful poke in the ribs. "Boo!" He grinned when she jumped, then his voice lowered. "I have something for you."

"No, Vincent. You don't need to bring me candy and flowers."

"No candy for you," he said. "I don't want you getting fat. No, this is something I gave the Baroness for Mother's Day. She left it behind when she moved to England. It's not really expensive, but I always liked it."

Margaret's eyes sparkled in anticipation as he opened the box. Nestled on a bed of creamy-white velvet sat a bumblebee brooch made of exquisitely carved jet in a gold setting, with two small diamonds for eyes on opposite sides of the head. The body and wings were brushed with real gold leaf — the entire piece reflecting brilliantly under the electric lights of the cozy room like an animated insect gathering energy for flight.

Margaret squealed. She'd never owned real jewelry before, especially anything this nice. Her arms slipped easily up and around his shoulders and she bent forward for a quick hug. Her eyes were even with his chin and the spicy aroma of his aftershave caught her nostrils. She leaned in and inhaled deeply of his scent.

Never one to waste an opportunity, Vincent stepped fully into the embrace, tipping Margaret's face up toward his and kissing her squarely on the mouth, just as Emily rounded the corner with Baby Jack.

"What's this?" Emily stopped short. "Excuse me, Mr. Sloane. Margaret, could you take Baby Jack for a moment?" She handed the boy to Margaret. "I need to get his dinner." Glaring sideways, Emily returned to the kitchen.

Margaret only shrugged and rolled her eyes. "Please, don't

say any more. It will only draw more attention."

Vincent stood silently in place, a slight nod his only affirmation, as she followed Emily into the kitchen. "It was perfectly innocent," she said. "I was merely saying thank you for a trinket his mother left behind." She set Baby Jack down on his blanket and held out the brooch.

"That *trinket* is likely worth several hundred dollars," Emily bit back. She'd warned Margaret repeatedly not to become involved with Mr. Sloane. It could only end badly.

Tuesdays were now the highlight of Margaret's week. She took special care with her hair, pinched her cheeks to add color and smiled dreamily as she prepared Madeline's tray and helped her dress.

"You seem distracted, Margaret. Is there something or *someone* I need to know about?" Madeline quizzed.

"Oh, no, ma'am." Margaret hurried to pick up the room and clear Mrs. Sloane's tray. She needed to freshen up the sitting room and bring in the coffee and cakes before Vincent arrived for the Sloanes' regular meeting.

After setting the table, Margaret stood in the corner of the large sunny room, standing first on one foot and then the other. Dappled sunlight stole through large windows on two sides of the room with black and white checkerboard tile creating a fresh backdrop for the family heirlooms collected across generations. A pair of huge Boston ferns stood sentry at the door to the hallway and kitchen, giving Margaret an unobtrusive vantage point from which to watch the Sloanes interact.

After dozens of surreptitious meetings in the front hallway, outside the kitchen door and behind closed doors throughout the huge mansion, Margaret no longer denied her fascination with Vincent.

She knew he was three years her junior, but she didn't care. She knew they could never be married, but it wasn't important. Margaret was falling in love with the charming, handsome young businessman and she simply let herself fall. After a lifetime in poverty, service and exclusion, it was her turn to be free-spirited, she decided.

She spent hours every Monday contriving excuses to be absent from Madeline's company the next day. She encouraged long lunch dates with Mrs. Sloane's friends. She told her boss she had agreed to watch Ryan, so the cook could mix up a special treat for Tuesday's dinner. One time, she even began sniffling that morning after breakfast and told Madeline she simply must take to bed for the afternoon, so as not to spread the germs to the babies or her.

After the interrupted kiss in the sitting room, Vincent and Margaret were more careful to hide their stolen moments. Often, after Madeline moved to the dining room for lunch, Margaret would stay behind to pick up in the sitting room. She carried the tray loaded with empty cups and saucers into the butler's pantry and slid them into a corner, closed the door into the kitchen, then stood quietly hoping to make herself invisible to everyone but Vincent.

Vincent entered the same way, closing the door to the sitting room and walking on cat's feet to the opposite corner. Margaret raised her lips to be kissed, not wanting to waste a single minute of their time together. His mustache tickled her neck as he nuzzled and moaned.

Margaret was careful not to give in too much. She needed to be alert — not only to his intentions, but she was always worried about Emily, Sadie or Jarvis walking in.

She'd talked to DeeDee about how she could keep Vincent interested, while preserving her virtue, but DeeDee only laughed. "Mr. Sloane isn't interested in virtue. You'll know when the moment is right."

Suddenly, she heard voices in the kitchen. "Where's Margaret?"

She breathed heavily and pushed Vincent away. "I have to get back to the kitchen with these dishes. Can I see you next week?"

Vincent trailed one finger across her bodice. His eyes suggested so much more. "I can't wait another week to see you. I'll make up some pretense to return on Friday. I know Madeline will be gone for a Halloween costume ball out of town, but I'll pretend I've forgotten. If you can wait for me in the library about this same time, I'll meet you there."

Hidden in the darker recesses of the library, Margaret waited for Vincent to appear after his meeting with Madeline. The heavy door to the room opened and Vincent slipped in with nary a sound. Floor-to-ceiling shelves crowded with books muffled any noise and heavy drapes at every window kept the room dark on an early winter afternoon, but Margaret recognized Vincent's footfalls.

"Margaret?" he called softly.

"Here," she replied from the corner near the dictionaries and a large ornate portrait of Ava Sloane. Each time she lingered in this spot, she could feel the first Mrs. Sloane's eyes boring down into her.

Ava had taken a $10 million settlement back to England with her, just after Vincent graduated from Harvard. She also received custody of Vincent's younger sister Alice.

Margaret was certain Madeline knew nothing of Ava's portrait still hanging in the library. Margaret knew Madeline never entered the library, allowing Vincent to manage the household affairs from the colonel's large rolltop desk near the wide window at the front of the house.

She'd tried to talk to Vincent once about his mother, but he was reluctant. "There's nothing to tell," he insisted. "She and my father were a poor match."

Madeline was seldom one to read a book all the way through. She preferred ladies' magazines and gossip columns like *Broadway Brevities* and *Town Topics' Saunterings*. This was one of the reasons Vincent chose the library for their assignation. If he were spied entering the room, the Sloane House records contained there gave him a handy excuse to be present.

In addition, the large bookcase in the corner near where Margaret stood now also served as a sliding doorway to a hidden passageway. Vincent pressed a button recessed behind a large volume of Chaucer and the shelf moved silently to one side. Margaret's head snapped back, then she slapped Vincent's arm playfully. He took her hand, and like schoolchildren, they ran up the narrow stairs on tiptoes, suppressing giggles.

Just before he died, Colonel Sloane had shown Vincent the passageway between the library where he kept his office and an attic bedroom where he met his mistresses. Vincent didn't tell Margaret about the mistresses, but there was no mistaking the wrought iron trundle bed covered with dusty old sheets in the corner of the room.

When they reached the top floor, Vincent pulled Margaret into him and loosened her hair. As it fell down over her shoulders, his kisses deepened, and his tongue found hers. Not a word passed between the pair, as he trailed one finger down the side of her face, along her neck and tugged at her neckline.

"We have to do something about this horrid black dress," he muttered under his breath. The stiff fabric rustled as his hands roamed up her back and nearer the difficult row of buttons marching from neck to waistline.

She leaned in and tilted her head, pulling him closer. "You chose the dresses."

"That was before I knew how anxious I would be to have it off of you," he breathed.

"Vincent!" Margaret gasped. She pulled back from his anxious embrace. "Not yet. I don't think I'm ready."

"I can't help myself, Margaret. I think I'm falling in love with you."

"What's that? A cookbook?" Margaret peered over Dee-

Dee's shoulder that evening after work. The two women's rooms were across the hall from one another and DeeDee lay on her stomach in bed reading.

"It's the *Women's Suffrage Cookbook*," DeeDee paused, turning the cover toward Margaret. A silhouette of Uncle Sam piloting the ship of state figured prominently on the bright blue cover.

Margaret was perplexed. "I don't understand. Why does a women's suffrage group publish a cookbook? Isn't the movement aimed at empowering women outside the home?"

"We use what we know to raise money and spread our message," DeeDee answered. "The cookbooks are also a strong tool for the jokes directed against us. We're painted as kitchen-hating witches."

Margaret snatched the cookbook and held it up over Dee-Dee's head. She moved to one corner and sat in the room's only chair to learn more.

One of the recipes was for graham crackers. She recalled DeeDee telling a story about a Reverend Graham, who believed rich food inflamed sexual appetite. He invented the graham cracker to help tame sexual desires. By the reverend's standards, some of the rich dessert recipes in the new cookbook were 100% dishonorable.

Other recipes were entirely playful, Margaret noticed. Like *Mother's Election Cake, Suffrage Salad Dressing* and *Parliament Gingerbread.* One recipe called for a quart of human kindness, mixed with tact and velvet gloves, using no sarcasm, especially for the upper crust.

She turned to DeeDee. "I didn't know you were interested in suffrage for women."

"Ireland is leaps and bounds ahead of America in women's rights," DeeDee said. "Ask your mother about women's rights to vote. Or, better still, there's going to be a march near here in April. Alice Paul, Carrie Nation and Helen Hunt will all be there. Do you want to go with me?"

Margaret dropped the book into her lap and lowered her

gaze. "I didn't come here to talk about women's rights or cooking. I need your advice on men."

Saunterings
Town Topics

September 9, 1914 A woman with a college degree in the Arts and a Quaker sensibility has brought her firebrand violence to fight for the women's vote back to American soil. Alice Paul, 29, is the oldest of four children and a descendant of William Penn, the Quaker founder of Pennsylvania. Her record of civil disobedience is legendary after a "conversion experience." Does this disobedience belong with the fair women of our New York City? Miss Paul has been arrested seven times and imprisoned three times. She has sought and received donations from our own Ava Belmont, a socialite of our fair city. It has to make you wonder, where are their husbands during these trying times? It is no wonder Paul remains unmarried, but Belmont has been married twice in socially prominent families in our city. Men, do we want the ladies voting for president, mayor or school board? I think not, as their emotions may sway the vote. I worry they look only for the most attractive face on the ballot.

Colonel William d'Alton Mann

130

Chapter Twelve

"**A**lice, please, *do* sit down!" Helen Hunt begged her friend. Normally, Helen spoke almost deferentially to Alice Paul, the outspoken and combative suffragist leader. While she usually avoided the popular idea of femininity — pastels, flounces and boned corsets — Helen was of the notion women could win more flies *and votes* with honey than vinegar.

Hunt dressed in menswear to promote her beliefs, as well. Her comfortable, cashmere tweed suit — jacket and trousers — was softened by a scarf at her neck and trained waves in her glossy auburn hair falling to her shoulders. And, her attraction to the cause of suffrage did not begin with her own fervent desire to vote. Instead she was attracted to the charismatic Alice Paul and their friend Lucy Burns.

While other ladies of their class sewed flags and wrapped bandages, Helen, Alice and Lucy led marches. Two days before Wilson's first inauguration, Paul organized a parade of more than 5,000 participants from every state in the union. Helen was quick to follow Alice's lead, carrying a sign and marching to the drumbeat of the older women's chants.

"Pray to God. *She* will help you." Helen's sign read in large letters, handwritten in blood-red paint. The energy of the crowd invigorated her as she stepped in time to their chants. At one point along the parade route, the chanting stopped for

Alice's speech. Helen was mesmerized by Alice's words.

"When the Civil War began," Paul told reporters, "Susan B. Anthony was told the same things we are being told today. If she'd only drop her suffrage work and become an abolitionist, women would be given the vote as a reward as soon as the war was over. She did, and as a result, all legislation in which women were interested was promptly dropped."

Suddenly, an overripe tomato hit Alice squarely on the bosom. Helen whipped her head around to identify the assailant. "Off with you!" she cried out.

A young ruffian grabbed her shoulder. "You're one of them. Be off with *you*, bitch."

Helen shoved the man, ducked away and ran toward the podium. Encumbered by the heels on her short boots, she clambered up the steps onto an impromptu stage, a flatbed wagon pulled by two draft horses.

"Alice, Carrie, make way. I've seen violence in the crowd. Surely you're the targets." At her urging, the horses — wearing gold tassels and white ribbons like many of the suffragettes — began to trot toward the front of the crowd. "You're driving into the fray," Helen cried. "We must move away."

The parade continued moving forward with the crowd close behind. Twice Alice stopped the wagon in front of the Waldorf-Astoria, where a small crowd had gathered for an international conference. "Mister President! How long must women wait for liberty?" Her shouts only brought more police to the front of the wagon.

The police shook their batons. "Move along, ladies, or we'll have you arrested for obstructing traffic."

Alice raised her fist and shouted, "We shall fight for the things which we have always held nearest our hearts." She stopped, cleared her throat and yelled as loudly as possible, her fellow suffragettes joining in. "For Democracy, For Women To Have A Voice In Their Own Government."

Helen continued to scan the crowd, trying to gauge the interest from different groups. She saw a trio of young women, all dark haired with pale skin standing at the back of the crowd near the hotel. They were dressed conservatively, but in similar black dresses with white caps, almost like a uniform. Servants from a nearby mansion, she presumed. The taller, more confident one of the three was carrying a sign saying simply "Suffrage for Women," while the other two hung back, unconvinced.

Meanwhile, the crowd surged forward, angry faces on all sides. Many of the women were dressed in white, a symbol of the suffrage movement, with blue banners or flowers on their shoulders. Helen saw one woman watching the show with wide eyes and frequent smiles, only to be pulled aside by a man, presumably her husband, and dragged back into the hotel.

"Many of the men feel threatened by strong women," Alice told Helen the next day, "and many of the women do, too. But I think we succeeded in our main objective, focusing attention on the issue of women's suffrage. Especially with President Wilson."

Emily refused to look Margaret in the face. She'd been trying for weeks to convince Margaret a relationship with Mr. Sloane was doomed. She watched Margaret find excuses to be in the same room as Colonel Sloane's son whenever he visited Sloane House.

Last week, taking Baby Jack to the sitting room for his mandatory public viewing by visitors, she watched Mr. Sloane take the tea tray from Margaret. His hand lingered when she passed the cups and his smile was a little too wide.

"He's using you," she told Margaret when she returned to the kitchen. "A Sloane and a servant girl? Don't be ridiculous."

When Margaret told Emily about Vincent's kiss, she chattered on like a schoolgirl. But, when Emily asked if she was embarrassed, she stopped short. "I'm not embarrassed," Margaret said. "I've done nothing to be embarrassed about."

"This will be trouble," Emily insisted. "Mr. Sloane does

not have good intentions. He'll take and he'll take, but he won't be giving anything back to you in return."

"We're neither one married," Margaret shot back. "And I'm not asking for anything in return. If Vincent *were* to propose marriage, I'd say no. I'm *not* stupid."

Emily drew back as if she'd been slapped. "I didn't say you were stupid."

"You called me ridiculous. You said he was taking me in."

"I just want what's best for you," Emily sat back in her chair and pulled Baby Jack closer. The boy required all her attention nowadays. He was toddling all around the kitchen and seemed fascinated by the flame from the gas stove.

Margaret stepped in and reached for the boy. "Emily, I'm not a child. I'm 28 years old and fully capable of taking care of myself. I know a man has needs, but I also have wants and needs of my own."

Now, it was Emily's turn to blush. "Wants? Needs?" she stuttered.

"I'm just saying, I'm a grown woman. I want to be married someday, so I'm careful. And, Vincent respects me. It's just a kiss, no promises of anything more."

Emily and Margaret sat quietly in front of the fire for several long minutes. "I love you, you know," Emily whispered, the baby's head tucked under her chin.

"I know. I love you, too Em Gem."

As Vincent led Margaret up the secret, dusty stairway into the attic, she held her breath, slipping one hand over her mouth to silence her thoughts from escaping into words and ruining the mood. Margaret had been thinking about her feelings for Vincent for weeks now, ever since she'd had the talk with Emily, but she was afraid to say anything.

Everything about her upbringing, her schooling in Ireland, and Emily's admonitions told her this was all wrong, what she was doing with him. But her body said it was all right.

As Vincent fumbled with the buttons along the back of her dress and untied the apron, Margaret pulled the frilly white cap off her head and loosened her thick, dark hair from its confines.

Dust motes lingered in the few shafts of sunlight entering the little room from the single north-facing window. The sun hadn't made an appearance in more than a week and now a light rain began to fall, but neither noticed the weather outdoors.

Margaret and Vincent were both breathing heavily, but she was the one to say, "Stop! We aren't married and we never will be. I'm not going to be your wife, ever." She tugged her dress tightly back across her chest and used the apron to shield the sight of her lace camisole from the devil's eyes staring back at her.

Vincent froze and his eyes bore into hers. "I am yours," he said. "I will always be yours. If marriage is what you want, I can arrange that."

Now, his movements became less hurried and he held Margaret close, her head nestled beneath his chin. His hands rubbed her back as he shared the warmth from his body. "I don't mean to frighten you and I'm certainly not trying to take something you're not willing to give. I've been a bachelor so long, I guess I wasn't thinking about marriage just yet. But I know I'm not willing to let you go, either."

The cold rain pattered against the window in the early darkness and the pair nestled deeper below the musty blankets. Quiet reigned.

Vincent was the first to break the silence. "I have to visit Europe for a few months on business soon," he said. "The situation there is tense, and my mother is concerned about her business interests."

He stroked her back as Margaret began to calm down. "I'll talk to my mother. I'll explain the situation and she'll understand. When I return in January, we can tell Madeline. Until then, you must keep quiet."

He began to kiss her again, softly this time. As her body warmed to his touch, she relaxed and began to return his kisses. They fell back onto the bed again and dust rose to the ceiling. "I love you," Vincent said.

And, I love you," Margaret murmured, as she slipped her hands beneath his shirt.

"That's all that matters," he reassured her. "We *will* be together soon."

17 November 1914

Dearest Margaret,

I fear the war is upon us. Redmond has declared in the House of Commons the government may withdraw troops from Ireland and leave us defenseless. He calls for a home defense from the Irish Volunteers, leading to another call for home rule. We were convinced a home rule would pass this year, but it left out the six counties of Ulster in the north.

Emotions are running high in Ireland as the Germans threaten Paris and even the volunteers are divided in support for the British war effort. I am worried for your brothers as they may be called to service. I am fortunate there are four boys still here, so one may be able to stay behind and help me with the farm.

Postal service is still hit and miss here, with more missing by far. Please write often, so I can stay current with your situation. Our financial situation is not dire and no travel will happen until the end of the war, so save your money there and we will talk about Celia's travel when times are better.

Yours,
Mam

P.S. This Sunday at Mass, Delia was there with her new baby. She and her husband have six children now. You remember Delia, don't you? She was in your grade in school.

Chapter Thirteen

One of the things Margaret loved most about her time with Vincent was when they just talked. Her Sunday afternoons were spent primarily with him, cooking a light meal, sharing passages from a book and talking about current events.

One day in early fall, the bees were buzzing lazily around the patio at Vincent's country estate, *Fairholme*. The couple had taken to visiting the country on weekends when Margaret was sure Madeline would be out of town for several days.

Margaret stretched lazily in a light cotton dress. She wasn't wearing any socks or shoes and her hair hung loosely around her shoulders on Vincent's lap.

"My mother wrote to me recently about the tensions in Europe. She said powerful men in Europe are struggling to maintain a balance of power. Since the Kaiser came to the throne in Germany, they are becoming more powerful, and Britain has not allied with France or Russia."

"Your mother is a student of international trade?" Vincent asked. In the past five years, the English monarchy — including his mother's new husband Thomas Lister, the 4th Baron Ribblesdale — had endorsed Parliament's race to build ships to expand their advantages over the Kaiser.

Only a week ago, Margaret heard a radio news account about an Austrian Archduke visiting the Bosnian capital of Sarajevo. "A group of six men had gathered on the street where the duke's motorcade would pass with the intention of assassinating him," the commentator read. "They missed, but when the duke was returning from a visit to see the wounded at a local hospital, he took a wrong turn that led to his death. Another of the assassins shot the duke and his wife."

Madeline was listening to the radio, too. "I don't think it matters much. The crowds in Vienna listened to music and drank wine, as if nothing had happened."

Margaret couldn't believe life could go on in Europe after the assassination, without any political impact. When Vincent visited Sloane House on Tuesday, she was boiling over with a list of questions.

"Emperor Franz Joseph was incensed," he agreed. "Riots broke out in Sarajevo, with Austria extraditing hundreds of Serbs from their country, imprisoning and executing hundreds of others."

The couple watched nervously as the assassination led to a month of diplomatic maneuvering between Austria-Hungary, German, Russia, France and Britain, called the July Crisis. Vincent canceled a planned cruise when additional countries joined the war, including Russia. Kaiser Wilhelm II of German was a cousin to Tsar Nicholas II, but the tsar refused to suspend mobilization and demands on France to remain neutral.

As the fall progressed, Madeline spent more time with the Goulds, giving Margaret and Vincent the opportunity to have time alone together at Fairholme, the Sloane's country estate. One weekend, Vincent pressed Margaret to travel with him to Boston the following Friday.

"I have a business meeting in the city. We can have dinner in the evening — someplace nice. No one will know you there. We can tell anyone who asks you are visiting from Europe. And, you can borrow a dress from Madeline's closet."

Margaret was vehemently opposed to borrowing a dress from Madeline. But she did have a castoff gown of Madeline's in her room. Earlier that month, Madeline had tossed a midnight blue paisley dress at Margaret's feet, asking her to donate it the rag man or have it burned. The dress had a red wine stain near the hem, so Margaret spent hours trying different formulas to remove the stain.

After several attempts of blotting, caking it in a salt paste and pouring boiling water over it, the dark red stain was nearly invisible on the dark blue dress. But *nearly* invisible wasn't good enough for Madeline. The gown, still lovely, was bound for the trash.

On Monday, Margaret pressed Madeline for her weekend plans, forgetting all about the holiday that week. "We're leaving for the holiday on Thursday," Madeline said. "Please pack my furs again, as I'm sure there will be sleighing. I'd invite you to come along, but there are no rooms for servants in the Gould's country house," she finished. "What will you do while I'm gone?"

Margaret smiled to herself. "I'll find something."

The weather in Boston was sunny and bright, but Margaret simply couldn't enjoy herself. She'd made a flimsy excuse to Emily and Todd for being absent four full days and found it difficult to pack a few items for an evening out, without someone getting suspicious. In the end, she told DeeDee she was meeting a friend from Ireland who had recently immigrated to Boston. To gain her cooperation, Margaret let her believe there may be a romantic liaison in the offing.

The carpetbag she'd found in the attic was small, but she'd placed tissue between the folds of the dress Madeline had refused after Margaret's hours of labor. She borrowed a bit of lace and a sewing kit from Sadie to create the finishing touches.

As a final touch, DeeDee shared a pot of deep red rouge for her cheeks and lips, along with blotting papers to complement her naturally pale skin. A gray-brown paste made from Vaseline and ash served as both eyeliner and mascara.

Although they were on the same train, they traveled separately so as not to arouse suspicion. Vincent asked Todd to arrange for his private rail car to be attached to a train out of Union Station for the business trip.

"I'll be staying in the city over the weekend," he told Todd. "I'm meeting with some old friends from college who still live in the area."

Margaret's ticket was on the same train, in coach. As they traveled, she daydreamed of the three days in Boston, alone with Vincent every night. "I'm sure I will mess it up," she'd told him when he made his weekly visit to Sloane House last Tuesday. "What will I say? How will I act?"

She was more worried about her Irish accent than anything, but she'd overcome that hurdle with a decision to say little, if anything, during their evening out.

"We're going to dinner alone," Vincent assured her. "I don't know a lot of people in Boston, so it's unlikely we'll come across anyone I know there. If we do, I'll introduce you as an old friend from my Harvard days. You can just speak quietly and they'll assume you're shy."

Margaret had two $20 gold certificates in her bag, with pictures of George Washington on the center of the face. She'd creased white bands on the back of the orange note bald, folding and refolding as the train clacked along the tracks.

Modern taxi cabs crowded the Boston railway station platform. She gave the name of a small, discreet hotel on Tremont Street Vincent had given her, and spent the drive across town raising her hand elegantly and repeating, "Good Evening" and "Good Evening, my name is Margaret Maginnis," without a trace of an Irish accent for a full half hour.

Margaret spent most of the afternoon alone in her room, pressing the dress and sewing a hook-and-eye to the ends of the lace to wear around her neck. Intent on her work, she jumped when there was a knock on the door.

"Who is it?" she asked, suddenly frightened.

"It's me, silly. Open the door." Vincent chuckled at her nerves.

As the door creaked open, Vincent pushed his way through and tossed his bag on the bed. "I've made reservations at Vincen... Whoa! Oh, wow!" He stopped, speechless.

Margaret had wrapped her shiny dark hair loosely into a coil at the nape of her neck. Small tendrils fought to escape from the knot at her every move. "Fasten my necklace?" she asked, turning her back as he looked up at her finally.

"The dress," he said slowly. "Your hair. Your face. You're stunning."

"Why thank you sir," Margaret replied. "You probably didn't know I could clean up so well."

"I don't care _if_ or <u>when</u> you clean up," he said. "You look lovely."

Vincent brought along a special gift, a cut glass bottle of fragrance from Max Factor. As Margaret dabbed a bit of cologne behind each ear, she continued to look suspiciously at Vincent's bag in the middle of the bed.

"Didn't you get your own room?" she asked. "It's not as if you can't afford two rooms."

He leered as Margaret hovered near the door. "I have a suite at the Godfrey Hotel downtown, in case anyone comes asking. I was hoping I might stay here, however. The bed looks comfortable enough."

"It's not as if, I mean, I just thought," she said. "I don't know what I thought."

"Margaret, darling. We've been together for nearly a year. What is it you're asking of me?"

"I'm not asking anything. Not really," she answered, her eyes cast down at the uneven wood floors.

Vincent crossed the room in two steps, reached into his bag and pulled out another small box, this one from King's Jewelers on the corner. Nestled on a bed of cream-colored velvet inside was a pair of jet-black earrings, dangling from a thin wire hoop. He raised the box up, near her face.

"I know it may not be what you were expecting," he said. "I do have a ring from my grandmother, I'd planned on saving for the right time. I hope to speak to my mother next month. We can call your mother then. Won't they be surprised?"

Margaret melted into him; her body pressed against his as she felt his heart beating like a bass drum. Softly, she kissed his neck and whispered. "Yes! Surprised is putting it mildly."

In the cab outside the Italian restaurant, a light snow was falling. Margaret wasn't sure what to expect. "I can order for the both of us, if you'd like," he said. "Do you like pasta? Red wine or white? Chicken or fish?"

Margaret was happy to let Vincent take the lead. Her eyes glowed in the candlelight from the stub dripping down a cut-glass holder at the center of the table. Covered with crisp white tablecloths, the heavy china plates were banded in dark blue with a gold rim. Three sparkling crystal glasses were near the tips of the myriad pieces of silver and Margaret was pleased she'd studied the arrangements of both at Madeline's last dinner party.

Margaret and Vincent's table was set for two in a secluded back corner of the main dining room. Vincent had arranged with management they would not be bothered on this special evening. As Vincent chatted with the wine steward, Margaret arranged the heavy cloth napkin in her lap.

When the waiter arrived, Vincent was prepared with his favorite dishes. "We'll begin with antipasti for two," he said. "Then I will have the Tortellini di Zucca and the lady will have Gnocchi di Palate for the first course, Dover Sole for the second course."

Madeline raised her hand to stop him. "Vincent, that's too much."

"I can't wait to share this meal with you," he said. "It's like an engagement party for two."

The waiter smiled and moved toward the kitchen, as Margaret sat staring at Vincent. "What if he recognizes you? He might tell someone what you said or who you were here with tonight."

Vincent took her hand across the table. "Darling, they're paid well for their discretion and, even if he does recognize me, it's not likely he will recognize you. We talked about this. Relax. Enjoy."

Margaret didn't withdraw her hand, but she continued to fumble with the napkin while she made small talk. "How was your train ride? And your meeting?"

"The meeting was canceled," he said. "My associate came down with a flu bug or something. I took the time to go shopping."

Her soft smile glowed from inside. She touched the jet-black bobs as they dangled from her earlobes. "You're so generous. I feel so beautiful."

"You are beautiful," he said. "The dress is lovely, as well. Was it something of Madeline's?"

"Yes, it's something she no longer wanted, so she asked me to take care of it. I think I'm taking very good care of it, don't you?" The tiniest of smiles crept from her lips.

Vincent paused as the sommelier approached with a bucket of ice and a bottle of wine. The steward poured a small amount of the sparkling wine in Vincent's cup. Madeline watched raptly as Vincent swirled the wine in the bowl of his cup, inhaled and then took a mouthful. He rolled the wine around in his mouth and then smiled at the steward. "Excellent."

The man poured a full glass for Vincent and another for Margaret. Smiling, he replaced the bottle in the ice bucket and left as quietly as he'd appeared.

Vincent raised his glass toward Margaret. "Let's not talk about Madeline, tonight. This evening is about us."

In turn, Margaret raised her glass and tapped his in salute.

She tried to imitate his learned way of tasting the wine but sputtered when her first drink was too large.

"Sip it slowly," Vincent advised. "It's an acquired taste."

Soft music drifted across the room, as Margaret looked around. "This is beautiful," she said. "I'd say it looks like we're in Italy, but I've never been to Italy. I'll have to take your word for it."

"This is the restaurant my parents rented out when I graduated from college." Vincent stared dreamily into his memories. "We had a wonderful time. I remember everyone drank too much wine. It's a happy memory for me, with both my parents. Probably the last time we were all together before the divorce."

"Are you close with your mother?" Margaret asked.

Vincent was quiet for a long time. When he spoke, his voice was filled with tension. "My mother pretty much raised my sister and I. Father was always at work or with his friends. After the divorce, he and I became much closer. The year before he was married to Madeline was one of the happiest in my life."

He took a deep, cleansing breath and leaned in. "I know you'll be a fantastic mother. I've seen you with Madeline's Jack and with Todd and Emily's boy."

Margaret laughed self-consciously. "I've always wanted a large family. Martin wanted five boys and two girls." She stopped suddenly. "I'm sorry, I shouldn't have mentioned Martin."

"We're being honest with each other, aren't we?" Vincent said. "I want to hear more about you and your life in Ireland. That's a part of you I've never heard you talk much about."

Margaret sat back in her chair and let her hands drop into her lap as the waiter brought their food. Slowly, she raised a spoonful of the creamy golden gnocchi to her lips. "Mmm-mmm." She sighed. "I've never tasted anything so rich, so heavenly. I want it to last forever."

"It's made with butternut squash," Vincent said. "I knew you'd love it."

"We did have squash at home, but it was baked with a lot of butter and sugar. My mother raised squash in her garden along with green beans, carrots and a dozen other vegetables."

Vincent smiled at the differences in their upbringing. "Do you like to cook?"

"No, not really. I take after my father in my hobbies. I love to read and to travel. Before coming to America, I'd never been further than Galway City, but my brothers visited Dublin and my father once went to England."

Vincent took her hand again. "When you are *my* wife," he paused to let the words sink in, "we'll travel as much as you'd like. I want to meet your family, so our first trip will be to Ireland once the troubles in Europe settle down."

Just then, Margaret and Vincent's reveries were interrupted by the waiter. "Excuse me, sir. Madam. Would you like to see a dessert menu?"

Vincent looked at Madeline and she nodded. Like a child in a candy store, Margaret was anxious to see what type of sweet treats were available in a fine restaurant like this.

The waiter pulled two dessert menus from behind his back and handed one to each of the diners. "May I recommend the Panna Cotta?" he asked. "It's a coffee and chestnut custard with caramel, poached pear and pine nuts."

Margaret nodded delightedly. She spoke softly, so as not to break the spell. "Yes, please."

Vincent nodded at the waiter as he took their menus. "Bring me a slice of the orange cake with sorbet. And two coffees."

He turned to Margaret. "We'll share."

But she looked worried. "What time is it?"

Vincent pulled his pocket watch, engraved with his father's initials, from his vest pocket. "About ten o'clock. Why do you ask?"

"I'm afraid this will all disappear when the clock strikes twelve."

"We'll be back in our room under the covers by midnight,"

he said. "I can't wait to have you all to myself. We can talk all night, if you want."

With all the unrest in Europe, Vincent had put off traveling to see his mother and sister much longer than he'd originally planned. He'd attended his mother's wedding to Lister, but he felt he was dancing on his father's grave.

He shivered, but not from the cold. It was a fabulous fall day in London as he boarded a train for his mother's estate in the country near Sutton Place.

His nerves seemed to be getting the best of him. While he'd become a more confident businessman since he was thrust into the management of Sloane Enterprises, seeing his mother had his nerves on high alert. As he settled into his private car, he looked at his hands. In the past week, he'd begun biting his nails again, something he hadn't done since he was a child.

He'd had a quick lunch in London before he boarded the train, but his stomach felt queer and his head ached. There had always been tension between Vincent and his mother. A controlling woman, she pushed at Vincent to move to London when she and Alice relocated there.

"Alice will be coming out soon. Perhaps you'd like an extended vacation in Europe while we're getting settled in. An apartment in London could be your pied-a-terre."

He had considered traveling more to Europe and perhaps staying with his mother when his father had remarried, gone on his honeymoon and then died suddenly. That seemed like a million years ago.

As the train steamed out of London into the countryside, Vincent cast about in his mind for how he might begin a conversation with his mother about Margaret. For the life of him, he couldn't recall a similar situation in his family or the gilded society that surrounded them in New York. Nothing.

He doubted any of his mother's friends had more than a

passing dalliance with a serving girl here in England. He knew his mother's penchant for looking down on the Irish, as well. "The only good Irishman is a dead Irishman," she'd once said to his father.

While he already saw his mission as doomed, Vincent was determined to forge ahead. His love for Margaret had only grown stronger in the year they'd been together. Well-read and well-spoken, Margaret's manner was not subservient, by any measure. Vincent was sure, properly dressed and coiffed for English society, Margaret might convince his mother she was a proper lady. Until she opened her mouth.

Vincent loved the Irish lilt of Margaret's voice and her laughing, loving way of speaking to others — from the small children in Sloane House, to her friends, the Roebkens. Even when they were alone, her soft voice caressed his thoughts, even as her hands caressed his body.

Pulling himself to attention, Vincent rehearsed the speech he'd planned to share with his mother. "I love her, mother. She's smart, pretty, funny. You'd love her, too, if you gave her half a chance."

"Come back to America with me and just meet her," he'd suggest, seeing his mother in his mind, smiling in agreement.

From the moment Vincent had stepped off the train at the small station near Sutton Place, his mother had peppered him with questions. She waited in the back seat of a Wolesely motorcar, while the chauffeur carried his bags.

"How is your business progressing?" she began, followed quickly by "What about that woman? His teenage harlot?"

Ava, divorced from Vincent's father less than a year before the Colonel remarried, had never liked Madeline Sloane. Vincent often thought his mother's marriage, shortly after his father's second marriage, was in response to their rushed ceremony and long honeymoon.

Never one to be outdone, Ava married the Baron of Rib-blesdale in late summer of the previous year at Saint Mary's, at Bryanston Square in London. They divided their time between Sutton Place in Surry and their townhouse on Grosvenor Square in the Mayfair district of London.

After two years in England, his mother fancied herself a close friend of the queen. Vincent's sister, Alice, was presented to King George V at court this past spring and was heavily involved in the social season. Her schedule was crowded with afternoon tea parties, polo matches, races at Royal Ascot and dress balls nearly every weekend.

"Your sister will be at home in Surry this weekend. I hope you will be able to spend some time with her before she has to leave again," the Baroness said.

Vincent took a deep breath. "Mother, there's something, or rather someone, I need to talk to you about."

"Stop blinking your eyes so often, Vincent. If you have something important to say, be a man. Stand up straight and look me in the eye."

Vincent drew his right hand through his hair and drew himself up to his full height. "Mother, I'm engaged. My fiancé is a young Irish woman I met through Sloane House."

"Irish!" she chortled. "You know how I feel about the Irish, mostly dirty left-footers, everyone. Is she a friend of Madeline's? What is her name?

His mouth was dry, and he felt a little faint, but there was no turning back. "Her name is Margaret Mannion. She met father and Madeline on the Titanic. She was a survivor and they met again after returning to New York City."

Vincent wished time would speed up and the afternoon's grilling could be over. He'd be on the first train out of Surrey when this ordeal was over. "She works for Madeline. She's a lady's maid."

An unnatural stillness settled over the drawing room and Vincent's pasted-on smile withered. "Mother, did you hear me? My fiancée is Madeline's maid."

"Oh, I heard you alright." Ava howled. "I was only hoping I had heard wrong. Are you out of your mind? A Sloane marrying a washerwoman? It's preposterous. Your father's fortune is only two generations old, so in some eyes, your money is new money. In English society, you'd be cast out. In the gilded age of New York, I'm sure they'd whisper."

"Oh, they'd accept your philanthropy, but all the while they'd talk about you behind your back. You would never be invited to the right parties. If you were to have children, God forbid, they'd be disinvited from every function, barred from the finest schools."

"Are you thinking they'd marry well? They won't!"

"B-b-but, mother." He trailed off.

"You may address me as Lady Ribblesdale," she barked. "If you want to act like a nobody, you're no son of mine."

Vincent spent three days in a London hotel, without ever leaving his room. During the day, he kept the heavy, velvet drapes closed — sunlight his harshest enemy. A competent businessman and until recently, a sought-after playboy. He operated self-assuredly in the boardroom and the bedroom. With a fleet of ships at his command, the young American tycoon appeared to have the world at his feet.

On the trip to England, his love lifted him even higher. He was now more determined to be a success in his personal life, as well. But, after visiting his mother, his life lay about him in tatters.

By the fourth morning it was even more difficult for Vincent to drag himself from his bed. His head throbbed, his eyes were bloodshot, and his mouth parched. He knew he had to use the bathroom to vomit and pee, or his bedclothes would stink even worse. He stumbled across the room into the marble and gold bathroom, and draped himself around the base of the toilet.

When he was finished, he passed out again, only to be aroused an hour later by a maid in the bedroom. She was humming softly to herself as she tidied up and changed the linen. From his perch at the bottom of the throne, Vincent saw the room brighten as she pulled the drapes aside and began plumping pillows and tossing empty wine and beer bottles.

"My God, woman!" He stormed into the room, nearly knocking her down, as his arms swung in her direction. She stumbled into a nightstand and knocked over a vase of flowers. As the nearby crystal decanter hit the window ledge, it shattered and cut her arm in several places.

"I'm so sorry." Vincent started to cry. "I didn't mean to cause a mess."

The maid stood stock still, then pulled a hankie from her pocket to staunch the blood and ran from the room.

"I'm sorry, mommy. I didn't mean to hurt her. I'll go to the closet."

Vincent walked into the large closet and shut the door behind him. He imagined the sound of a key turning in the lock and huddled in a corner, near a pile of dirty laundry.

He could hear his mother laughing as she left the room, her little boy sobbing in a dark corner because he wasn't allowed to go outside. He burrowed deeper into the darkness of the dirty clothes littering the floor, trying to escape the pain. But it would not go away — it was embedded in his brain.

Todd knew the story of Margaret's possible pregnancy from his wife, but he'd been suspicious long before. "She disappears every weekend," he'd told Emily on the long Fourth of July weekend. "It isn't just coincidence Mr. Sloane is going to Boston for four days at the same time."

Emily warned her friend again and again to stay away from Vincent Sloane. She'd watched DeeDee flirt with Vincent in the past, only to be rebuffed. She knew his reputation as a playboy in New York society circles. But growing up, mother often said, "It's nobody else's business," and she was determined to step back until Margaret sought her advice.

Saunterings
Town Topics

September 23, 1915 Friends and neighbors, Town Topics will spare no expense in reporting all the news that is fit to print. Our intrepid reporters tell us a Millionaire Playboy was seen with an American Beauty, in Boston this month. The newsman at a Boston restaurant recognized young Vincent Sloane, out of circulation for more than a year, at a secluded table in a popular eatery near his alma mater, Harvard College. The woman has not been identified by name, but our source tells us she was a dark-haired beauty, well-dressed and finely coiffed. The pair dined at the famous Vincenzo's, having both a bottle of fine wine, two main courses and two desserts from the fine dining menu. Saunterings attempted to contact young Sloane to verify the account and get the young woman's name — they appeared infatuated. But Sloane's secretary, here in the city, tells us he has gone to Europe to meet with his mother. Are wedding bells in the offing?

Colonel William d'Alton Mann

Chapter Fourteen

For the weeks surrounding Vincent's absence, Margaret was in a stupor. Her body was in a constant state of alert, listening for the sound of Vincent's voice in the hall or word from Madeline that he had returned. By the fourth week, she wandered in and out of Madeline's room in a trance. She carried the breakfast tray up from the kitchen and set it in the bathroom.

"What's got into you lately, Margaret?" Madeline wore a pinched, unhappy expression. She demanded the maid begin again on a complicated plait they were copying from a lady's magazine.

"I'm sorry, Mrs. Sloane. I'm distracted by the bad news out of England and Ireland. Have you heard anything from Mr. Sloane?"

"No, and I don't expect any transatlantic calls either. He went to see his mother, you know. She's not exactly my greatest fan." Margaret began to fidget. "Ouch, you stuck me with that comb."

Margaret's distracted, dream-like fantasies morphed into a real illness the week before his return. While she was often tired after a long day with her employer, the past week things had worsened. Once, while she was waiting in the car with Todd, she dozed off in the middle of the day.

She and Todd were debating the situation in England

and its possible effect on Ireland, when the chauffeur started a lengthy tirade on English rule in Ireland. Nodding agreeably, Madeline felt the warmth of the car's interior envelop her in a hug beneath the blanket she always carried. She woke an hour later with the imprint of stitches riding up one side of her face like a scar from Frankenstein's monster.

Todd grinned, "Sleep much last night?" he asked. "Or am I that boring?"

The next morning, she was preparing Madeline's breakfast tray. Standing near the gas stove, she carefully spooned an egg into a pan of boiling water. The raw egg fell to the bottom of the pan — a fragile pebble in a stream of swirling water, cracking and spewing much of its insides into a milky mess.

Margaret turned her head and put her hand to her mouth. "I need a cup of tea, Sadie. Can you pour me a cuppa while I finish Mrs. Sloane's tray?"

Later that day, the smell of coffee brewing on the stove drew the entire staff to the kitchen for teatime. As the maids gathered 'round the giant wooden table where Sadie made her magic happen, Margaret came into the room. Quickly, she pivoted and made a beeline for the basin in the staff toilet behind the kitchen. When she emerged a few minutes later, her cheeks were red, and her eyes swollen. Everyone in the house had heard her retching.

"I think I'm coming down with a cold or the flu," Margaret told Emily. Ryan and Baby Jack had been sick a lot recently and she frequently shared spoons, cups and kisses with the little ones.

"You go on upstairs," Emily said. "I'll bring you some soup."

When she got to Margaret's room, her friend was in her nightgown standing beside the bed, but still looked peaked. Emily set the tray down and paused with a knowing look. "Margaret, isn't it obvious? You're pregnant!"

Margaret swayed, holding tightly to the table beside the bed. "Pregnant? I can't be."

"You can't be, or you don't want to be?" Emily countered. She looked around the room before whispering under her breath. "I know you've been spending a lot of time away from the house. Todd thinks you may be involved with Mr. Sloane. You have to tell him."

Margaret played the thought over and over in her mind. She was both terrified and ecstatic. She'd always wanted to have a houseful of children, but she was quite sure this wasn't a good time.

Oh, Vincent would be over the moon. He wanted children too. They'd discussed marriage before he left for England, but now it would have to happen as soon as he returned, for everyone's sake.

Margaret was ready to be a wife and a mother. She couldn't wait to tell Vincent.

On the day before Vincent's return from England, Margaret was tidying up Madeline's bedroom while the lady of the house was in the adjoining bath. The maid picked up a newspaper, the columns crowded closely with heavy black type, like ants marching across the folds.

The *New York Post* was folded open to the society page — Madeline's favorite. There at the top was an engagement announcement for Helen Hunt and Vincent Sloane.

Margaret fell to the chaise lounge where Madeline's clothes were laid. The bismuth-pink room dipped and swayed. Her head was as light as the gauzy curtains, but her stomach was a rock. She closed her eyes and tried to center her thoughts.

From the adjoining bath Margaret could hear Madeline calling, but she seemed so far away. Her pulse sped forward like a racing locomotive and she tried to reply, but she could not answer.

"Margaret, the water is growing cold," Madeline called. "Bring me my robe and a warm towel, right away, please."

Margaret roused herself and stood up unsteadily. In the bath, a roaring fire helped keep Madeline warm as she soaked in a foamy soap-filled tub for more than an hour. As the fire died down and the water cooled, Margaret's employer declined to dawdle, however.

Margaret helped her dress and arrange her hair, but told her employer she was feeling ill and asked for the rest of the day off. Madeline had hardly touched her breakfast tray, one that Margaret had struggled over for nearly 45 minutes, between bouts of morning sickness.

"I hope you are feeling better this afternoon, Margaret, but no matter. I plan to stay in after the ladies leave. Perhaps we can read together later in the day."

Madeline had found many new authors at Margaret's suggestion. Sharing books and authors was a favorite pastime of both women and one that usually brought them together on an intellectual level. But Margaret was in no mood for sharing anything with anyone, any longer.

She vacillated between wanting to kill herself and wanting to kill Vincent. At first, she wanted to forgive him. He didn't know about the pregnancy, she rationalized. Then, she decided he didn't care. He'd never loved her.

By day's end, Margaret couldn't understand what might have happened to the man she'd wished a fond farewell three weeks ago. Something had changed in England and he'd become a society playboy once again. But her child needed a father, not a playmate.

Since Vincent's return from England, Margaret had seen him only once. It was the day after his engagement was announced in the newspapers. She was in the kitchen, sitting quietly with the other women from the staff and enjoying a cup of tea one afternoon, when Vincent strolled in from the dining room without a care in the world.

The room went silent. Slowly, Margaret rose stiffly from her chair. "Excuse me," she said to the others. "I need to see to Mrs. Sloane."

"Margaret. Miss Mannion," Vincent called after her. "May I speak with you for a moment, please?"

As she reached the hall, Margaret whirled to face him. "I don't want to talk to you. Ever again."

He grabbed her arm and whispered. "Margaret, let me explain."

"I don't want to hear your explanations. You've made your bed, now lie in it." Margaret's voice started to rise.

"It's my mother," he bit out. "She doesn't understand. I love you. We can still be together."

"No, Vincent! No, we cannot!"

She wrenched free, twisting her arm as she escaped the conversation. "I never want to see you again *and* I never want to speak to you *or* hear your name."

Tears tracking rivulets down her face, Margaret ran back through the kitchen and out the back door into a driving wind. Pulling her arms closely around her body, she raced over to the garage and away from the boring eyes of the kitchen staff gathered near the windows on the back of the house.

She hadn't counted on Todd being in the garage, cleaning and polishing one of the cars. The snowy streets of New York City played havoc on the shiny black Bentley, but Todd was not one to let dirt sit on a Sloane automobile. He always carried a soft rag in the boot and another in his back pocket, folded neatly as a handkerchief.

Todd pulled his hands from the soapy, acrid-smelling bucket of water. Without a word, he pulled Margaret into his arms and held her close while she sobbed.

"But..., But, I ..." she started to explain.

"Ssshhhhh." He patted her shoulder. "I know. I know."

He patted Margaret's shoulder in time to the raindrops starting to fall outdoors. "Looks like we may have snow before nightfall," he offered.

Margaret grimaced. "Thank you, Todd, and thank Emily, too. She tried to warn me, but I wouldn't listen. I just don't know what to do."

She sniffled and squared her shoulders as Todd stepped back to his job. "I'm going to go in," she said, turning to go.

"But, as God is my witness, I'll never love another man again."

Madeline Sloane had made a conscious decision not to attend Vincent and Helen's engagement party. Not that she had been invited, but had Helen and her mother overcome Ava and Vincent's aversion to her presence, she was determined not to be present at what was billed as the city's social event of the season.

Instead, she chose to remain in the city and meet with her friend, Richard Gould, for dinner at Sloane House. She'd coached Emily on how Baby Jack was to be fed early and put to bed in the nursery for the evening. On those nights, Emily slept in the room attached to the nursery.

Margaret spent most of the afternoon fussing with Madeline's hair and wardrobe. It helped to keep her mind off her troubles. "Your gown for this evening is especially becoming, ma'am," she said, as she warmed a curling iron by the fire. The wooden handle was embellished with nickel-plated floral designs and was the fanciest piece Margaret had ever seen.

"Tonight, *is* special," Madeline confided. "I promised Dickie a special dessert after drinks in the salon. It's a fine summer's evening and I want my new lavender nightgown laid out near the bath. Mr. Gould will be spending the night."

Margaret feigned ignorance of Madeline's intentions. "I'm not sure I understand. Do you want me to ask DeeDee to prepare a guest room?"

"Don't be a goose," Madeline scolded. "Dickie has been nothing but a gentleman so far, but I think he needs a little extra push to make it official. I'm hoping he'll propose. In *my* room, in *my* bed."

Margaret's eyes grew wide. Madeline was always frank — she was able to trust Margaret. "I'd like you to pick up a package for me at the druggist this afternoon. It's called a pressary and is the most modern method for preventing pregnancies and improving hygiene."

Margaret set the curling iron aside. "Yes, ma'am. Will there be anything else?"

"Yes." Madeline slipped her wedding band from her hand. "Wear this. He may ask if you are married. Say yes, and mention five children. These devices were designed for working women like you. Don't hesitate. We don't want him to be suspicious."

Margaret took the ring and Madeline's leaf of stationary with the name and address of the apothecary. As she turned to leave the room, she couldn't pass up the opportunity for more questions. "What if you were to become pregnant, ma'am?"

Madeline lowered her voice conspiratorially. "There are ways of handling that. With the right connections. Now, get on your way. I need you to be back before five."

Margaret thought talking to Emily about the pregnancy and Vincent's engagement may have been the most difficult conversations she'd ever had. She certainly had no intention of telling her mother or sisters.

But those tearful confrontations paled to the holy terror that rained down when Margaret shared the information she'd gleaned from Madeline that afternoon. DeeDee, the housemaid, filled in some of the blanks on Margaret's return from the druggist.

Now, Margaret and Emily were sitting in the nanny's room next door to the nursery. Baby Jack was asleep, and Todd had driven Madeline and Mr. Gould to dinner at Le Coucou, near Chinatown. As Margaret took up the knitting Emily was teaching her, she began hesitantly. "Mrs. Sloane asked me to pick up a package for her today at the druggist. I was too embarrassed to tell Todd what she asked me to buy for her. It's birth control."

Emily set down her knitting and frowned. "I don't suppose we're the ones to judge, but it's just not right."

"The French have been offering periodical pills for 70 years." Margaret watched Emily's face. "It's kind of the same."

"No, it's not!" Emily replied angrily.

Margaret pulled one of Madeline's ladies' magazines from behind her back. "Look at this!" She held the glossy inside back cover up for Emily's inspection. The full-color advertisement showed two pretty young women wandering the beach in bathing suits, with stripes from shoulder to ankle. "It says they assist nature in her wondrous functions. What could be more natural than that?"

Emily was not to be cajoled. "They're marketed as a laxative, Mags. They're for sick headaches and constipation, not for getting rid of unwanted babies."

Margaret ignored Emily's response. "Surgical abortions are much safer since doctors began using a method of flushing the uterus. DeeDee told me you can pay the $25 fee on an installment plan." She paused to catch a breath. "The Post had this ad listed under medical services — *'Strictest confidence on complaints incidental to the female frame'* she read. *'Experience and knowledge in the treatment of cases of female irregularity, such as to require but a few days to effect a perfect cure. A simple, easy, healthy and certain remedy is within our control.'* Medical services," she reiterated, sounding less confident.

"Surely you can speak to Vincent again before his wedding," Emily said. "It's four months away yet. If he knew you were pregnant, everything would change."

Margaret paced the room. The volume in her voice rose several decibels "Vincent doesn't know I'm pregnant and he never will. No one will ever marry a woman with a child hanging on her. I'm not some poor, young widow who's lost her husband in battle. I'm a whore!"

Emily pulled Margaret close. "You're not a whore, darling. You're a young woman, alone in a new world, who fell for the wrong man. We'll make this work."

Now the terror had passed, Margaret was forced to make a decision she knew would be best for her *and* for her baby. She sat ramrod straight in a pew at St. Joshua's. Dozens of candles flickered in the darkened sacristy as she prayed for hours to gather the courage to go it alone. She had never seriously considered an abortion; her Catholic upbringing wouldn't allow her to get rid of the baby.

Despite Madeline's assurances about modern women and inconvenient pregnancies, Margaret remained convinced she was carrying a child in her belly. She and Martin had talked dozens of times about having children. As soon as they were married, they would start a family. Margaret wanted six children — three boys and three girls, like her parents. Martin wanted five boys and a girl.

Meteorically, Margaret crashed back into reality. Martin wasn't here anymore. Vincent wasn't really here anymore, either.

She had come to the church to throw herself on the mercy of the priest and ask his assistance in finding a couple to adopt the baby. But, after hours of contemplation, she'd changed her mind again.

Emily's words that evening were a comfort. "Ryan would love a little brother or sister. I can raise your baby as if he's my own. With you living in the big house next to ours, you could visit all the time. You'd be his second mother and, when he's ready to hear the truth, we'll tell him together."

At first, Margaret was relieved to have Emily offer to assume all the responsibility for the baby. But her fear gave way to anticipation and impending motherhood.

Most evenings, Margaret would lie alone in her room and

talk to her baby. "You are a wondrous person," she would say as she sank deeper into the thin mattress. "I don't need a husband to make us a family."

She pulled the covers closer, cocooning herself and her child in safety. "I want to be your family. I can be that person. I want to be your mother, your only mother."

The next morning, Margaret was anxious to see Emily. "I'm ready to be this baby's mother. I am his first mother and his last. You are my best friend and my baby's auntie. We'll raise him together."

29 August 1915

Dearest Mam,

Mrs. Sloane has become engaged to be married to a Mr. Gould, also of New York society. I am undecided what I am going to do next, but I have several possibilities for new employment in service. I am also considering manufacturing as Ellie did when we first moved to the city.

Colonel Sloane's son is engaged to be married, as well. His fiancée is Helen Hunt. They will live in a smaller home near Sloane House, but I will not be surprised if they choose to move into the big house when his stepmother leaves.

There are many exciting new things happening in my life. I read carefully of the unrest in Ireland and England. Is everything well with you? Tell me more about Celia and her marriage plans with Sean Kelly, please. I was surprised to learn of her engagement, but I will send the savings I have accumulated to you to help with the costs of the wedding and the farm.

Much love,
Margaret

Chapter Fifteen

Vincent had slept very little since his arrival back in the United States and not at all on the days he visited Sloane House. Margaret had avoided him at every turn and messages sent through Todd and Emily were returned unopened.

He'd hoped for a chance to explain his decision — his mother's decision and his acquiescence, actually. After four days dead drunk in the London hotel room, Vincent left England a subdued man. The strength and vigor he'd maintained following his father's death and his ascension to the throne of the Sloane estate, disappeared.

At every opportunity since he'd arrived back in America, he tried to send word to Margaret; tried to explain the circumstances behind his sudden engagement to Helen. It was all about his mother and Helen's mother. Miss Hunt as simply not his type.

He had known Helen since childhood, but the imagined romance their mothers had cooked up was a new wrinkle in their relationship. The Huntington estate adjoined the Sloane's and the engagement marked the uniting of two families of great wealth. The society columnists were agog.

After all, the baroness had explained during Vincent's visit, Helen is the granddaughter of a multi-millionaire and a descendant of a signer of the Declaration of the Independence.

On her mother's side were two justices of the United States Supreme Court.

It was a match made in the diseased heaven that was his mother's mind. His bride's athletic, outdoorsy style was in sharp contrast to Vincent's more ethereal interests in books, writing and ... Margaret, dear Margaret.

Vincent's fevered mind traveled where his body could not. He was confined to his bed for more than three weeks with what doctors diagnosed as an abscess of his lungs. And now Margaret was wiping his brow, mopping his sweaty chest and changing cool cloths around his swollen neck.

He opened one eye. "Margaret?" But the private nurse only smiled back. The baroness had hired the nurse to care for her son in his own home to avoid gossip.

For most of his laying in, Vincent's throat was on fire. He'd grown two additional Adam's apples, one just in front of and below each ear. He was embarrassed to have the nurse apply warm compresses to his genitals, as well. The pain in his testicles was wicked and the drugs prescribed by the doctor did little to soothe the swelling and inflammation. Even after the swelling had subsided, the fever persisted, and he was allowed no guests beyond his private nurse.

The nurse had little formal training, but she did have the good sense to wear a mask at all times when she attended his sickroom. Waking from a nap near the end of his convalescence, Vincent heard the doctor who visited each afternoon. "Only one in four males has the problem," he said. "We can cut back on the opiate injections, but continue analgesic creams and aspirin powders."

When he asked the nurse why the doctor had changed the pain medications, she said the testicular inflammation probably wasn't as severe as first thought. "Don't worry, Mr. Sloane, we'll have you better in no time."

A month later, Vincent's wedding day dawned gray and muggy, much like his mood. By the time the ceremony was performed, a fine rain was falling, and the temperature had taken a nosedive. It was cool enough to have a fire going in one of the living rooms of Hopehouse, a 35-room Tudor Revival Mansion, built by Helen's father.

Two stories tall and built of red brick, it was a picturesque enough setting for a society wedding. Weakened by his recent illness and abed for three months, Vincent had adopted a certain pallor making him appear ghostlike beside his new young bride.

Two years his junior, Helen was the society girl his mother had dreamed of, even before she'd destroyed his dreams of marrying Margaret. Vincent spent the morning building up the courage not to leave Helen at the altar. He simply couldn't believe he was marrying Helen; she was not the type of woman he was attracted to. Two strong bourbons just before the ceremony sealed his fate.

Just as the sonorous tones of a grandfather's clock chimed the appointed hour, the bride, leaning on her father's arm, descended the grand staircase. Vincent's younger sister, Alice, was a bridesmaid and Helen's sister, also Alice, was the maid of honor.

The bridal party passed through the library and into a large, cheery room at the southwest corner of the house, paneled in white with a large marble mantelpiece, banked with rambling roses, where Vincent awaited his fate.

Fortified by the bourbon, Vincent looked toward his mother in the front row, across from Mrs. Hunt, another Helen. "My God," he thought to himself, "it's as if all these women are reinventing themselves, over and over. Alice, Helen. Helen, Alice. Same old women, day after day."

The baroness smiled archly, and Vincent knew the day would continue in the same vein. His best man, Herman Oelrichs, smiled grimly. The strains of the wedding march died away and the old priest, a relic of his mother's time in New York City, read the vows.

The couple knelt before a white satin and gold prie dieu. Framed above them in flowers and set in the wall above the mantle was a large oil painting from a scene in the Austrian Tyrol.

Helen smiled up at her groom. Her simple dress, a creation of rare old lace and tulle, was also worn by her mother at her parents' nuptials. The satin train was edged with a ruche of tulle and she wore real orange blossoms from the Hopehouse conservatory. This morning they were still in bloom. She carried a bouquet of lilies of the valley and white orchids. Her only ornament, a rope of pearls, Baroness Ribblesdale had chosen as her son's bridal gift.

After the ceremony, the 50 family and guests moved into the sun porch for a bridal breakfast with a splendid view of the Hudson. The smell of hydrangeas, sweet peas and daisies filled the air.

At the baroness's insistence, the bride's table was placed in the library for Vincent's protection. He had not been out of the house since he was taken ill nearly a month ago.

The screened orchestra struck up a medley of popular tunes from the hall as the plates were cleared away and Helen left to change into her going-away dress — a dark blue serge and a black hat with wings. The bridal couple ran the gauntlet of rice and old slippers to a horse-drawn covered cab which bore them away to Fairholme, the Sloane's country estate.

The family's yacht, *The Norma*, was anchored in the Hudson, but Vincent's health didn't permit a honeymoon or even a short cruise for a month's time. Plans had been hatched for a Mediterranean cruise during the summer.

The baroness and Vincent's sister, Alice, meanwhile would sail for London tomorrow, newspapers reported. Vincent hadn't bothered to speak to his mother since her arrival a week earlier. Wedding plans didn't require his input and Vincent simply no longer cared.

During his convalescence at Fairholme following the wedding, Vincent despaired of reconciliation with Margaret. He busied himself with reading the newspapers and toying with his private railroad, complete with narrow-gauge railway running around three-quarters of the estate and a unique train station.

It was news of the war in Europe that kept him from dwelling on his estrangement from Margaret. In May, German U-boats sank the British liner *RMS Lusitania* with 128 Americans among the dead. One of those killed was Alfred Vanderbilt, a friend of the family.

Vincent attended the Vanderbilt wedding near the same time as his father's second wedding. It was a nagging reminder — the Vanderbilts had planned to sail on the *Titanic*, but were delayed. Fate plays cruel tricks, Vincent thought, smiling grimly.

Later that year, the British ship *The Britannic*, a sister ship to the *Titanic*, sank after hitting a mine in the Aegean Sea. The *Britannic* served as a hospital ship for the British forces. More than 30 people were killed, but 1,000 others were rescued.

It was the type of story Vincent longed to share with Margaret. The two seldom talked about her experience on the *Titanic*, but she would be happy to hear the modifications the White Star Line made on the *Britannic* after the Titanic went down had saved many lives.

The *Britannic* had made five successful voyages bringing wounded British troops back to England from various ports around the world. It made Vincent even more determined to become involved in the war effort.

He wrote to President Wilson, encouraging him to join the fray. But Wilson declared "America is too proud to fight," demanding an end to attacks on passenger ships. Germany complied. His pandering to European forces kept America out of the war and won him a second term in the White House, but Vincent lost all respect for the man.

New York Times
Monday November 20, 1916
WILSON NOW FREE TO ACT

Intends to Push Various Foreign Problems to Issue at Once

U-BOAT WAR THE WORST

BLOCKADE ALSO PRESSING

WASHINGTON, Nov. 19 -- A portentous and complicated international situation faces President Wilson, and for the next few weeks it will engage his attention and that of his advisers to the practical exclusion of all except the most urgent of domestic subjects.

In the last days of the campaign, Robert Lansing, Secretary of State, frequently spoke of the necessity of postponing action on the more delicate international questions because of the uncertainty of the outcome of the political contest, which had a direct bearing on the success or failure of some of the Administration policies.

From now on the President expects to deal with all foreign questions without embarrassment, and he is receiving from his advisers a summary of the outstanding issues so essential to taking stock of the basic situation which must be met, now that international relations have returned

to their place of prime importance. While it is not evident that there will be any fundamental change in policy, freedom from fear that any move at all would be misinterpreted inspired by an internal political struggle has been removed. President Wilson and Secretary Lansing feel that they are able to act with a single eye to the international situation, and their immediate conferences on the President's return to Washington indicate how pressing they feel the situation to be.

The President must decide how the United States shall meet the German submarine situation, on the one hand, and the Entemte allied trade restrictions, on the other; whether the retaliatory legislation shall be entered, whether the traditional theory of isolation shall be abandoned for commercial neutral action, and whether the country shall have an aggressive or a passive polity toward the peace conference, the trade war after the war, and the Permanent League of Enforce Peace, which the President has accepted in theory, and, during the rest of the war, whether America's attitude shall be governed by a decided benevolence in the interpretation of international law according to its own best interest, or shall it be strictly legalistic, regardless of whom it affects.

Chapter Sixteen

All through the spring and summer, Margaret wore several layers of loose clothing to help hide her pregnancy. She made it her practice to always be carrying a bundle of clothing, dishes or newspapers in front of her belly. Some careful stitchery helped her let out the clothing she already owned, and, in the end, Emily borrowed an older one of Sadie's black dresses to take in.

Margaret felt fortunate Mrs. Sloane joined the Goulds in the Hamptons for the summer and even more lucky she was able to beg off, under the pretense there wasn't room for an extra lady's maid in the summer house.

To compensate, Margaret kept herself busy around Sloane House. *"Idle hands are the devil's playground,"* her mother always said. What would she say now, Margaret wondered, if she knew of her situation?

Margaret was certain no one in the house, outside of Emily and Todd, knew she was expecting. She'd begged Emily not to tell Todd, but her friend wouldn't consider keeping a secret of this magnitude from her husband.

Todd was on his way to the Hamptons one weekend to drive Mrs. Sloane to the beach. The car was crowded with hampers of picnic food, blankets and a swimsuit that no longer camouflaged Madeline's figure.

Madeline had purchased the suit to show a little more of

her figure and allow from some exposure to the sun. She chose a garment for the actual sport of swimming, she told Margaret.

As Margaret packed the suit on top of the picnic hamper, a cover up and additional outfits Mrs. Sloane had requested, Todd lingered. "Emily has explained your situation," he offered kindly. "Please know that we are here for you no matter the outcome. I will be happy to treat him as one of my own. But, I'm not sure how we'll explain it to Ryan."

"I doubt he's noticed my pregnancy." Margaret blushed. "When the baby arrives, we'll fall back on the stork's surprise delivery." She scurried back into the house to avoid Todd's questions.

She didn't want to talk about the problems they might encounter. A positive attitude, plenty of hard work and a constant smile were Margaret's way of dealing with difficulties in the past. She was sure she could continue in the same vein in America.

The summer heat had become too much for Margaret to bear. She still thought she was fooling other staff into believing she'd gained a great deal of weight, by padding her bosom and her sleeves and eating constantly.

In Madeline's absence, Margaret only relaxed her daily routine in early July as the city's heat index rose. She took advantage of the deep tub in the servant's quarters on the third floor to cool down and took frequent naps while Sadie thought she was watching Jack in the nursery.

Emily was happy to pick up some of the slack for Margaret. She'd hand off Jack each afternoon for a shared nap time, sneaking down the back stairs and out the kitchen door while the cook was taking the scraps out to the dogs in Colonel Sloane's kennel behind the garage.

Mrs. Sloane was forever asking Todd to walk the dogs, to sell the dogs and, one time, even to shoot the dogs. She was not a dog person, Emily understood, but Jack would want a pet in a couple of years and one of his father's retrievers would be the perfect companion for the boy.

Emily tiptoed across the gravel yard, walking slowly so as not to alert Sadie of her passage. As she rounded the corner of the garage hiding the stairs leading up to her apartment, the cook came around from the other side.

"I thought you were putting young master down for a nap," Sadie said. "Who's watching after him?"

"Margaret offered to help me out." Emily averted her eyes. She was not accustomed to lying.

Sadie nodded. "It's good of Margaret to help. Doesn't lying down with the baby just make her more tired?"

"She's reading." Emily compounded the lie by offering up the title of a book she had in her own reading pile upstairs.

"It's a book, for goodness sake," she muttered under her breath.

"I heard that," Sadie retorted, returning to her kitchen and a sink full of dirty dishes.

With Vincent and Helen confined to Fairholme, Margaret spent most of her days helping in the kitchen and putting together a plan for the future. One Friday, she took the chance to sit down in Madeline's study to rest her swollen ankles and enjoy a ladies' magazine.

Just as she'd become involved in a serial novel with juicy details and color illustrations, she was surprised to look up and see Sadie standing there watching, observing her without a word, but a seriously judgmental look on her face. "Oh, and aren't you a fine one to be sitting in the parlor on this warm summer day. Is there anything I can get for you, milady? Will you be needing dinner in the sunroom this evening?"

Margaret nearly cried. She yanked her feet from the needlepoint stepstool with the doves, hearts and vines stitched around the perimeter. As she rushed to stand up, her head swam. She caught hold of the chair.

"No need to be so spry. You don't want to hurt the baby," Sadie said.

Margaret froze. "You know?" A tear escaped the corner of her eye.

"I've known for months," Sadie continued. "I'll help you and Emily to keep your secret. And, I was serious about the light supper. But, of course, I'll expect your help."

Just then a gush of water flowed between Margaret's legs and onto the stool.

"Cancel dinner plans, Margaret. It's off to bed with you and your wee one. I'll call Emily from the nursery. Do you plan to lie in at the hospital, like Mrs. Sloane before you?" Sadie mocked, but she had a grin on her face, too.

"DeeDee's cousin is a midwife," Margaret felt panic creep into her voice. "Emily said she'd call her when it's time."

Sadie lumbered toward the back stairs, leading to the nursery. "It's time, alright."

For hours, Margaret labored alone in her room. Emily and DeeDee had both offered to sit with her, but she wanted to carry the load on her own back, to remember the day. Riding the crest of a wave in the oceans of pain, she rested in the valleys of fear between. Based on stories she'd heard from Cathleen O'Dey, a woman was more likely to die in childbirth than on the dangerous New York City streets at night.

But, as the pains increased, Margaret nearly reveled in her suffering. Much earlier in the pregnancy, she had decided she needed to atone for her sins and suffer on her own the consequences of her misdeeds.

Emily had discouraged the isolation, but Margaret was dogged. Instead, her friend sat just across the hall with DeeDee by her side, ready to call for the midwife when the pains were closer together.

"Ohhhhhhh!" Margaret wailed. "Help me, St. Gerald!" She thrashed from side to side on the narrow bed, holding onto the head rail with both hands as the contractions put her belly in a vise grip. "Emily, help me, please!"

As her friend rushed to her side, Margaret's face was again torn in suffering. Emily had a short, easy labor with Ryan and the sight of Margaret's snow-white complexion and shiny eyes crying out for relief tugged at her heart. "Call the midwife," she barked at DeeDee. "And bring me more towels."

Margaret's bed was soaked in sweat and Emily could see her natural instinct to push was kicking in. "Wait, baby. Wait for the midwife."

Margaret's eyes drilled into Emily's face. "No! I can't wait. He's coming! Now!"

With a shudder, she screamed out as Emily picked up the covers to see the top of the baby's head, covered with hair, presenting between Margaret's legs. Blood stained the linens.

DeeDee came rushing back into the room. "She's on her way, but it will likely be a half hour. Can you wait?"

"This little baby is not going to wait for anyone," Emily told DeeDee. "We're going to have to do it ourselves. Have you ever seen a baby born before?"

"My mother had six children," DeeDee said. "I'm the oldest."

She tore a wide swatch from her apron and wadded it below the baby's head to help staunch the flow of blood. "She's already torn. She'll need a doctor afterwards. We should have called for the midwife earlier."

Emily turned to her friend. Margaret's eyes were closed, and Emily shook her shoulder. "Okay, Margaret, on the next contraction, push as hard as you can. *Push*."

Margaret panted as she felt the crescendo rise from deep inside. "Is he here?" Just then another contraction hit, and she bore down.

Emily gripped Margaret's hand and looked anxiously toward DeeDee. "Well?"

The maid smiled as she wrapped a clean towel around the slippery body and placed him on Margaret's stomach. "Hand me the thread, there." She pointed to the basket that had appeared out of nowhere at Emily's feet. "I need to tie off the cord."

As DeeDee wrapped the umbilical cord in two places with a heavy band of sewing thread, the midwife arrived. "Just in time," she said. "And I see your little one couldn't wait."

Carefully, she pushed DeeDee's hands to one side and removed a sharp knife from her pocket. With one quick swipe, she cut the cord and sat down to deliver the afterbirth. She was the only one in the room who wasn't crying.

The baby stopped wailing for a moment as Emily helped Margaret bring him closer to her breast. He nuzzled and gulped air, opening his eyes and looking directly into his mother's eyes. The two younger women gasped.

Emily's tears matched Margaret's now. She remembered the day Ryan was born and how quickly he'd bonded with her and Todd. She bit the corner of her lip as she wondered if Margaret's baby would ever know his father.

"You'll need names for the birth certificate," she told Margaret.

Margaret pulled her eyes from the baby's face to search Emily's face. "Is it okay to call him Danny? I know you were planning on another boy someday."

"Of course, sweetheart. Danny, Ryan and Jack. The *Three Musketeers*."

Margaret, Emily and the remaining household staff hadn't seen Madeline Sloane in months. She spent most of her time in the Hamptons, touring from one family estate to the other, seldom with her son Jack in tow.

While Madeline was away, Margaret was able to move freely about Sloane House. Danny occupied Ryan's cradle in the kitchen, where Sadie spent much of her time rocking him near the fire.

Without Danny in the carrier she had fashioned from some old blankets, Margaret moved quickly from one room to the next, tidying up, mending Madeline's clothing and ironing the same blouses and scarves repeatedly.

At the end of the summer, she had decided she would give Mrs. Sloane her notice. What good was a lady's maid when the lady of the house was never at home?

She chose a blistering hot Sunday afternoon to move her things into Emily and Todd's apartment. She was melting in the attic room on the third floor and Emily's offer to help with Danny during the night was a Godsend. As the sun beat down, she carried her belongings from house to garage. She was surprised to find in the three years she'd been living at Sloane House, her wardrobe was now full.

Friends among staff had knitted, sewn and even bought little blue booties, caps and sleepers. Margaret squared her shoulders as she dropped the last box of baby items at the foot of the stairs and returned for her bedding.

Margaret struggled with the thin, gray-striped ticking, stuffed with cheap, cotton batting. Down three flights of narrow stairs and out the kitchen doorway, she hoisted it onto a wheeled cart and across the gravel path between the house and the garage.

Each turn of the wheel was two steps forward and one step back. The hard rubber tires needed more weight to make purchase in the small pebbles.

Danny would be waking up momentarily. He'd been asleep for four hours, since the family returned from Mass where he'd cried for more than an hour. A colicky baby, Margaret had difficulty nursing and was embarrassed to hide in the church's nursery with a blanket thrown over his head.

When she got to the garage, she stopped to relish the cool interior of the dark building. At the base of the stairs, she called out softly to Todd.

"Can you help me with this mattress?"

Todd rushed down the steps. "Sorry, I was playing with Ryan and Danny," he said.

"The baby's awake?" Margaret's nap was a distant memory already. "I was really hoping to get a couple hours of shut-eye today. I'm expecting Mrs. Sloane back this evening and I wanted everything lined up, so I could tell her I'm leaving. I have applications in with several of the finer homes along Fifth Avenue. I hope she'll give me a reference."

"You can tell herself, soon," Todd chuckled. "She just called, and I'm headed to the train station to pick her up. She couldn't wait to tell me she's engaged and will be leaving Sloane House next month."

23 April 1916

Dearest Mother,

Today is Easter Sunday in America. Mrs. Sloane is away with friends, but she left her son Jack in our care.

The entire staff celebrated together in the Sloane House kitchen, as we must all return to work in the morning. So few of their holidays are religious, so not everyone attends Mass, but Emily, Todd and myself took Baby Jack. I pray Mrs. Sloane does not uncover our little side trip to St. Matthew's.

I am anxious to hear more of the rising unrest in Europe from your vantage point. Are you able to escape the misfortune and mistrust as Irish men and women? Tell me all is well, and you miss me.

Your loving daughter,
Margaret Mannion

Chapter Seventeen

Throughout her pregnancy and Danny's birth, Margaret kept up on the growing unrest in Europe and the effect of the United Kingdom's involvement in the great war. Her mother's letters were full of war stories, the most frightening being the uprising on Easter Monday 1916.

Bridget said Germany sent a shipment of arms to the rebels, but the British intercepted it just before the uprising began. There was fierce street fighting on the routes into Dublin and heavy casualties.

Margaret's mother and her neighbors saw isolated fighting about County Galway and the British seized property in County Wexford. The uprising lasted for six days, but with much greater numbers and heavier weapons, the British Army suppressed the Irish efforts.

"Leaders agreed to an unconditional surrender on Saturday," Bridget wrote, "but some fighting continued another 24 hours until word reached those here in the country."

Bridget stayed inside her home, cooking and reading by candlelight. After the surrender, the country remained under martial law. Several of her friends were taken prisoner by the British, but Bridget was sure they had played no part in the uprising. One, a friend since childhood, was sent to an internment camp in Britain, and another executed following a court-martial.

Bridget heard talk in town of increased popular support for Irish independence. "It has been more than 100 years since the Kingdoms of Ireland and Great Britain were united. Now the Irish parliament may be abolished, and our government given token representation in the British Parliament. Many more are considering immigration to America."

In the evenings, Margaret, Emily and Todd often talked about returning to Ireland after the war. Todd felt strongly there could be no return for his family until Ireland achieved home rule.

He was a walking encyclopedia on the issue. "Home Rule Bills in 1886 and 1893 were short-lived, but many Irish men and women still dream of an independent Gaelic Ireland, called Sinn Fein."

"About the same time we came to America, a third Home Rule Bill was introduced by the British prime minister. Of course, Protestants opposed the idea. They just don't to be ruled by a Catholic-dominated Irish government."

Margaret was less defiant. "My mother insists the Irish Volunteers want to secure the rights of all the people of Ireland, without attention to creed, politics or social group. When the volunteers smuggled rifles into Dublin, my mother read, the British army stopped them by firing into a crowd of civilians."

War was no longer a distant booming of rifles on the continent, Bridget told Margaret. "By now, Ireland seems to be on the brink of a civil war. One of the ladies from Loughanbouy, Susan McCurry was openly hostile to the volunteers. Her husband and her son were in the British Army and she depended on her army allowance. Food supplies coming in are also disrupted by the rebels."

Margaret wanted to support the Irish Volunteers. But there was little she could do from where she lived. "Some of the volunteers are hissed at and pelted with refuse. My mother's neighbors call them murderers."

Bridget was saddened by the ugly remarks and cat calls from her friends, as the volunteers marched to surrender.

Bridget Mannion had always been a worrier. She worried about her sons trying to raise a potato crop and herd sheep on the Irish countryside. The absentee landlords and heavy mortgages only contributed to poor crops and small landholdings.

But, most of the time Bridget worried about Margaret, held captive in America by the Great War. She wrote letters on a weekly basis, addressing them to the Sloane House as Margaret had said three years ago. But the last she had heard from Margaret was a year earlier when her daughter had many friends, but no husband. If her sons were drafted into the war effort, Bridget would be lost and likely to perish as the war's casualties extended into Ireland.

In 1916, Great Britain had passed a law requiring military service to extend conscription to Ireland. The UK was dangerously short of troops on the Western Front.

The Irish Parliamentary Party opposed conscription. Large numbers of Irishmen had willingly joined Irish divisions in 1914 and the likelihood of forced conscription created a backlash. Some linked home rule and conscription, causing further outrage. Similar campaigns in Australia and Canada seemed to target Irish Catholics.

In Bridget's estimation, Irish units continued to suffer the heaviest casualties in the British Army. "It is no wonder Ireland was opposed to the war and British conscription. The actual number of Irish casualties is argued at every pub and on every street corner," she wrote. "This summer, Dublin's Mayor Laurence O'Neill, wrote to your American president asking for support. Perhaps we'll see support from that front."

Margaret didn't hold out much hope for American support in Ireland. President Wilson had introduced his own Selective Service Act a year ago, to enable the registration of all American men, ages 21-31, as eligible for the draft.

12 November 1918

Dearest Margaret,

The newspapers are full of war! Is it the same there? The first engagement in Europe by UK troops was the Royal Irish Dragoon Guards!

Since Britain joined the war four years ago, I have worried daily about your well-being in America and any hope of your return. Then, America declared war on Germany last year and my worries ratcheted up.

My largest concern throughout the war has been the Pope's call to end the war. Even the Irish bishops declared conscription oppressive and unjust. A sign was posted to the church door Sunday, denying the right of the British government to enforce compulsory service in this country. They asked we pledge ourselves to one another to resist conscription by the most effective means at our disposal. There were anti-conscription rallies nationwide last spring.

I still hold out great hope for the coming years and your return. At the end of this 'Great War,' I am hopeful Ireland will rise again and make a final declaration of independence from England. I am also hopeful you will return with a husband and children in the end. A mother can hope, right?

Your mother,
Bridget Mannion

Chapter Eighteen

Madeline paced the floors at Sloane House for days. Confined by a recent downpour of rain, she wasn't able to visit her friends — the Rockefellers, the Vanderbilts, the Carnegies and, especially the Goulds. In September, according to Jack Sloane's will, Madeline would lose her annual stipend from his trust fund.

Richard was a banker, the vice president of a large manufacturing company in New York, and part owner of the Brooklyn Times. In the past four or five years, he had done business on occasion with both Jack and Vincent Sloane.

"I respect your late husband," Richard told her. "Not only for his business sense, but for his choice in women."

"Thank you, Dickie," Madeline replied. "I was a child when I married the Colonel. I'm a grown woman, now."

Gould ran his eyes up and down Madeline's trim figure. The gossamer fabric clung to her body, with a low-cut bodice to allow an ample display of both her jewelry and her bosom. "That you are. It's not time for games any longer, Madeline. Would you marry me?"

Madeline's champagne glass shook. This was the moment she'd been waiting for, to escape Sloane House and marry a man of his own wealth and standing in the community. A chance to get out from under Vincent's thumb.

"Of course, Dickie. Would you mind a small ceremony

this fall at your home? I'm anxious to be your wife — to be out from under the Sloane curse."

Gould smiled. "Yes, darling, on one condition — call me Richard. I'm not a boy any longer, either."

He kissed her greedily on the lips and his hands roamed her backside, anxious to learn more about the topography of his new possession.

Madeline sighed and leaned into his kiss. "Not so quickly, *Richard*," she emphasized. "I really don't want to wait any longer. I think I can have the ceremony arranged within the week. Do you mind if the minister is not Episcopalian?"

He frowned. "I'll arrange the priest. The Gould family has always given generously to St. Matthew's on Fourth Avenue. It's time the rector there gave back."

With a quick squeeze, Richard refilled both their champagne glasses and stepped into the hallway to call his parents. He wanted to share the happy news with everyone. His mother was especially adept at putting together an impromptu party on short notice. She'd have a guest list for Madeline in days.

Alone in the Gould family sitting room, Madeline breathed a sigh of relief. She'd call Vincent in the morning and give notice. She smiled grimly. After a forced marriage at only 19, she'd hoped her second marriage would be for love. Richard was a nice enough fellow; his looks were on the border of pleasant and portly. But there was just no spark.

A pleasurable diversion at first, perhaps at best, she supposed. It was time to get on with business. She trailed into the hall and wrapped her arms around Richard's waist as he chatted with his sister on the phone.

Vincent was dissatisfied again. And bored. "I aspire to be more like my father," he told his new wife. Vincent's father was not just a businessman and a financial wizard. He was also an inventor and a novelist. Among his many accomplishments was a science fiction novel about life in the year 2000.

In real estate, everything Vincent touched turned to gold. As a talisman, he carried his father's gold pocket watch, engraved with his initials — the one his father had worn the night he died. The fact his father's body was one of the first to be recovered only added to the cachet of the piece.

But, like his father, Vincent wanted to be more than a leader in business and society. He jumped at the opportunity to enlist in the United States Navy Reserve a year earlier. A reservist, he called himself, and served full-time as support to the U.S. Navy, however much he felt they were sitting on their hands waiting for Wilson.

Vincent's father had personally financed a volunteer infantry unit during the Spanish-American War. He had also donated his yacht to the U.S. government. This gave Vincent the idea to volunteer the *Norma*, his yacht to help patrol American waters during The Great War. He dreamed of commanding a naval force overseas aboard the *Norma*, but his pressure on Wilson had not yet borne fruit.

During his absence on one of the patrols, Helen had telegraphed Vincent with good news. Madeline Sloane would be married to Richard Gould in October. This meant Vincent and Helen could move into his parents' house right away. But Helen was certain there would be some redecorating to be done before the move could take place. Her tastes were so vastly different from Madeline Sloane. She didn't think she had seen Madeline at any of the charity events she sponsored.

Helen loved music and opera and helped found the New York City Center and the New York Opera Company. She was a patron of the Metropolitan Opera on Broadway and owned two boxes at the house, one for Vincent and herself, a second for guests.

An accomplished pianist, Helen had placed three or four

grand pianos in each of their homes. Each time she strolled by one of the instruments, she paused to play a full show tune or a bit from an opera.

She was also a trustee of the Metropolitan Museum of Art, making it her mission to support emerging artists and create teaching and performing jobs for artists of every ilk.

Vincent was certain the entire home might have to be redone before they could move in. He was glad he was out of town so often, on patrol. While he liked his townhouse on East 80th, The Sloane House was the rightful home for the family's leader.

Originally constructed for Vincent's mother, its early French Renaissance architecture was similar to a chateau. The ballroom could hold 1,200 people, compared with his grandparents' earlier mansion at Fifth Avenue and 34th Street.

Helen's best estimate for the move was Spring of 1917. The ballroom hadn't been used since Vincent's mother moved to England. His father had the home updated during his holiday with Madeline, but the style was rococo.

Helen didn't like the crystal chandeliers with pearl strings drooping from one to the other, Persian rugs and peacock feathers. The small marble waterfall would be replaced, and the Louis XVI candelabras brought over from Europe swapped out with more modern pieces.

Vincent shrugged. It wasn't about money, he decided. While he'd never had to work a day in his life, Vincent had learned, under Margaret's tutelage, there were others more deserving of money than the disgustingly wealthy socialites that redecorated family mansions to suit the season or the hostess's whims.

He decided then and there he would remain on patrol until the house was complete. The icy waters surrounding the city were no discomfort aboard *The Norma,* safeguarding the Brooklyn and Manhattan bridges.

Vincent had been anxious for the United States to join the war for years. As soon as the Germans started bombing passenger ships, he wrote to President Wilson, insisting America declare war on Germany. Not only was he unhappy with his marriage, he was itchy to prove himself to his mother and his family. His only responsibility with the reserves was to help guard bridges and aqueducts against possible German sabotage.

One morning at breakfast, Vincent slammed his fist on the table. He shook his newspaper in the air, fanning the flame of his passions. "Listen to this, Helen. 'When the Germans resumed unrestricted submarine warfare, they invited Mexico to join them as allies against the United States and promised to help recover the territories of Texas, New Mexico and Arizona. The UK intercepted the message and proudly presented it to the U.S. embassy in London.'

"But, Congress didn't declare war until now. By God, man, it's April."

Helen looked away, contemplating her soft-boiled egg and toast as if it held the secrets behind the entire conflict. "Vincent, please, control your temper. You'll get your chance soon enough. Why don't you call Franklin for advice?"

Franklin Delano Roosevelt's half-brother was Vincent's aunt's husband. "Volunteer for active duty," FDR told him. "Offer to take The Norma overseas."

Vincent jumped at the chance to lead his own yacht on patrol. After a month of additional training, he led a full crew overseas, but was later assigned to an armed yacht, at his own request. He wanted to fight the Krauts or die trying.

He was promoted to lieutenant in January and received another promotion in July. In France, Helen joined him to do charity work at the YMCA naval base in Bordeaux, while he served as a port officer at Royan.

Carefully, Vincent asked about Sloane House. "Who's in charge? Did you keep any of the maids Madeline hired?"

"Yes," Helen offered, eagerly. "There are two younger ladies I was certain would go with Madeline, her nanny and her lady's maid. But, since you had asked the driver to stay on, the nanny remained as assistant cook. Her husband is the driver."

"And, the lady's maid?" Vincent's voice trembled. "What responsibility did you find for her?"

"My own maid, Rozella, has decided to move to Chicago to be nearer to her family," Helen went on. "I needed someone I could trust, and Margaret seems very devoted to Todd and Emily."

Vincent's ears picked up at the mention of Margaret. After nearly two years, he still held out hope for reconciliation with her. Despite his marriage, Margaret was still single and might be willing to resume their relationship.

"I also appreciate her open manner and strong voice," Helen continued. "She has become involved in women's issues that are important to me. She has friends among the Irish she has drafted to join our cause."

"I was talking to Alice Paul and Carrie Chapman Catt just the other day ..."

Vincent had already shut out the background noise that was his wife's voice. Margaret was living in his house. She must still have feelings for him. If not, at least he could see her on a regular basis.

New York Times
March 19, 1917

EXPECT ACTION BY WILSON TODAY
President May Call Congress to Meet at Once or Declare a State of War Exists.

NO DOUBT OF OVERT ACTS

Officials, Though Cautious, Are Convinced That Germany Is Challenging War.
Special to the New York Times.

WASHINGTON, March 18 -- Technically the sinking of three American merchant vessels by German submarines has not changed the international situation; actually, these sinkings have given a more critical turn to it and paved the way for the initiation of a state of war between Germany and the United States.

Whether the Government regards the sinking of the three ships as the overt act which President Wilson mentioned in addressing Congress as cause for taking more drastic measures than a break in diplomatic relations is not being disclosed tonight. It is doubtful if it has been determined. The President, as far as known, has not consulted with any of his advisers, and there have been no conferences between members of the Cabinet. But officials who have been aware all along of the attitude of the President, expressed the opinion of this evening that the situation was "grave" and cautiously indicated that the overt act had been committed.

What is meant by the statement that technically the sinkings have not changed the status of the international situation is that they are merely repetitions of other offenses by German U-boats since relations between the two countries were broken off and President Wilson served notice that he would be obliged to adopt other measures if Germany carried out her declared intention of resorting to sinking merchant vessels on sight.

Chapter Nineteen

I t was a shame their move into the Sloane House had been spoiled by his trip overseas on *The Norma*, Helen mused. While she admired her husband's patriotism and unflagging service to his country, she had hoped as an officer, he would be able to delay his departure until the move into the big house on Fifth Avenue was complete.

Madeline's marriage to Richard Gould last year left little impression on Helen. She had made her decisions about marriage and a new home before the mansion became available. She agreed to live at Sloane House to appease Vincent, but she visited the huge home with a discerning eye toward activities geared more toward fundraising and social awareness than over-the-top society balls.

A huge crystal chandelier hung over the large dining table and cast a soft glow into every corner. Heavy drapes covered the windows along the south wall. "Draw the drapes open, please," Helen asked the lady's maid who'd followed her about the house, making notes of her decisions.

"Yes, ma'am." Margaret struggled with the weighty red velvet floor-to-ceiling curtains.

"It's okay," Helen rushed to help and bumped Margaret's arm. She took the clipboard from her. "What is your name again, dear?"

"Margaret, milady," she answered quickly.

Helen guffawed. "You mustn't call me milady," she chuckled. "I'm just a woman like you, making my way in this world as best I can. I may have started life in different circumstances, but we're all in this together, we girls."

The tour continued into the ballroom. Four massive crystal chandeliers anchored the center row of the huge room. At one end was a massive marble fireplace that went all the way to the ceiling. On the mantle were two massive marble nude men holding a built-in picture frame, containing a painting of a gala at the palace of Versailles. At the other end was a musician's balcony opening off the second floor, where a wall of Chinese screens blocked the musician's view of the ballroom.

"Please make a note for the movers, Margaret. The statues and painting may be auctioned for charity — either the ballet, the opera or the performing arts. After we get rid of some of these ghastly paintings lining the walls in the same manner, we'll have them replaced with new pieces from up and coming young artists from the Metropolitan Museum of Arts. I'm on the board there."

As Margaret trotted up the stairs behind Mrs. Sloane, she was surprised at her vigor. Helen was exactly the same age as Margaret, but she'd lived a charmed existence with no heavy lifting and toting to keep her strong.

"Come along, dearie," Helen called back. "You'll never keep up with me on a tennis court."

On the second floor, was Madeline's suite of rooms — a domed boudoir, dressing room, bathroom, closets and her pink sitting room. Also, on this floor was a guest suite and the linen closet. "Was this Madeline's or Ava's room?" Helen inquired of Margaret as they stopped just inside the master suite.

"Yes, Mrs. Sloane."

Helen frowned.

"I mean, yes, Helen, both the previous Mrs. Sloanes used this suite."

"Gut it," Helen replied. "Even if it hadn't been used by those dreadful women, Vincent and I could never sleep in the same room."

"Please, ask the builders to create two adjoining master suites, with a shared sitting room at the center and adjoining doors. Bathrooms at the rear and dressing rooms to either side."

"Vincent's room will be done in brown leather and heavy wood; my room will have similar colors, but in a lighter version all around. As befits my sense of femininity," she laughed again, lightly this time.

The guest rooms on the third floor and servants' quarters were not of interest to Helen today. She was in a hurry to prepare for a gala at the Met that evening to benefit her beloved Musicians Emergency Fund.

"Keep me informed, Margaret," she said. "I hope we'll be great friends."

Margaret's growing comfort around Vincent's wife made her decision to stay at Sloane House easier. She was always looking over her shoulder for signs of his return on leave, but Helen's easy manner and frequent enlistment of Emily and her attendance at non-work-related events made the work less drudgery. In addition, Helen was a refreshing change of etiquette, with little fussiness in clothing or dress.

On occasion, Margaret wondered why Helen kept her on, since there was so little for a lady's maid to do. Not one to look a gift horse in the mouth, Margaret chipped in more often around the house, especially in the kitchen, and as a personal secretary to Mrs. Sloane.

With her chores at Sloane House easing up, Margaret took every opportunity to spend free time with Danny. She relished the bed and bath time routine she had with Danny and Ryan.

Ryan was five years old and much fairer than Danny, but treated him like the younger brother he was. As they shared the large metal tub, Emily relaxed with a book and Margaret heated more water on the stove to add to their bath and keep them comfortable. When the water was a muddy gray, the boys pranced about the apartment naked, until their mothers wrapped them in large, white, fluffy towels — hand-me-downs from the Sloane House.

But books were a special private time for each of the boys with their own parents. Danny's favorite was a classic Emily had introduced to Margaret shortly after her arrival at Sloane House. *The Emerald City of Oz* was above Danny's head, but Margaret favored the colorful scenes of Oz and glossed over the scenes with Growleywogs and Phanfasms.

She liked Dorothy, the dreamer, and identified sadly with her lack of parents. Danny liked Dorothy's animal friends, including the Cowardly Lion and Billina, the yellow hen. He fell asleep, his dark, curly locks shading his eyes now — reminding Margaret she needs to get out the scissors this weekend. Sleepily, she caresses his cheeks, no longer those of a chubby toddler.

Just as she drifted off to sleep herself, Todd deposited a dozing Ryan in the bed beside her and nudged Margaret. "Mags, it's a bit crowded here. Do you want to move onto the bed?"

"Mmmmm," she groaned. "I'm good."

Helen had moved into Sloane House in April and May. She made no short work of taking the staff into her confidence, making sure she knew each one's story, their family and their responsibilities around the house. Emily and Margaret had worked out their stories ahead of time. Danny and Ryan were brothers, they told her, and Margaret, as Emily's best friend, stayed with the family to help care for the rambunctious pair.

Todd, who'd already been vetted and whole-heartedly approved by Vincent before he left for the war, was a talisman for the pair of women and Margaret had an easy go of it with Helen, as well. Mrs. Sloane had taken a shine to Margaret on their first day, as they toured the house before she moved in.

While it was still difficult for Margaret to call Mrs. Sloane by her given name, she did feel comfortable in assuming many of the lady's duties during the remodeling project at Sloane House. Helen was occupied with her charities and her work with women's suffrage, she told Margaret. Housework, even choosing materials and ordering carpet layers and painters about, were not duties she enjoyed, so she was happy to have Margaret take over in that department.

For her part, Margaret found great joy in finishing the interiors of the public rooms and Mrs. Sloane's part of the bedroom suite. The clean, simple lines and colors Mrs. Sloane had chosen as guidelines, gave Margaret a great deal of latitude in choosing fabrics, textures and patterns to compliment the entire suite.

The only part of the project that stopped her was the completion of Mr. Sloane's bedroom. Margaret had decided early on she would never refer to Mr. Sloane as Vincent again, either when she was speaking with Mrs. Sloane or her friends. It was her way of distancing herself from his memory. As time passed, she was able to pretend, at least to herself, Vincent Sloane was merely an absent landlord and not the missing father of her child.

Helen Sloane, while a similar age to both Margaret and Madeline, was the polar opposite of Madeline. Easygoing and casual, Helen often wore men's trousers, not just the tailored, evening gown-like slacks Madeline favored, but true menswear.

"Why should men have the easy way with clothing?" she asked Margaret one day. "If I'm wearing a dress and hat and boots, I'm hobbled to no end. I have work to do and I cannot do it in elaborate, fussy trimmings. My wardrobe, like yours, should consist of outfits chose for freedom and convenience."

Where Madeline had changed for morning, afternoon, dinner and then evening wear, Helen might wear the same stockings two days in a row. She often went without a corset. Neither woman had the type of figure requiring exaggeration of their lines, but Madeline wore a corset all day, every day. Margaret often carried smelling salts to help her recover if she wore her corsets too tight or skipped meals to fit into a tighter gown for an evening at the theater.

Once she'd moved into Sloane House, two of Helen's fa-vorite activities directly involved Margaret. Todd was teaching Helen to drive an automobile and she wanted Margaret to learn as well.

Helen cut quite a figure when out for a spin. If it was a wet or snowy day, she might even wear a duster over her entire cos-tume to keep the mud and grime off her clothing.

That summer, Margaret had often worn clean, castoff jackets borrowed from Todd. The cut was similar to Helen's car coat, but the quality and style of the jacket left a lot to be desired. Standing side-by-side, Helen and Margaret looked the part of mistress and poor servant girl. It was not a look Helen approved of.

"My dear girl," Helen scolded. "If you won't dress well for yourself, think of my reputation. I've ordered a new car coat for myself. And, as I expect you to learn to drive, you may wear this coat. If something were to happen to Todd or myself while we are out socially or on work detail, I'd expect you to take the wheel."

Within minutes, Margaret and Helen had joined Todd in the gravel area in front of the garage. Each day, when he put the car away, he raked the gray and brown pea-sized gravel to a beach-like smoothness. Today, he was dressed in his dark liv-ery suit, but without the jacket. His sleeves were rolled up and there were patches of oil on one arm.

"Just checking her out, to be sure she's ready for you ladies to take a spin," Todd said. "Mrs. Sloane, if you'd sit behind the wheel and Margaret in the passenger seat, I'll begin."

Todd was a patient teacher. "The three pedals on the floor here are, right to left, the brake, reverse and the clutch. The lever to your right, is an emergency brake. But move it straight up and you're in neutral. Forward, you're in drive."

Margaret was already confused. She'd never paid attention when Todd was driving her to and from the Kelly's, never realizing she'd be learning to drive one day soon. She furrowed her brow and concentrated harder.

"To stop the car, put the lever in neutral and step on the brake," Todd intoned. He put the lever in the center position.

Mrs. Sloane stepped on the middle pedal and the car lurched back. "The brake is the one on the left," he reminded her. "The middle pedal is reverse."

Helen made five or six short turns around the large graveled area, then stepped out and urged Margaret to take her turn.

Margaret quickly picked up on the rules necessary to go in forward and reverse, but one time stopped just barely short of running into the garage. "Can we go out onto the street?" she asked, anxious to be on her way. "I want to try the levers on the steering wheel column. I can remember how you used them to rev up the motor and speed up the engine."

Todd's smile faded, as he cautioned Margaret and Mrs. Sloane to stay in the yard for today's lesson. "Tomorrow, we'll try driving on a straight away country road," he offered. "The secret when you come to a curve is to reduce power before you apply the brake, by pulling the lever forward. That's important."

A light, drizzly rain was falling the next morning when Margaret took Mrs. Sloane's breakfast up to her room. The lady of the house wore a sad expression. "Today's lesson will have to be postponed," she said. "Perhaps we can go shopping for my new car jacket. Would you like a new jacket, too?"

Margaret's face colored and she hid her old jacket behind a large potted fern in the corner of the boudoir.

"I insist," Helen continued. "Tomorrow, we'll be attending a women's suffrage meeting and I'd like you to sit behind me and take notes. Your involvement is required to help me stay current. Perhaps you'll learn to take up the cause and share your knowledge with Emily, DeeDee and the other girls. I'm convinced women will be allowed to vote by war's end."

Chapter Twenty

As the days progressed, Margaret and Helen became more like friends than she and Madeline had ever been. The new Mrs. Sloane had completely redone the second floor where they stood now, and it certainly made life easier for the servants.

With fewer tchotchkes lying about, cleaning was easier. Helen wore fewer gowns, lotions and laborious hairstyles, as well. Margaret's job included fewer changes of clothing to prepare, fewer lady's bits to launder and Helen required absolutely no assistance in dressing.

More importantly, the new Mrs. Sloane was not one to ask leading questions. Margaret was concerned her new boss would learn about Danny and throw her out of the house. When Vincent's name came up in conversation, she found a way to busy herself downstairs. She was just about to leave with the tray and a week's menus for Sadie, when she heard Helen call her name.

Helen stood and tugged at her trousers. "Did you hear me?" she snapped. "Our Women's Suffrage Association is meeting today with a group of leaders for free negroes. Are you coming along? The national association wants to join with the blacks to attain the vote for all Americans. We can't be treated like secondhand citizens any longer."

Margaret fumbled with the breakfast tray. She had always been curious of the large number of black people she saw around the city. There were very few black people in Ireland, most in major cities. The few black women she'd seen in Queenstown were more familiar. Like her, they worked as servants of the wealthy families, but enslavement was rare in Ireland.

Helen was still lecturing. Her hands fluttered around her face, knotting and unknotting her scarf, as she dressed for the meeting. "Their right to vote runs parallel to our own concerns."

Margaret turned and rushed out the door while Helen finished patting her hair and added a pot of lip stain to her bag. Her employer always acted jumpy when they attended suffrage meetings. Margaret hoped the quick, high-pitched laughter apparent at the last meeting would be less obvious this time.

Weekends and evenings were the only time Margaret had with her son. During the week, Emily was able to keep Ryan and Danny in the apartment, the Sloane House kitchen or in the yard. On occasions, when she was needed in other parts of the big house, the two little boys busied themselves in the kitchen, looking at simple children's picture books or playing with blocks left behind by Jack Sloane.

Often, Helen would go out of town for the weekend with Alice, meeting with suffragettes in Philadelphia, Boston or the like. Margaret didn't really care for the trips. While Helen often invited her along, she always got the distinct impression Mrs. Sloane would rather travel alone. She was an independent woman and Margaret admired that about her.

In fact, she had begun to pattern many of her behaviors after Mrs. Sloane. Unconsciously, she put her shoulders back and her chest out. She smiled more often now, despite Vincent's absence. In the 18 months since Danny's birth, Margaret appeared more relaxed and Emily caught her smiling and laughing more often.

Margaret hoped to become entirely self-supporting in

raising her son, not relying on the uncertain chance of a good marriage any longer. She was more at ease taking the lead in conversations at meetings with Mrs. Sloane, leaning in to listen and occasionally initiating contact with another person of her class.

Her interest in women's suffrage grew as she spent more time with Mrs. Sloane, but she was sure it was a cause she'd carry long after she left Helen's employ.

On Saturday, Margaret and Danny took a picnic to a new American graveyard at the city's center. Designed like a garden, the flowers were beautiful in the spring and summer and the public was welcome to enjoy the grounds.

They unpacked their basket in a quiet spot, away from the graves. Emily and Todd said this was a gruesome activity, but they had not been touched by death as often as Margaret in the last two years.

She knew their bodies weren't here at this pretty cemetery, but somehow, she felt closer to them. She used the opportunity to talk to Danny about his Papa Lawrence, back in Ireland. And, while she was embarrassed to tell Emily, she encouraged Danny to believe Martin Gallagher was his father.

Danny was fascinated by the gravestones. "Daddy's stone?" he asked. "Daddy in da ocean?"

Margaret sidestepped Danny's questions with a jam sandwich and two cookies Sadie had saved from Friday's tea. "Look at the pretty flowers."

She pointed down the hill. "See the red-breasted bird hopping just over there? What kind of bird is that? A robin?"

Todd and Emily invited Margaret and Danny to visit Central Park with them the following weekend. It was an hour's walk from Sloane House, but Danny's short legs made the jaunt difficult. Todd had considered asking Mrs. Sloane if the family could use her car, but hesitated in ever asking for too much from his employer.

Instead, Margaret decided to use her proximity to the boss to beg the favor. But first, she needed to hear from Mrs.

Sloane about working in munitions on weekends to help bring in some extra money for Danny's future.

Margaret gritted her teeth. She'd rehearsed today's speech to Mrs. Sloane through much of the night, tossing back and forth in her narrow bed above the garage. This morning, as she brought the tray to Mrs. Sloane in the dining room, she choked out, "Mrs. Sloane, there's something I'd like to discuss with you."

Helen smiled cautiously. "Of course, dear. Can it wait until after I've had my coffee? By the look on your face, it's serious and I always thought light conversation better aided in digestion."

In the sitting room after breakfast, Helen called Margaret. "Now, what is it you wanted to talk about?"

Margaret shifted from one foot to the other. "Some of the staff have been talking," she began nervously. "With Mr. Sloane, the butlers and other housemen away in military service..."

She stopped, swallowed hard and began again. "I mean there are just a few of us not able to serve. We're not American citizens. Yet."

"Vincent has told me there are Irish nationals serving in the United States military," Helen said. "There are also more than 10,000 American women enlisted in active duty in the Navy, serving stateside. They are paid identically to the men."

"Yes, ma'am. We were wondering, I mean we would like, if it's okay with you..." Margaret stuttered to a halt again.

Helen tilted her head toward Margaret. "Spit it out, girl. We haven't all day."

Margaret forged ahead. "We'd like to find positions outside Sloane House, perhaps in the munitions factories or as railway guards or ticket collectors. Todd might be able to find work as a police or fireman."

Helen thought for a minute. "When the men return from the war, they'll want their jobs back," she said. "I'll have to give

Mary Wernke

this some thought."

7 August 1917

Dearest Mam,

I am in high hopes this letter will reach you as we have heard posts are not faring well between America and Ireland during the war. I do know there is some postal censorship in the United States and Great Britain, but I will say nothing of interest to the soldiers.

Several of our number have entered the U.S. Army from New York City. Vincent Sloane, the owner of the Sloane House, volunteered his yacht as a hospital ship. Sister Mary Eleanor, our sweet Ellie, is working in hospitals on the coast with returning soldiers.

Mrs. Sloane has taken a shine to me, I believe. She often asks me to accompany her around the city in her campaign for women's suffrage. Can you imagine, Mam, women voting? I hope to be among the Americans who are able to vote for president in 1920, if I'm allowed to become a citizen.

How is the war affecting you there in Loughanboy? Are there any local boys gone to war? Please try to write to me. I know your letters will take longer to arrive, but they cheer my soul upon receipt.

Yours,
Margaret

Chapter Twenty-One

M argaret hadn't come face-to-face with Vincent since shortly after his marriage to Helen. Following his extended convalescence at Fairholme, he'd only come to Sloane House a few times to tie up loose ends with his stepmother. By the time he and Helen had decided to move into the house, Vincent was a member of the U.S. Navy and commander of his own ship, his former yacht *The Norma*.

As she rounded the corner of the back stairs that morning, she hadn't anticipated his presence. Instinctively, she clutched the bundle of sheets and towels near her midsection.

They were not alone in the kitchen. Emily hovered near the fire with Ryan, teaching him to count beans and drawing simple letters on a slate board.

Margaret clung unsteadily to the door frame leading to the garden. Danny was playing in the dirt, between rows of green beans and lettuce. As his mother looked back, he plucked a lettuce leaf from the ground and popped it in his mouth.

"Margaret, are you okay?" Vincent asked. There was sadness in his voice, but neither of the women felt any remorse.

"My health is of no concern of yours, Mr. Sloane," she replied icily. "Please, step aside. I have produce to wash."

Emily merely shrugged and turned her back on Vincent as he stumbled from the kitchen. He bent over like an old man and his gaze was clouded. Shortly, she heard a door slam and Vincent didn't appear in the kitchen again until his return on leave from the Western Front two years later.

He was surprised to see a second little boy with Emily this time. He had a heavy shock of dark, bristly hair and startling blue eyes.

Danny looked up at the uniformed man. "SO-JER!" he pointed at Vincent. "Look, SO-JER!"

Emily hushed the boy and turned to Vincent. "Todd is in the garage," she offered, inclining her head toward the back door.

Vincent wasn't here to see Todd, she knew.

"Mrs. Sloane is out for the day. Margaret has gone with her to a meeting."

Vincent turned abruptly at her name. "Is she well? Does she speak of me?"

"Mrs. Sloane seems in fine fettle, most days," Emily replied. "She speaks of you often and fondly."

"You know what I mean," his eyes bore into Emily's.

She leveled her gaze at him and, with absolutely no affectation, replied calmly, "Margaret's fine, too. She never speaks of you. She has no need to. She's met a fine Irish man and is planning to settle down, start a family."

She glanced knowingly at Danny.

Vincent lowered his eyes. "Tell her I asked after her," he begged. "Tell her I still love her." His features twisted in pain.

Within minutes, Emily heard Vincent and the butler in the front entry debating the merits of parquet floors and muddy footprints. Then she heard the front door open and Vincent returned to his men's club. Minutes later, the back door opened.

"Anything to report?" Margaret asked her friend. She was loaded down with clothes and pamphlets for Mrs. Sloane.

"No, nothing. Mrs. Sloane was here earlier, but she was alone and had no time to chat. She said she would see you later in the week. She had a meeting in the capital."

Margaret proceeded up the stairs and Emily made the sign of the cross with one hand. "Forgive me, Father. For I have sinned," she muttered beneath her breath.

As America became involved in the war, Vincent had not been unaware of Eugene Creel's role in the propaganda campaign and applauded the role of American celebrities. He was invited to become one of the "four-minute men" lecturers delivering talking points in neighborhood movie theaters across the country. Once the agenda became clear, Vincent demurred only because he wanted to serve in the Navy, on board *The Norma*.

Others of Vincent's society friends spoke not just in theaters, but at churches, lodges and colleges. They became messengers from the government at Washington. One of Creel's speeches was distributed throughout the world, making it harder for German propagandists to distort the President's messages.

But Vincent was shocked when Creel enlisted Helen in his stead. The suffragist was well-known in the New York State Woman Suffrage Party for using the telephone to call potential voters to ask their views on suffrage. She also led an incredibly successful fundraising campaign, making large donations herself and soliciting a sizeable sum from the Astors and the Goulds.

In her letters to Vincent overseas, Helen spoke constantly of Jane Addams, Alice Paul and Carrie Chapman Catt. "Even five years ago, President Roosevelt was a champion of women's rights. He is considered one of the great feminists of our time, advocating for corporal punishment for wife beaters and women in executive positions in the New York City police department."

In early 1917, Helen and some of her friends joined Alice Paul and a group of suffragists in picketing the White House. They called themselves the Silent Sentinels, a rotating cluster of women who stood at the White House gates for months, carrying signs intended to challenge and embarrass the president.

At first, Wilson seemed amused by the picketers. He tipped his hat and smiled. He even invited them in for coffee.

Today, Helen and Margaret stood sedately near the gate, holding a sign on two six-foot poles Todd had fashioned from lumber lying about the garage. "To the Russian Envoys," it read in large black letters, "President Wilson and Envoy Root are deceiving Russia. They say we are a democracy. Help us win a world war, so that democracies may survive."

The Russian banner reflected Alice, Helen and Margaret's growing desperation as war distracted both the nation and the Congress from the suffrage campaign the two older women had been leading for four years. But they had no intention of giving up.

"Clearly they believe we are nothing more than brood sows to raise children to get into the army and be made into fertilizer," Helen told Margaret. By November, Margaret and Emily had become firmly entrenched in Helen's National Women's Party.

Together with Lucy Burns and Helen Sloane, Alice was determined to ignite a fire for a constitutional amendment granting women's suffrage. Their first big event was a suffrage parade, similar to one the women from Sloane House had been involved in last January.

Helen spoke fondly of Alice to Margaret. "While she clashes often with President Wilson, she is from an affluent New Jersey family and has degrees from Swarthmore and the University of Pennsylvania."

"She studied for a short time in England and I'm certain that is where she learned her militant tactics. British suffragettes were already marching on the streets of London, making public speeches and forming picket lines near public venues 100 years ago."

Margaret looked over Helen's head at Emily and smiled

knowingly.

With Helen and Alice pushing for high visibility and controversial new tactics, tensions continued to grow between the leaders of the party and the new women. Last year, when Alice proposed watch fires, where they burned copies of Wilson's speeches, the women's party split into two factions. Margaret followed Helen, who in turn followed Alice.

While many thought of the Silent Sentinels as a joke or a curiosity, public sentiment changed after the U.S. entered the war. Police began to arrest the women on charges of obstructing traffic.

Today was Helen and Margaret's turn to hold the large sign near the White House gate again. Margaret remembered the day was November 14, 1917, because it was Emily's birthday. Later, she was happy Emily had chosen not to attend.

Inspired by the British suffragettes who were already taking more radical steps, Alice was in prison and was being forcefed while on hunger strike. The prison superintendent ordered 40 male guards to arrest Helen, Margaret and the other women to teach them a lesson.

Margaret and Helen went docilely enough to the Occoquan jail. Their hope was to be reunited with Alice and to offer comfort. As they walked toward their cell, a guard attacked Helen and Margaret, beating them with a club and dragging them into the cell. Others reported being choked, punched and kicked.

Dora Lewis told Margaret her arm was twisted behind her back and she was slammed into an iron bed twice before they left her unconscious on the floor. Her cellmate thought she was dead and suffered a heart attack, but she was denied medical treatment until the next morning.

Alice started a roll call. "Helen?"

"Over here," Sloane answered from the other side. "Margaret is with me. We're okay."

"Dora?" Paul called out.

No answer.

The guards ordered Alice to stop and handcuffed her arms to the cell bars above her head, leaving her standing, bleeding all night. In solidarity, the other women stood holding their arms above their heads through the night.

After the first night, the women refused to eat for three days. The guards tried to tempt the women to eat with fried chicken.

Paul called out to those on the cell block, "They think there is nothing in our souls above fried chicken."

As the hunger strike continued, the warden began to worry some of the prisoners may die, leading to more negative publicity. He ordered Paul be moved to another jail, where she was force-fed.

Later, Helen told Margaret that Alice was held down by five men as a tube was forced through her nose, causing painful, severe nosebleeds.

Helen and Margaret felt lucky to have escaped injury and resolved to share few of the details with Emily, Todd or Vincent.

After the Night of Terror, Margaret was frightened to picket outside the White House. Eventually, a White House attorney, who had served as a campaign adviser to Wilson, resigned his political post to represent the Silent Sentinels in court. Once the story broke, it received broad coverage in the media, outraging many readers and contributing to the growing public support for their cause.

But much of the damage had been done. Margaret begged Helen to allow her to find a job outside Sloane House.

"As long as you're here first thing to prepare for the day ahead and at the end of the day, to report in, I'm willing to work with you," Helen agreed.

With additional tutelage from Todd, Margaret was able to find part-time and temporary work delivering packages to various government agencies. She also worked as a driver for one of Mrs. Sloane's friends whose chauffeur had enlisted, driving an ambulance for the New York City hospitals and delivering messages for a courier service.

Many of her employers provided a car similar to the one Todd had taught Margaret to drive. She was an excellent student and willing to take many of the jobs other women weren't able to handle. Farm women drove tractors while their husbands were away at war and Margaret read of one pair of upstate New York women working as carpenters, but the majority of NYC women served as telephone and wireless operators, railroad conductors and making flags at the Brooklyn Navy Yard.

Emily wanted to work as a nurse or volunteer with the Red Cross, but Todd and convinced her she was needed to care for Ryan and Danny and to oversee the other servants. Many of the younger girls, like DeeDee, had escaped the house for higher paying positions in airplane factories once the U.S. joined the war last spring.

25 December 1917

Happy Christmas, Mam!

Today is a day for rest. I have taken on another job as a driver, helping to deliver patients to hospitals after serious accidents or illnesses.

I have less involvement with Mrs. Sloane's women's suffrage movement. We are still involved in letter-writing campaigns and Mrs. Sloane attends conferences and offers stirring speeches. There have been some occasional suffragists being hauled off to jail, but I have avoided trouble for the most part.

Since the U.S. has entered the war, we look for a swift end to hostilities. When the war has ended, I hope that I will be able to visit Ireland once again. I miss you so much!

Yours,
Margaret

Chapter Twenty-Two

Vincent liked being in charge on *The Norma*. The yacht had been converted to a small hospital ship, moving quickly in or near war zones. Covered by the Hague Convention Act of 1907, his ship must give medical assistance to wounded personnel of all nations, must not be used for any military purpose and could not hamper enemy combat vessels.

However, hospital ships were frequently attacked, both on purpose and by accident. *The Norma* displayed a large Red Cross both forward and aft.

Vincent's second officer saluted and handed him a telegram. "German High Command has ordered its submarines to destroy hospital ships, suggesting illegal shipments of arms may be on board. The HMS Britannic hit a mine last month. Thirty people were killed, but the rest of the crew and passengers were able to escape."

The war was hitting back on all fronts. Vincent recognized the Britannic as a sister ship to the Titanic, opening old wounds. Already in a sour mood after his short visit to New York, he might have welcomed a German U-boat on *The Norma's* tail. His mission to dart behind enemy lines and pick up wounded soldiers was certainly welcome.

Nicknamed *The Comfort*, the Sloane yacht had insufficient capacity for safe transatlantic navigation and was confined to the waters off England and France. As the end of war neared, many of the patients suffered more often from disease than mortal injury.

Vincent's final days on *The Norma* were filled with sleepless nights as he comforted dying men and helped them write their last words in letters home. He read his letters from Helen aloud to some of the men.

"Life here at home is quiet," she wrote. "The music halls and theaters keep people amused with acrobats and conjurers. Tickets are very cheap and attract a working class. A band played the Colonel Bogey March, made popular in England. It is a handsome, patriotic tune sure to keep your toes tapping."

At first, the spread of the new flu virus set off few alarms. There were fewer deaths than in previous epidemics, despite the enormous numbers of soldiers infected.

In the daily reports Vincent received by telegraph, he read more than 10,000 sailors had reported to sick bays in May and June, but only four died. "French and Spanish troops are sickened, too, but it was dismissed out of hand, until the King of Spain became ill," one telegram read. "The press has christened the disease the Spanish Flu. Report incidents on board *The Comfort* ASAP."

Many of the American soldiers Vincent met had trained together in Kansas, but there was no camaraderie aboard *The Comfort*. The virus seemed to mutate rapidly, changing enough from one man to the next that Navy doctors had a hard enough time identifying it, much less fighting it.

As *The Comfort* steamed toward home, Vincent received a second telegraph claiming the disease had originated in the United States and spread to France with the arrival of American troops. In addition, a giant tsunami wave of illness had returned to wash over the U.S.

As *The Comfort* docked in Boston Harbor, Vincent reported only 15 patients. Three had died en route, but several of the Navy doctors, nurses and Red Cross workers had taken ill. In a hospital at Camp Devens, an Army training base 35 miles from Boston, accommodations were set up for 1,200 patients.

On September 1, they had 84 patients. Within the week, dozens more fell ill, and the diagnosis was the Spanish Flu. Vincent remained on his ship, hoping to avoid the contagion, but within the week, he was delirious and screaming in pain when touched.

A doctor visiting the ship diagnosed meningitis and ordered he report to the hospital at Camp Devens. But, by now the hospital was overwhelmed — doctors and nurses were too sick to treat patients and there were too few workers to help feed patients and staff. The hospital ceased accepting new patients, no matter how ill.

Vincent remained alone on his ship, certain he would be dead by nightfall. He rewrote his will to include not only Helen, but Margaret, as well. Delirious with pain, Vincent reasoned Margaret would forgive him for his indiscretions, if she were to inherit much of his wealth.

During the night, Vincent's fever broke. He stumbled along the pier, ashen and bedraggled, his clothes soaked in sweat. Fear had emptied the streets. The only other human Vincent spied was an equally sick man driving a horse-drawn cart, loaded with bodies, destined to be buried in mass graves.

Shipbuilders watched from behind shuttered windows. Vincent hoped to hail a cab, visit a motel for a hot shower and take a train back to New York. But the streets were empty, the large hotels were all closed and no one would come near the dirty young man who just yesterday commanded a Navy vessel.

He stopped along Battery Park and napped on a park bench. He begged food from a hobo nearby and hitched a ride on a garbage truck to a flophouse near the beach. There he was treated to a cold bath, some equally cold gruel and a wormy apple.

He was finally able to befriend a worker at the YMCA hostel. Surrounded by black men and women, the YMCA offered a clean, safe dorm room with food and basic hygiene facilities. The social worker was able to call the Sloane House and relay Vincent's recovery and presence in Boston.

Within two days, Todd had arrived in Boston with face masks, blankets and new clothes for Vincent. He arranged his boss, hardly recognizable from the day two years ago when he'd left New York City to serve his country. Vincent had abandoned the ship in Boston's Harbor with orders to have it sanitized and donated to the U.S. Navy.

As they motored south, Vincent dozed and then woke fitfully. Cosseted once again, Vincent was uncomfortable with comfort now. In the last 18 months, he'd seen hundreds of men die. Some with arms or legs blown off, others blinded by mortar fire and now, thousands coughing up blood and expiring overnight.

"You've changed, sir," Todd said.

"My God, I hope so," Vincent replied. "I want to help others. Why should I live in luxury while others live in abject poverty? I'll speak to Helen straight away about an idea that came to me during the past few days, staying in a hostel and unrecognizable by anyone. I want to create a foundation to help others, build public housing, not luxury apartments. Basketball courts and..."

Vincent was asleep again and didn't awake until Todd pulled into the drive at Sloane House.

On the 11th day of the 11th month, at the 11th hour, the Sloane House was draped with flags. Spirits were high as much of the staff joined Vincent and Helen on the veranda along the front of the house for a patriotic parade. Margaret, Emily and Todd kept the children indoors.

Fireworks, bells and whistles filled the air. Young men in uniform danced and sang along the parade route and women stopped them to offer cake, lemonade and kisses.

Vincent sat in his chair and reviewed the last two weeks, since his arrival back in the U.S. Alone and afraid on *The Comfort*, Vincent was sure he was going to die. His last will and testament were still folded carefully in his ruck sack at the back of his closet upstairs. His plan was to burn it in his bedroom fireplace, but he hadn't had a moment alone.

Helen and Sadie hovered at his bedside every waking moment. They were often there when he was asleep, too. Helen had hired a private nurse to care for her patient at great expense. Due to the continued flu outbreak in the city, nurses were very hard to come by, as most were attached to the military or a large hospital. But Helen was not sparing any expense to regain Vincent's health.

He waved wanly at small band making their way up the avenue. Vincent hadn't expected traffic on the street. Many were still trying to emerge from the pandemic that had claimed 70,000 lives in the U.S. and 500 million worldwide. The highest death rates were among otherwise healthy people between the ages of 20 and 40 years old. It was a miracle he had survived.

After returning home, Vincent had spent nine weeks in the hospital, his breathing still labored. He fussed at the prospect of 11 weeks reporting as an outpatient, but with Todd's support he made the tiring trip every other day for breathing exercises.

Many of the sick and wounded men returned home needing medical treatment. The treatment was free, along with financial support in the form of a pension and assistance in finding employment. The process was not an easy one and many described the disability suffered after the battle as more terrible than its wartime counterpart. Many relied on pensions that were difficult to acquire but were unable to work.

One of the soldiers recognized Vincent from his time on *The Comfort*. "The medical board I've been to talk to seems almost hostile," he said. "You have to have proof positive or you don't get anything. I suspect the doctors were chosen to suit the circumstances. They don't want to be too sympathetic or it will cost the country too much."

Vincent's nurse told a similar story. She'd been discharged from service entirely when she asked for two months sick leave. "I'm really a very strong person," she told Vincent. "I'm suffering from war strain and just wanted a short time before returning to work."

The government administrators were ambivalent toward shell shock. With the pressure on doctors dealing with physical wounds, men sufferings from psychological damage didn't even report their illness. A pension for a non-physical complaint was doubly difficult and most were discouraged from even applying.

The more war stories Vincent heard, the more he was determined to create a fund of sorts to help returning vets, the poor and hungry, the soldiers struggling down Fifth Avenue with missing limbs, blind or otherwise disabled.

As his recovery progressed, Vincent sought out the advice of not only his wife, but the staff he trusted most, Todd and Margaret. While he saw Todd every day, on their trips back and forth to the hospital, Margaret refused to visit him in his room.

Todd had been stingy with information about Margaret's well-being and supposed marriage. He seemed perplexed Vincent was asking so many questions about his friend and took his concerns to Emily. Once she'd 'fessed up about her stories to Vincent when he was home on leave, Todd asked the obvious, "Does he know about Danny?"

Since Vincent's return, Margaret had hidden in the kitchen and the apartment garage she now shared full-time with Emily, Todd and the boys. Danny called both women mama and Todd was papa, but the driver was pressuring Margaret to tell Danny and Vincent the truth.

Margaret was nearly apoplectic. "Danny is too young to know the circumstances of his birth and Vincent has no right to his beautiful son."

"That's just it," Todd said. "Danny is Mr. Sloane's son, no matter the circumstances. Letting him believe I'm his daddy is not just sad, it's sinful." He crossed himself as an added protection and to push Margaret toward the truth.

Not one to pile on, Todd had been saving this last comment since the drive back from Boston. "If you tell him you know this, I'll deny on my deathbed I was the one that told you. Mr. Sloane knows, since the terrible illness just before his wedding, he's not able to have children."

"Mrs. Sloane knows, but she's reconciled herself to remaining childless," he finished. He stood, watching Margaret and hoping for a reply.

A silent tear snaked its way down one cheek and she dashed it away with her balled fist. "Now, isn't that the devil's handiwork," she cried. "He gains a son by our evil deeds, but loses it all in a marriage his mother arranged. It doesn't change anything. I'm still not going to share my Danny boy with Mr. Sloane."

Just then, Emily entered the room with the boys to begin work on their morning's lessons. Ryan was more than two years older than Danny, but the two were as thick as thieves. Danny looked up to Ryan as a younger brother might and imitated him at every turn. If Ryan could count to 20, Danny wasn't far behind. If Danny needed help with his ABC's, Ryan was there to lend a hand.

The air in the room was thick enough to cut with a knife. Emily looked questioningly at her husband and then at her best friend.

"Don't ask," Todd said, pulling both boys on to his lap for a hug and a kiss on the tops of their head. It was time to take Mr. Sloane to the hospital for his breathing exercises. The two men had become close, like the boys, but it was difficult to tell who the mentor was and who was the mentee in the pair.

Often Vincent turned to Todd for advice, not on women as that topic was taboo since his wedding, but Todd was reveling in the younger man's desire to learn more about Ireland's rich culture, the problems of the working class and the antics Danny and Ryan enjoyed on a regular basis.

"Your little one sounds sharp as a whip," Vincent told Todd. "Do most three-year-olds even know their alphabet, much less the spelling of their first names?"

"Emily taught him D-A-N, right off," Todd said.

"But you call him Danny Boy, correct?"

"It's an ancient ballad, but the words are recent," Todd said.

"Oh, Danny Boy, the pipes, the pipes are calling,
From glen to glen and down the mountain side.
The summer's gone and all the roses falling,
It's you, it's you must go and I must bide."

"Some have interpreted the song to be a message from a parent to a son going off to a war or leaving as part of the Irish emigration. I'm guessing that's where Margaret came up with the name."

As soon as the words escaped his mouth, he bid them back.

"I mean Emily, of course. I don't know what I was thinking. Margaret loves little Danny so."

"It's okay, Todd," Mr. Sloane said. "You don't have to censor your words around me. I've made my bed, as it were, and now I must lie in it. One day soon, Margaret will find her true love, be married and have a son of her own. That's a joy I'll never know."

With Mr. Sloane in the back seat, Todd was able to grimace without alerting him something was off.

"Someday, Mr. Sloane, perhaps you will have a niece or a nephew. Hasn't your sister Alice married a Russian prince or some such thing?"

"Now you're changing the subject, Todd," Mr. Sloane replied. "When we visit England next to see Alice and her young princes, I'd like you to come along. I hate to drive in England — the cars and the roads are all backwards. Maybe you can meet your family there or take a side trip to the Emerald Isle, if I tarry

Mary Wernke

long enough."

"That's kind of you to offer, Mr. Sloane," Todd answered quickly, relieved to move away from the subject of Margaret and her son.

25 January 1919

Dearest Margaret,

A Happy Christmas to you, my darling daughter! I am so happy to have the boys and their families — 14 grandchildren — around me at the holidays. John's son is already six, so I'm hoping more babies by next Christmas.

I have been breathing easier since the war ended in Europe. In Ireland, more than 200,000 men and women served, but only half will return. Unemployment is still rampant in our country and many who served in the British forces don't feel welcome here any longer.

In the general election, the Irish Parliamentary Party was defeated by the Sinn Fein party for the first time. It was my first time to vote and I thought of you and your American suffrage groups. The new law allows women over the age of 30 to vote now and all men over the age of 21, including working-class men.

I fear another war with all this unrest. I had wished for your return to Ireland, but now I am unsure. Just this past week, the assembly issued a Declaration of Independence and two members of the Royal Irish Constabulary were killed by Irish Volunteers. They are now calling themselves the Irish Republican Army.

Yours,
Mam

Chapter Twenty-Three

Margaret hummed softly under her breath, as Danny drifted in and out of sleep. They snuggled deeper beneath the pile of blankets on Margaret's pallet near the fireplace and she struggled to stay awake. She needed to talk to Emily about something important, but the thought kept floating out of her grasp.

It was a difficult conversation Margaret had with Todd earlier that day. She was still adamant she would not tell Danny the true nature of his parentage. The little boy was comfortable with Todd as Papa. Todd was a great papa and Vincent need never know.

"Mama?" Danny's voice drifted up from beneath Margaret's chin. "How come Ryan has only one mama and I have two?"

Margaret cast about for an answer, as if one would pop up out of the flames. "I don't know Danny. Go back to sleep, now."

This was a development Margaret and Emily hadn't considered when they'd hatched their plan to raise the boy with three parents, instead of one or two. Ryan already knew Margaret by name at that point, so it hadn't occurred to either of them to have Ryan call her mama, too.

The point niggling at the back of Margaret's mind took on a sudden sharpness. Todd had planted the seed of guilt in Margaret's mind this morning. Vincent was not ever going to be a father, she knew that. She'd always expected Helen and Vincent would have children someday. They were still young. They had years ahead in their marriage and Helen would make an excellent mother for sons and daughters.

"Oh, Danny." She released the boy and slid from beneath the covers. "What have I gotten us into?"

Margaret slipped silently into the apartment's one large kitchen and living room, not wanting to interrupt Emily and Todd on their night off. The three took turns putting the boys to bed each night, allowing the remaining pair to enjoy a quiet cup of tea, a good book and some easy conversation. In the married couple's case, the conversation often turned to canoodling and tonight was no exception.

Margaret cleared her throat. "Excuse, me," she offered. "There's something we need to talk about." She hesitated, then blurted it out, "It concerns our sons." Now, she had their undivided attention.

"Todd has probably told you about our talk this morning," she began. "He suggested once before I need to tell Mr. Sloane about Danny and I resisted. But today he told me Mr. Sloane will never father another child. It's got me thinking."

Emily stared into Margaret's eyes. "Mags, honey, it's a difficult decision and don't we all know it. It's the right thing to do."

"I'll have to talk myself into it some more," Margaret replied. "But, I'm willing to think about it. Maybe we can introduce Mr. Sloane to Danny and see if there's a connection."

"That sounds like a good first step," Emily said. "You'll know when the time is right."

"I'm back to bed." She turned back toward the room where the children slept peacefully by the fire. "You two can go back to your snuggling. A little sister for Ryan and Danny would be nice."

"Mr. Sloane." Margaret's voice startled Vincent's reverie.

"Margaret, I'm so happy to see you, to speak to you again.

Is there something I can do for you?"

"No, sir. It's I who would like to share something with *you*." Margaret's words were no less startling than her appearance in the study between his and Helen's rooms on the second floor.

Vincent spoke cautiously. He didn't want to ruin the moment alone together. "I'm afraid Helen is out for the afternoon. I rather thought you would be with her at her suffrage meeting. She tells me Wilson is ready to come around."

"I'm here to speak to you, Mr. Sloane. It's a difficult thing I've come to tell you and I need you to *not* look at me." She glanced down herself as she spoke. "And, please don't ask any questions until I'm through."

"I'm listening." He spoke softly and kept his eyes turned away.

"When you chose to be married," she said, "I respected your decision. I've come to accept it was, perhaps, the best thing for you."

"Margaret..." He looked up, then lowered his eyes again as he saw her reproach.

"Let me finish," she went on. "What I couldn't tell you then, what I am having difficulty telling you now, is that I was with child." She paused, not knowing if she could go on.

This time Vincent looked at her with awe. "A baby?" he whispered. "We have a baby?" His voice quavered.

Again, silence. "Not a baby, exactly. Danny's nearly four years old."

"Todd's younger boy? Danny is your son? Our son?"

The confirmation was in her eyes. She nodded, the silence broken only by her labored breathing. "I didn't intend to tell you, ever. But I think you have the right to know."

"Sweet Jesus, yes!" he breathed. Tears filled Vincent's eyes. "May I meet him? Have you told him about me? What's his favorite color? Is his last name Sloane?" The questions poured out of him, jumbling up and not waiting for an answer.

"Stop!" Margaret cried out.

"I'm sorry," he said. "You're right. It's too soon to say anything to anyone. I'd just like to meet him, perhaps hold him on my lap or play with him."

"I'll think about it, but you mustn't tell Mrs. Sloane and you certainly can't tell Danny. He's much too young. Maybe he can think of you as a rich uncle."

"How appropriate." He grimaced. "A rich uncle."

"I didn't mean it that way," she said. "I don't want anything from you. Simply getting to know Danny is my gift to you, my apology for not telling you four years ago. I didn't know it would all come to... to this."

"To my inability to ever have children?" he snapped. "Did Todd tell you about my, my problem? Of course, he did. But now I have Danny. I have a son."

"Your name is not on the birth certificate and, I repeat, I am not asking for your financial support. I don't need your money and neither does Danny. Your father's son, Madeline's Jack, is your heir as it should be."

"Let's not argue," Vincent pleaded. "Just let me meet my son. I won't say a word to anyone."

Danny's first meeting with Vincent took place on a Tuesday afternoon. The event was more carefully orchestrated than the Armistice agreement a year earlier. Vincent struggled to stay quiet and give Margaret time to think, but in the end, his patience sped the process along.

Emily and Todd were his unforeseen allies, as well, keeping the secret from Helen while acting on Vincent's behalf behind the scenes. All three of them knew not to push Margaret on the plan for the father and son reunion. If she dug in her heels, it might never happen.

Within days of Margaret's surprise announcement, Todd and Vincent had been to FAO Schwartz twice. On the first trip, Vincent purchased two life-size Teddy Bears, one for Danny and another for Ryan.

Named after President Theodore Roosevelt, a close friend and distant relative of Vincent, the Teddy Bear followed a cartoon in the New York Herald depicting a time Roosevelt refused to kill a tied-up, beaten black bear in 1902. The next year, the Ideal Toy Company wrote to the president asking for permission to market a Teddy Bear and the rest was history.

Against Todd's wishes, Vincent purchased a bear for Ryan, so as not to raise questions among the staff or with Helen. On the second trip, Vincent picked up Tinker Toys, bird whistles and a train set with 15 feet of track.

Vincent was like a kid in a candy store. He'd examined a pedal car based loosely on the Sloane's Cadillac, but settled on the train set. "This is something Danny and Ryan can play with together," he told Todd, when the driver pulled the car around to load the purchases.

"Respectfully, NO sir. My boys will not be spoiled and there's no room in our apartment for a 15-foot train set."

Vincent was about to correct Todd on the "my boys" comment. But it did beg the question that had hung in the air between them for days now. Would Danny and Margaret remain in the apartment over the garage?

"I had assumed Margaret would move back into the house and Danny would take his rightful place in the third-floor nursery," Vincent replied.

Todd stopped the car and pulled over. "I must disagree. Margaret will never allow Danny to live at Sloane House."

Vincent's voice was sharp, but measured. "It's not yours or my decision to make, Roebken. It is up to Margaret. Now, let's hurry home so I can push Helen out the door to one of her interminable meetings."

Todd frowned and eased back into New York traffic, taking the long way back to Sloane House.

Danny hid behind his mother's skirt as they left the kitchen and moved into the front hallway of Sloane House. He'd never been beyond the kitchen in the main house, without using the back stairs to visit Sadie and DeeDee in their servant's quarters on the fourth floor.

On one occasion, Emily took Ryan and Danny to the third-floor nursery where she used to spend so much time with Baby Jack. John Jacob Sloane VI was eight years old now and living with his mother, stepfather and two half-brothers.

Emily followed Madeline's new life in the social pages of the Herald and knew she'd had two more sons by Richard Gould, but left him for an Italian movie star and body builder just before the war broke out in Europe.

Emily took them to the nursery to see the mountains of toys Baby Jack lived with, as a lesson in the evils of excess. Jack was never happy, she told them, despite the wagons, stuffed animals and whistles piled high about the nursery. But when they arrived the toys were all missing. Helen had them packed away and donated to charity, attempting to erase every vestige of Madeline's presence at Sloane House and that of her son.

Today, Emily and Ryan set out to visit the garage. She told the little boy he could watch his papa work on some wooden toys Todd was making for a Christmas party at church.

As they stepped out the back door, Danny ran after them. "I want to go with Ryan and Papa," he bellowed. "I don't want to meet Sloane man."

Emily chuckled, but remained firm. "Mama wants you to meet Mr. Sloane. He's the nice man who owns Sloane House. He likes little boys, just like you."

"He likes Ryan, too?" Danny asked through crocodile tears.

"Yes, he likes Ryan, too. But he can only meet one boy at a time. Run along, now; your mother's in the kitchen."

Indoors, Margaret was finishing the touches on a tray of cookies, milk and tea. She set the tray down and grasped Danny's hand firmly as they moved toward the sitting room, where Madeline Sloane had greeted so many of her guests. A fire burned brightly in the fireplace.

In one of the two easy chairs near the fireplace, Vincent fidgeted. He stood when Danny and Margaret entered the room, then sat down again, his hands working up and down the chair's arms. In the other chair, the six-foot Teddy Bear loomed.

Danny took one look at the bear and raced toward the fireplace, pulling up short when Vincent reached out his arms.

"Slow," Margaret cautioned them both.

Vincent moved his hands to his side, again fingering the doilies on the armrests. His cheeks were bright pink, whether from the fire or his anticipation, Margaret couldn't be sure. She moved quickly to Danny's side.

"It's okay, Danny Boy. You can touch the Teddy Bear. It's a gift from Mr. Sloane."

Now Vincent hesitated. "Call me Vincent."

Margaret shot him a warning glance, as Danny reached for Teddy. A pair of small gaily wrapped gifts sat to one side of the bear.

"Mama?" He looked back, unsure now at seeing the gifts. Christmas was months ago, and his birthday wasn't until summer.

"They're for you, son." Vincent leaned forward. "I missed your birthday the last three years while I was away. I want to make it up to you."

Danny tore into the packages, uncovering the Tinker Toys — small wooden balls, threaded on strong chords, thin dowels with slices in each end and round connectors, covered with holes."

"You can build things with them." Vincent pushed a red dowel into the connector's center hole. He chose three shorter blue dowels to create a windmill effect, while Danny watched in fascination. "Do you like to build things, son?"

"My papa and Ryan are building in the garage," Danny told him. "Do you know my papa?"

"Yes, Danny," Vincent said. "Your papa and I are very good friends. He's told me so much about you."

"Can you whistle?" he asked the boy, as he pulled a bird whistle from his coat pocket and popped it into his mouth. "This whistle sounds like the doves at the park. Perhaps we can visit there someday."

Danny crawled onto Vincent's lap and looked up. "I like birds," he said. "And parks. I think we can be friends." He looked back at his mother, seeking her approval. Margaret nodded.

Vincent saw Margaret bob her head. "I do, too, son." He relaxed into his chair. "I do, too."

Margaret exhaled and stepped back into a corner of the room. Seeing the two together, she was struck at the resemblance. Danny's dark hair mirrored Vincent's cowlick and the near curls around the ears. His blue eyes, something she'd always attributed as a throwback to her grandfather Michael, were an uncanny reflection of his father.

She was not ready to share her news with the world, but she'd made the right decision in sharing Danny with Vincent. If things continued in this vein, she decided, a telling letter to her mother was a good next step.

Chapter Twenty-Four

Most afternoons in the past week, Danny and his new friend Mr. Sloane would play together in the sunny sitting room while Margaret looked on. By the fourth day, she felt comfortable moving to the hallway and by week's end, she was back in the kitchen, mixing up cookies for Mrs. Sloane's Friday bridge club when Danny came tearing in.

"Mama!" He was out of breath. "Vincent wants me to go to the park to feed the birds. Can I? Can I, momma?"

Margaret looked up to see Vincent enter the kitchen. His face was even more flushed than Danny's.

"I'm not sure you're well enough to be going to the park," she said to Vincent, more than Danny. His breathing had become more labored with the cold weather. "Danny has been coughing a little bit at night, too," she said. "Perhaps it's better to wait until another day, to see if you both feel better."

As if on cue, Danny barked twice. "I'm a puppy, momma!"

Vincent shrunk from the room, as if he'd been beaten. His daily romps with the little one had taken a lot out of him, more than he cared to admit. At the hospital this morning, the doctor had advised he stay close to home.

"There are still traces of the flu virus out there," he cautioned Sloane. "In your weakened condition, you are especially susceptible to a relapse."

But Vincent was in love with Danny. All of the love Margaret refused from him was funneled into their boy. If Danny wanted a new toy, Danny got a new toy. If Danny wanted to go to the park to see the birds, it was off to the park for the both of them. Margaret's admonitions to take it easy put a damper on his plans, but he didn't set them aside.

When Helen arrived home from her dinner with the suffrage ladies, he would tell her the truth. He hadn't discussed the idea with Margaret, because he knew she'd say no. Helen would understand, he was sure. Since they weren't able to have a family of their own, his son would become their heir. The nursery would be Danny's kingdom and Helen would dote on the boy, just as he did.

Vincent settled back in his chair and began to doze. His dreams were filled with a happy threesome — Margaret, Danny and himself — feeding the ducks at Central Park, flying a kite on the back lawn, Vincent leaning in for a kiss and Margaret . . .

As if on cue, Margaret shook his arm.

"I'm going to have to go home to take care of Danny," she told him. "Emily said he's running a fever and she has to finish the meal for this evening. Will you be okay alone until Mrs. Sloane returns?"

"Of course," Vincent replied. "May I help with Danny?"

Margaret was not ready for such intimacy between her son and his father. But her thoughts were immediately replaced by a bigger concern as Todd came into the room.

"I think we should call a doctor," he told Margaret and Vincent. "Danny's coughing much harder now and he's burning up with fever. Emily's packing him with cold compresses, but we can't take any chances."

Dr. Phelan's face was grave when he stepped out of the nursery at Sloane House. Unbeknown to Margaret, Vincent had asked the housemaids to clean the nursery from floor to ceiling, chasing away the cobwebs, vacuuming the upholstery and generally disinfecting the room for a possible new occupant.

This wasn't the homecoming he'd had in mind. When Todd told Vincent that Danny was coughing up drops of blood the morning after he'd taken ill, Sloane wasted no time. He called the family physician back to the mansion and ensconced Danny in the upstairs nursery.

He'd convinced Margaret, Todd and Emily to keep Danny home last night, but isolated from Ryan. Dr. Phelan had been caring for Vincent since he was a child and the foursome agreed this was the best course of action for Danny.

Vincent jumped up. "Doctor?"

"It's the flu, alright," the doctor said. "But he's young and strong and the virus is in a weaker form. You are blessed with an immunity, Mr. Sloane. The rest of the boy's family and your staff should avoid contact. It's still highly contagious."

Margaret ran past the others, into Danny's room. The nursery retained its pale blue walls, deep blue rag rugs and striped nautical prints on the drapes and furniture. Danny's little body thrashed restlessly on the bed once belonging to his young uncle, Jack Sloane.

She'd been wearing a mask when the doctor arrived, but removed it to talk to the physician. Dr. Phelan had ordered respiratory sprays, sneeze guards and masks for all of the staff, as well as Mr. and Mrs. Sloane. Vaccinations were dispensed in the front hall the same day, but the doctor said it was not likely to spread without direct contact with the infected boy.

Quarantine seemed the only recourse.

Margaret heard Emily talking to the doctor outside the nursery door. "We thought it was a cold or maybe bronchitis," she said. "We are always careful to be sure the boys take in fresh night air; I know bad air can bring on a disease like the flu."

Dark spots, the color of the mahogany, shadowed Danny's face. The doctor had used a mercury thermometer to record Danny's temperature in his armpit at 103 degrees. Margaret watched her son doze, then held him to her as he resorted to another coughing fit. They'd already put him back into diapers the night before; he couldn't control his bowels.

"Mama," he whimpered. "Daddy."

"I'm here, Danny," Vincent answered from behind Margaret. Quickly, he knelt at Danny's bedside and put his head in his hands. Danny was sleeping again.

"He's asking for Todd," Margaret hissed. "Get out!"

"Please, Margaret, let me stay. I'm his father."

Margaret felt weak and so very tired. She didn't have the will to fight with Vincent and, in truth, felt sorry for his missing so many of Danny's younger years. She promised God then and there, if He would spare her son, she would never deny Vincent the joy of knowing Danny again.

Vincent stretched out on the floor next to Danny's bed. He cradled the boy's head in one hand and tried to take Margaret's hand in the other. She shook him off and crawled in beside her son, oblivious to the danger of the flu virus.

For the rest of the day, Margaret and Vincent stayed by Danny's bed. Emily and Todd had returned to the garage apartment to console Ryan and help him understand what was happening inside Sloane House.

Emily's heart was torn between Ryan, who seemed healthy and Danny, who was battling for his life in the nursery. Her best course, she decided, was to care for her remaining family and lend support to Margaret in whatever form she was able.

As Ryan finally dozed off for the evening, Emily excused herself and made her way up the backstairs to the nursery door. She knocked softly, donned her mask and entered.

Margaret was asleep, lying across the bottom of the bed and Vincent dozed in a nearby rocker. Emily stepped closer to Danny and caught her breath. A blue-gray tinge extended from his ears and was spreading all over his face.

"Surely the devil has come into this house to take our poor Danny Boy," she said to herself. She shook Margaret awake.

"Hold him," she said. "There's nothing more we can do."

As the women murmured to one another, Vincent stirred and opened his eyes. He looked at Emily and she shook her head sadly.

This time, Vincent sat behind Margaret and held her and Danny together, locked in one embrace. The little boy continued to wheeze and cough, but never regained consciousness. As the sun peeked over the horizon on April 3, 1919, Danny breathed his last and slipped away.

Vincent gently pulled Margaret's arms from around Danny's lifeless body. She allowed him to hold her, as she could not hold herself. She sobbed into his shoulder, her entire body shaking with grief. Her arms raised, she pounded them against Vincent's chest. "This is your fault," she said. He could only nod.

Margaret's despair racked her body as she gasped for air. Her son, her life and her reason for being was gone. The only man she'd ever really loved was her boy. Not Martin, not Vincent. No one but Danny.

No one could heal the gaping hole Margaret felt growing inside her. She pushed Vincent away and stumbled toward the door. Emily took her arm and led her to the nanny's room next door. The cornflower blue and cream quilt Emily had used when Jack was a baby was still there.

She wrapped the coverlet around Margaret and her own shoulders and pulled her best friend down onto the narrow bed. Emily held her tightly as Margaret wept until there were no tears. No crying could comfort her.

As she started to fall asleep, Margaret could hear Emily singing under her breath.

"But come ye back when summer's in the meadow,
Or when the valley's hushed and white with snow,
I'll be here in sunshine or in shadow,
Oh, Danny boy, oh Danny boy, I love you so!"
She pulled Margaret closer and leaned in. "Margaret?"
"If I am dead, as dead I well may be,
Oh, Danny boy, I love you so."

Margaret finally slept, her last thoughts following Danny's journey home. She dreamed of clouds and sunshine, a toddler running among gravestones, searching for his Papa and Martin, reaching out from a watery grave.

Vincent staggered down the stairs to the second floor and into the master suite. He poured himself two fingers of Scotch in a heavy glass tumbler he kept in his bedside table. He hadn't had a drink since his return from Boston, but this was a special occasion.

He swallowed the rare Dalmore 62 whiskey in one gulp. Pouring another, he moaned. "Danny. Boy."

He slurred his words, intelligible only to himself and his wife, standing at the door between their rooms. "Special." He drew out the word in his grief. Exhaustion overtook him as he sank to the floor.

Helen stepped into the room, but she didn't move to help Vincent from his spot on the ground beside the huge mahogany four-poster bed Margaret had chosen for the master suite. "The boy." She paused. "He's dead?"

"The boy's name is Danny. *Was* Danny. And, yes, he's gone."

"Why would you care? You're a dried-up old prune!" he lashed out, his arms flailing into the air separating them.

"You'll never have children. We're a fine pair, aren't we? I'm sterile and you prefer other women. The Sloane line ends here, tonight."

Helen was not surprised. "The Sloane line ended years ago, Vincent. It's just taken you this long to realize it."

"Margaret's son was mine, too," he choked out.

"I know," she said. "I've known for a long time. Margaret and I became friends while you were away fighting Germans. Her face is an open book. She flinched whenever I mentioned your name. It didn't take long for me to put two and two together."

"Why didn't you say something earlier?" he shouted. "I could've known my son years ago."

"It was not my story to tell," she shot back. "Margaret will always be your first true love. Let it be said, you were never mine. You were a means to an end and I'm there now. I'll be staying in the guest room today and tomorrow," she finished simply. "I've made arrangements to travel to Philadelphia with Alice for a suffrage conference there. My attorney will be in touch."

Vincent didn't bother to respond. He'd anticipated an angry response at first from Helen, when he broke the news of his son's parentage. He hadn't expected Helen had known for years, however. How she must've lain in wait with that news, choosing the right day and time to spring it on him, to grind him under her shoe.

She was a grand old lesbian and she was happier than he'd ever been. Vincent threw the tumbler across the room and it shattered against a heavy chifforobe in the corner. Drinking straight from the bottle was faster. He'd rather death or unconsciousness come sooner, than later.

Margaret didn't leave the nanny's room for a more than a week. Emily brought in food, but the trays went untouched. Her eyes sunken and her hair lank, her tears had run dry, but she was able to sleep much of the day. Finally, Emily pulled Margaret from the bed. The graying sheets were soaked with sweat, tears and the food stains from the offerings of well-meaning friends.

Propped in a chair, Margaret winced when Emily softly sponged her body with a soft, warm cloth. She moaned softly in simple pleasure, as her friend lay her head back and lathered her hair in the wash basin. Warm water dripped down her shoulders and a bit of soap leaked into her eye.

There were no tears, which further concerned Emily. She left the room for a pitcher of orange juice and some fresh biscuits Sadie had made to try to tempt Margaret further. As if she were preparing a breakfast tray for the lady of the manor, Emily set a fresh, pink rose in a bud vase to one corner. Cloth napkins and fine china gave an air of well-being to the biscuits slathered with creamy yellow, just-churned butter and blueberry preserves. Two slices of thick, crispy bacon stood guard to one side.

Almost as an afterthought, Emily sliced a small tangerine and added it to the tray. Oranges were Margaret's favorite, but Emily doubted she'd notice. But she was determined to get Margaret to drink something; perhaps even to force-feed a bite or two.

When Emily returned to the nursery, Margaret was sitting up in the wing chair near the south dormer window. Her hair showed a comb had been applied with little attention to style, but Emily was impressed.

"I've brought you a little something," Emily smiled brightly. She began to hum, and Margaret's ears perked up.

"In Dublin's fair city," Emily started to sing. *"Where the girls are so pretty, I first set my eyes on sweet Margaret Malone."*

Margaret smiled wanly.

"As she wheeled her wheelbarrow through streets broad and narrow," Emily continued. *"Crying, Cockles and mussels, alive, alive, oh...!"*

"I'm alive, alive, oh," Margaret finally admitted. There was no sparkle in her eyes and her voice petered out on the last word.

"Sweetie," Emily went on. "I don't expect much from you today, but it's important you get outside and get some fresh air. I can ask Todd to bring around the car, if you aren't up to taking a walk."

Margaret frowned, but she stood shakily and walked toward the stairs. Emily rushed to her side, taking an arm and steering her toward the sitting area just outside the baby's bedroom.

"Have a little drink, Margaret," she said. "If you can, take a bite or two, but it's more important you drink as much as you're able. You're dehydrated."

Mary Wernke

Again, a wan smile and a weak shake of her head as Margaret sunk into the wing chair in the opposite dormer. "I do love orange juice, Em Gem," she said. "You're the best."

15 May 1919

My dearest mother,

My time in America has not been kind to me, after all. I miss you all desperately and long to return home. I have left Sloane House and booked passage on a liner home in early June. Two of my very best friends and their son will travel with me. Todd and Emily grew up in County Galway, near Ballinasloe and dream to start their own business there, as well. Emily is expecting a second child this fall and wants to be in Ireland for his or her arrival.

There is so much to tell. I will let you know my date of arrival in Queensland, the same port I departed so many long years ago. I will travel with Todd and Emily to Galway. See you soon!

Your daughter,
Margaret

Chapter Twenty-Five

Bridget rushed around the cottage. She'd baked brown bread three days in a row in preparation for Margaret and her guests' arrival later today. Fresh-churned butter was cooling in the larder and she'd butchered two chickens on Saturday, so the meat would still be fresh for today's celebration.

She wanted to invite the entire village to welcome her home, as they had bid goodbye seven years earlier, but Margaret insisted only family be there at their first meeting. Thomas and Patrick were in the fields until supper time, Ellen and Celia would be traveling together from nearby Loughaunboy. Celia would be anxious to hear more about Sr. Mary Ellen, Margaret's friend who'd joined the convent. Celia was saddened her sister-in-law would not be allowed to return to Ireland to visit.

Bridget's youngest son Lawrence was the postmaster — he boarded in Castle French during the week, but promised to stop by on Sunday after Mass. His was an important civil position and the family's main source of income since the farm was still doing poorly.

Gravel crunched outside and Bridget froze. She knew it wasn't the boys coming in for dinner because the tires were smaller on the vehicle she heard now. The dogs started to bark furiously, and Bridget's beloved cat, Martha, meowed as she stretched and gazed outdoors.

The car's horn blasted, and Bridget rushed to the door,

nearly colliding with Margaret outside her rustic kitchen.

"Mam!" Margaret gathered her mother into her arms. "How are you?"

"Oh, just a little bit grayer," Bridget's muffled voice seemed distant, as she cried into Margaret's shoulder.

Margaret moved to hold her mother at arm's length. "Let me get a look at you. You've changed."

"Of course, I've changed. It's been nearly 10 years. You said you had news," she prompted. She hoped Margaret was engaged. She could not understand why Margaret had never married. There were plenty of opportunities to meet young Irish Catholic men in America.

Margaret was anxious to change the subject. "Meet my friends, Mam."

Ryan bounded out of the car door Margaret had left open. Emily and Todd followed. "Mrs. Mannion," Todd touched his cap. "This is my wife Emily and our son, Ryan."

"Please, call us Todd and Emily," Emily said. She pulled her son away from the dogs gathered around the car. "Say hello to Mrs. Mannion, Ryan."

"G' day, Mrs. Mannion," Ryan offered, before turning his attention back to the mutts at his heels.

"Come in, come in. Where are my manners?" Bridget shooed the foursome into the cottage. She put the pot of potatoes and cabbage on the stove.

"Dinner's in the oven. It will be ready shortly."

She turned to Margaret. "Tommy and Patty will be home when the Angelus bell at St. Mary's rings this evening." She glanced at the grandmother clock in the corner. An inheritance from her parents, it was the only factory-made piece in the room.

"Do you need to wash up?"

Emily glanced at her husband, then toward Margaret and finally, at the door. "Todd and I would like to take a walk before dinner, if you don't mind, Mrs. Mannion. It's been a long drive and Ryan has a lot of pent up energy to burn off before sitting down to eat."

Bridget didn't know what to make of the knowing glance passed between Margaret and Emily. She knew Margaret had important news and she'd assumed it was happy news. She was no longer so sure. "Stay on the road," she told Emily and Todd. "Dinner should be ready in half an hour."

Margaret turned to her mother. "Mam, sit down and let me set the table. We have a lot to talk about."

Margaret caressed the old crockery plates from the cupboards her father had built when she was a child.

"They're not much," her mother apologized. "You're probably used to fine china at the Sloane House."

"Mam, I'm happy here. I want to be here. There was nothing left for me in America."

Bridget pressed her daughter, probing for more information. "You said when you were rescued from the ship, you felt as if your legs had been chopped out from beneath you. But, based on your letters home, I'd gathered you got your sea legs back and were busy making something of yourself."

"I found a good job, Mam, working for a woman I met on the ship. She was a widow. Much like me, she lost her husband on the Titanic. She had her baby a few months later, but wasn't happy as a single woman. She married again two years later. I told you this in my letters."

Bridget frowned. "It's been seven years, Margaret. I'm an old woman. I forget things."

"I'm sorry, Mam. I was making a point. Mrs. Sloane was unhappy because she was no longer married. She had health, wealth and every reason for happiness. She had a beautiful son, a beautiful house, but she wanted a husband. She didn't think she could be happy on her own."

"We *both* recognize that pain." Bridget still mourned her husband who'd died the same year as Martin and Colonel Sloane.

"A woman, without her husband, is nothing unless she has children."

Margaret paused in stirring the potatoes and cabbage on Bridget's stove. "Mam, I'm a 36-year-old woman without a man, without children. Am I nothing to you?"

Bridget was unapologetic. "It's how I was raised, Margaret. How I raised you. It's not natural for a woman to remain alone. You will always have a place here, in your brothers' home. After I'm gone, you can care for them, since they seem to be perpetual bachelors."

"That's not who I am anymore." Margaret drew up a chair and took her mother's strong, wrinkled hand in hers. "I've known love with Martin and maybe with another man in America."

Bridget's head came up to meet Margaret's eyes. "You're in love?" Margaret's words held promise.

"I *thought* I was in love," Margaret corrected her. "I had a son and I lost him, Mam."

Margaret's eyes filled with tears and she watched her mother take it all in. "You had a child?" Bridget was incredulous.

"He died three months ago from the Spanish Flu. One day he was healthy and playing with his stuffed Teddy Bear. Two days later, he was gone. Taken from me in the very home where I'd worked nearly all the time I was in America."

Margaret took a deep breath. She had to remain calm until she'd told her entire story. Her mother had the right to know.

The clock ticked in the corner. Margaret smelled scorched potatoes on the wood stove, but she didn't move from beside her mother.

"A son?" Bridget repeated her question.

"Yes, Mam. Danny was four years old when he died in April. He's buried in the country, in a family cemetery in upstate New York. It was a kindness of the Sloane family to keep him there."

Bridget's incredulity gave way to tears. When she spoke, there was a finality in her voice. "I'll never meet Danny," she said.

"I'll never visit his grave."

"No, Mam," Margaret replied with the same determination she'd chosen to begin this difficult conversation. "We will have to carry him here," she tapped her chest, her sad smile beating alongside her heart. "And, I'll be here for you, always."

August 10, 1919

Dear Margaret,

I beg your forgiveness, as I was not able to bid you goodbye before moving from Sloane House to stay with my parents for a short while. I am also distraught for the loss of your son Danny. While I've never had children of my own, I can imagine the sadness and horror of losing someone so close, so young and so suddenly.

You are likely wondering if I bear any ill will, knowing Vincent was Danny's father. It was not news to me. Simple math and your starry eyes told the story soon after my arrival at Sloane House. Because ours was an arranged marriage, children were not part of the discussion until after the fact, so Vincent had wrongly assumed we would have a houseful.

Your revelation of Danny's parentage resolved that matter rather neatly. But of course, he's devastated. But I digress. I have always admired your intelligence, your strength as a woman of few means. Your life was always much different than mine. I want you to continue your good work after I leave. Vincent will be of no help with his little foundation. He still believes careers are for men. I have sent instructions to my attorney and Vincent to pay out the sum of $2,500 to your account upon your visit and signature at The Bank of Ireland. Please visit the bank soon before my divorce complicates my instructions, as funds could become tied up in the legal system.

Your friend,
Helen Hunt Sloane

August 17, 1919

My dear Miss Mannion,

I am writing to assuage your concerns regarding perpetual care for your son Daniel's grave. For your many years of service and in thanks for all you've done for this family, we are honored to care for his place of eternal rest. I have sold Sloane House, as it is too large for a single man and I have no plans to marry again. I have created the Sloane Foundation with the proceeds from the sale. Our guiding principle is to serve those who have served others. One of the first recipients of the foundation's largess will be your friend and mine, Mr. Todd Roebken.

I have wired $2,500 to the Bank of Ireland in his name. Prior to her departure, Mrs. Sloane told me she wished an equal amount be deposited in your name, to help you make a new start in your home country. Mr. Roebken had related to me you were an excellent driver in your own right, so I'm hopeful the two of you will be able to work together.

Yours truly,

Wm. Vincent Sloane

Chapter Twenty-Six

Margaret had been distant since the letter arrived from Mr. Sloane on Friday last. After the postman arrived at her doorstep, Margaret disappeared from the house she now shared with her mother. She showed up at Todd and Emily's cottage an hour later, somewhat tear-stained, but no less determined.

Todd showed her into the living room. Emily was lying on the floral couch, a blanket over her legs and her belly straining the fabric of the one maternity dress she owned that still fit.

"She's not moving around as quickly. She swears there's more than one baby in there." He smiled wanly, a man without a job and nearly five mouths to feed. Then he noticed the odd look on Margaret's face.

"What's up, Mags? Bad news?"

"No, not really. Just odd. I have a letter from Mr. Sloane. He wants us to buy a car and start a business here."

"No one in Loughaunboy owns a car," Emily piped up. "A farm truck, maybe, but not a car. People will frown on a woman driving around unchaperoned."

"Emily, it's 1919. Women have the vote in Ireland and will soon be able to vote in all 48 United States, if President Hoover can convince Congress. Plus, think about it — I learned to drive alongside Mrs. Sloane when I was in America. I'm quite good at it."

Margaret turned back to Todd. "I'm pleased Mrs. Sloane remembered me, too, even if it required Vincent's money to make amends as she saw them. She knew we were breaking down barriers and others might have been deemed us unwomanly."

Margaret and Todd spent the next hour at the kitchen table devising a plan while Emily and Ryan napped. Unable to wait any longer, Todd jostled Emily awake and helped her into the kitchen. As he set a cup of coffee in her hands, Margaret rushed in. "We can provide a taxi service in all of County Galway. There's room for motoring instructors, garage owners and even mechanics. It' a chance for Irish women to be involved in fundamental and far-reaching ways."

"Slow down, Margaret," Todd cautioned. "I don't want to work for someone else anymore. Not even you. I want to be my own boss."

Margaret hurried ahead. "It's an opportunity for us *both* to be partners. Mr. And Mrs. Sloane were clear the money would belong to *both* of us. Nothing more and nothing less. There's training available for women in Galway City on driving and making a business of it — proper dress, deportment and just getting dirt under our fingernails. We can buy an older car and fix it up. Then, use the rest of the money for training and a second car someday."

Todd could feel the wind in his hair, the liberty the idea of a car service presented. The old-fashioned prejudices of female masculinity associated with women drivers in America were not the same here, except perhaps with Margaret's mother.

On the ship's crossing, Todd had been reading about business opportunities in his homeland. Clearly, images of the independent, mobile female motorist had chimed a strong symbolic chord in Great Britain and Ireland. However, there was the serious matter of money to consider, he'd thought at the time, resigning himself to a lifetime in service to others.

Within minutes, he was scanning the past two weeks' newspapers looking for used cars with low miles.

For weeks, Margaret and Todd scoured the countryside looking for just the right car to get their business venture off the ground. Their only investment to date was two gray and navy serge uniforms, complete with fine Irish driving caps and an accountant's course, offered by mail out of Dublin.

Just today, they had settled on a 1915 four-cylinder Model 43 Buick with a collapsible soft top, electric lantern lights and running boards. The pair had taken turns driving in circles around Bridget's family's farm with Emily and Ryan in the back seat, hollering out encouragement. By the end of the day, they were tired but still anxious to work on their business plan.

Margaret spent most evenings at Emily and Todd's, working through the accounting lessons with the pair and playing with Ryan. The young family was her only true connection to Danny. It hurt to see Ryan healthy, happy and quite alive, when she knew Danny rested cold and alone back in America. But she was resolved to make something more of herself for Danny's sake. She knew he would be proud to see his mother take control of her destiny, moving along a path of her own choosing.

Margaret seldom thought of Vincent, alone in his house in New York City. She had read news articles about the Sloane Foundation and the good work done there, but they were always punctuated with small bits about Sloane's own descent into alcoholism and despair. She wondered if Danny ever realized what Vincent was to him in his short life, but she hoped against it.

"Three multiplied by 10 is 30," she pulled herself back into the rows and columns of figures they'd developed for income and expenses. "What is the cost of petrol per gallon, again Todd?"

"Thirty-seven pence and three-quarters," Todd responded, without pausing a beat.

She licked her pencil and added the 37.75 to 30 pounds.

"Do we need to factor in an auto laundry?"

Emily was intrigued. "What is an auto laundry?"

Todd enjoyed teasing his wife. "It's a station where *you* can wash the car and clean out the inside with a Hoover. That will be *your* job."

"That can be *my* job," Ryan interjected. At seven, Ryan was a a big boy with golden curls and dimpled cheeks that drew all the young mothers to gather around him.

"A good idea, son." Ryan had been despondent for weeks following Danny's death and was just now coming out of his shell.

"What do you think, mama?" Ryan turned to his mother, resting comfortably near the peat fire.

"Momma, did you hear me? What do you think of my car washing business?"

Emily hadn't heard Ryan's entreaties. She wrapped her arms tightly around her large belly. "I think it's time we take a ride of our own," she said. "There are no hospitals in Loughan-boy, and the midwife is in Dublin with her daughter's new baby. It's a long drive to Galway City, but I think we'd best be on our way."

"The baby's coming?" Ryan vibrated with excitement. "Can I come along?"

Emily looked imploringly at Margaret.

"No, you'll stay here with me," Margaret said. "We'll stay up late and drink hot chocolate. I can make popcorn on the stove. Your parents will call when your new little brother arrives."

"How do you know it's a boy?" Ryan asked.

"Just a feeling," she said. "A mother knows these things."

It took three hours for Todd and Emily to drive the distance on the two-lane highway completed since their departure for America. It was dark outside, and Todd was thankful for the lanterns at the front of his "new" car.

When the phone rang just after dawn the next morning, Margaret beat Ryan to the receiver.

"Daniel Mannion Roebken was born at 5:37 a.m.," Todd announced proudly.

Margaret wept, as she offered up a prayer in thanksgiving. Danny would be here with her again, soon.

Since her return to Ireland, Margaret had lost her resolve to visit Martin's family in Currafarry. Residual survivor's guilt and her shame at finding a new love in America after Martin's death, haunted her even now.

Martin had three sisters in New York. Mary Gallagher lived in White Plains, Margaret and Martin's original destination in Westchester County. Erin Toomey and Nora Gallagher lived and worked in New York City, but Margaret didn't make time for them after the sinking of the Titanic, nor did they seek her out. It simply hurt too much to face his sisters after his death. Martin's parents, Patrick and Catherine, remained in Ireland.

After Martin died, Margaret had never expected to see his family again. She understood his parents had asked Mary to administer the estate in White Plains. His personal property was estimated at $800, but she had no claims on him before their marriage.

Martin owed the previous store's owner $1,600 for the store and the adjoining lot where they'd planned to build a home one day. The two were valued at $6,000. She hoped his parents or his sisters were able to recover some of the value of the property Martin had worked so hard to secure, but she didn't want to come begging.

As she drove, Margaret revisited the pain and heartache in the last seven years since she'd left the shores of Ireland on the Titanic — the ship sinking, Martin's death followed so closely by her father's death, and finally the loss of little Danny. Her heart was broken again and again, but she was a stronger woman, too, for her time in America.

She had learned to put herself first in some instances —
allowing for love and long-term happiness with another man,
even if it didn't work out in the end, she had held Danny. She
wouldn't trade those four years for any other time in her life.

Deciding to return to Ireland was a moment of strength
for Margaret, not a moment of weakness, as some suggested. She
wasn't coming home to lick her wounds. Not to burrow into
the sadness of a hidey-hole in her mother's cottage. Margaret returned to blossom and grow as an independent woman, full of
hope for the future on her own and the ability to hold her head
high among family, old and new friends.

Only one thing remained on her plate before moving
into the future, alone or with a special someone, someday. She
needed the closure in her life that might come from saying
goodbye to Martin's family. Returning to Currafarry brought a
lump to her throat. It had been seven years and she'd had only
the one letter from Martin's parents after his death.

The White Star Line told Patrick Gallagher that Martin's
body, if discovered, was never identified. The family's grief, like
her own, rested somewhere in the North Atlantic. Today, driving along the road on the east side of the village Martin called
home, Margaret pulled to one side of the narrow lane, overcome
with emotions.

She could almost see Martin ambling down the lane to
meet her the last time she'd visited. *His dark hair falling in his
eyes. His crooked smile. "Hey, missy. Just in time for supper, I see."*

Martin would always tease Margaret about her insatiable
appetite for his mother's cooking. Kate's scones, dotted with
cranberries and orange peel, were a special weakness for Margaret. She like to drench the little biscuits in pools of soft, sweet
butter from the dairy cows on the neighboring farms.

Immersed in her memories, Margaret startled to hear a
horn blast as an older green truck rounded the curve ahead of
her. She let her foot off the gas and the clutch at the same moment. The car lurched forward and died.

Margaret cursed her luck, engaged the hand brake and

turned the key twice, before stepping out to open the hood. One of the pneumatic tires she and Todd were so careful to care for was as flat as the Irish driving caps they wore. She yanked the jack from the boot, hoisted the car's body and began to loosen the tire from its wooden wheel.

As she continued her work, a tall blonde man in greasy gray coveralls shot from the seat of the truck she'd been surprised by moments earlier. He'd turned around and came back to check on her welfare. "Hey, missy, need some help with that tire? I'm a mechanic here in town. My name is Martin, what's yours?"

Margaret jolted, nearly hitting her head on the fender of the car as she turned 'round. "What did you say your name was?" she asked.

He tried to look friendly, his timid smile meant to disarm her fear. Or was it anger? One side of his mouth curved up more than the other, forming a lopsided, but earnest smile.

"Martin Hopkins," he replied, dipping his head and lowering his eyes. "At your service."

Book Club Questions

1. How did you experience the book? Were you immediately drawn into the story — or did it take a while? Did the book intrigue, amuse, disturb, alienate, irritate or frighten you?

2. Which characters were easy to admire and/or dislike? What are their primary characteristics?

3. Early in the book, Margaret tells Ellie she never wants to talk about the Titanic again, to anyone. In fact, the real Margaret seldom spoke to anyone about it and only talked to the media once, late in life. Have you, a friend or a family member ever had an experience that you simply refuse to discuss?

4. Do you think Vincent's decision not to marry Margaret is justified or ethical? Could they have made good life partners?

5. Do any characters grow or change during the course of the novel? If so, in what way?

6. Who in the book would you like to meet? What would you ask, or say?

7. If you could insert yourself as a character in the book, what role would you play?

8. Consider the ending. Did you expect it or were you sur-

prised? Was it neatly wrapped up — maybe too neatly? Or was the story unresolved, ending on an ambiguous note?

9. What similarities did you see between the three men in Margaret's life – Martin Gallagher, Vincent Sloane and Martin Hopkins? Were the physical and personality traits endearing or off-putting?

10. If you were writing the epilogue, what would happen to Margaret (the real Margaret or the fictional Margaret) in the next 10 years of her life?

11. If you were to talk with the author, what would you want to know?

Author's Note

The real Margaret Mannion traveled with her fiancé, Martin Gallagher, who died in the accident and she did return to Ireland seven or eight years later to meet and marry Martin Hopkins. That is where the facts end, and the fiction begins.

I have made every attempt to be accurate with historical facts and timelines. I know some Titanic enthusiasts may find small errors in the details of the Titanic loss. I wasn't there, and I tried to stay close to historical accounts, while inserting a fictional account in the middle of the chaos.

If you enjoyed this book, please leave a review at www.amazon.com.

Please join my Facebook page for Mary Wernke, Writer or follow me on Twitter. You can also subscribe to my blog at marywernke.net for more fun stuff about books and travel.

Reviews and word-of-mouth are the two single best ways to promote my work and make it possible for me to continue writing. *The Young Irelanders*, my free prequel to this book, will be available soon at www.marywernke.net, along with future books, already in the works.